THE INN AT WILD HARBOR

GRACE WORTHINGTON

CHAPTER ONE

ASPEN

Never say never. Or even, never ever. That was the exact warning Great-Aunt Lizzie had given her years ago. "As soon as you say it," the older woman had instructed, "life will hand you something you least expected, and you'll regret those words."

It was the type of advice Aspen had taken to heart. After all, her life seemed to be punctuated by following a list of nevers: Never quit one job before you have another. Never date a guy who is your friend unless you want to ruin the friendship.

Because of her fear of breaking the rules, she was still stuck in the same soul-crushing job for the last five years, while everyone else in her life had seized their life-changing moment. Her best friend, Megan, was engaged. Her sister had married. Her parents had moved.

Aspen glanced around the bland white-walled marketing office where a dozen zombie-like workers huddled behind cubicles, entranced by their computer screens. The office smelled like burned coffee and warm copy paper. Even her sweet-and-salty trail mix bar tasted like a limp cardboard box.

She clicked over to her email, hoping that Matt had sent his daily roundup of funniest memes. Only he understood that a random picture of lip-syncing cats was the way to make her smile. His messages were unequivocally the best part of her day, like a dopamine hit that helped her survive until five p.m.

But instead of a delightful meme, her inbox flooded with emails from her boss, one office complaint about the workroom's dirty microwave, and three spam messages promising her a rockstar body (an overpriced weight-loss program), the man of her dreams (a dating app with mostly scumbags), and a legal-sounding letter ensuring a hefty inheritance from an African prince. She was pretty sure the last email had been circulating since 1997.

After deleting all three, another email slid into her inbox. *Win $5,000 with your original photo of a hometown hero. Enter today!*

Photography contests were ridiculously enticing, like Ben and Jerry's chocolate chip cookie dough ice cream. She simply couldn't stop dreaming about a life outside of the office, especially pursuing a more creative life while traveling the world. Never mind that she'd be hopelessly broke—at least she'd be happy. No memes required.

The idea of entering the contest spun around her mind like a wobbly top. If she could win five thousand dollars, she could leave her job at the Hartford Marketing Agency, a job that had completely sucked every ounce of good energy from her brain molecules daily.

She had taken the office administrator job five years ago, hoping she could move into the art department once she proved her talent for photography. But each time she tried to hint about her experience, they ruthlessly ignored her. The boss would give her a curt nod, like she was a child presenting her latest crayon drawing.

Her shoulders slumped as another email appeared from her boss, Mr. Vincent Hartford, a brusque man who had only smiled twice in the last five years. Not that she was counting.

Like usual, his message didn't bother to include a greeting, only a quick, *Don't let anyone bother me. No interruptions unless the building is burning down.*

Even though his personal office was mere steps away from her desk, he preferred email rather than walking the ten steps to where she sat.

As the phone gave a shrill ring, she cleared her throat and forced herself to sound chipper. "Good afternoon, Hartford Marketing Agency."

"I need to speak with Vincent Hartford," a gruff voice with a strong East Coast accent demanded.

She hesitated, her heart squeezing uncomfortably. She knew Lou Mattichelli's voice from the luxury car dealership because their agency handled his marketing. Although he was a reliable client, he had terrible manners, especially with lowly receptionists like her. He often steamrolled right over her attempts to direct the conversation.

"My apologies, Mr. Mattichelli, but Mr. Hartford is in a meeting—"

"You gotta be kidding me," Lou chided. "I've been his client for years, and he gives me the runaround?" He didn't care if the building was burning or the entire world was on fire. His goal was to gain Mr. Hartford's undivided attention.

Her shoulders tensed. Of course, Lou wouldn't let her off easy on a Monday. No was never an acceptable answer for the man.

"I'm sorry, but he gave me strict instructions," she pleaded, hoping he'd hear the quiet desperation in her voice. It was not her fault, but Lou made her feel like it was. "I can have him call you first thing when he finishes, okay?" Her voice shot up higher, ending on a brittle note of hope.

"You put me through to him, or tell him I'll send my business elsewhere," Lou demanded.

Aspen pushed air through her clamped teeth. Lou was forcing her into an awkward position—to obey her boss or bend to a client. Aspen rubbed the back of her neck. Clients that made her the bad guy were the bane of her existence, but she couldn't risk losing a major account.

"Let me check to see if he's available," she said, trying to appease him.

"Okay, but it better be—" Cutting off his response with the hold button was mildly satisfying, even if approaching Mr. Hartford's door brought terror to her heart. Aspen tilted her ear toward the door and gave herself a pep talk. *He won't be upset when he finds out it's Lou. He'll understand this time.*

Slim chance of that happening.

Her cheeks puffed out as she exhaled. *You can handle the wrath of Hartford.*

As she held her hand to Mr. Hartford's door, she paused. A few staffers were staring at her back. She could feel their eyes boring into her. She gave a weak tap that sounded like someone had bumped the door.

From within, a deep voice shouted, "I'm in a meeting, and I asked *not* to be bothered!"

"Um, Mr. Hartford?" she asked weakly. Scattered glances drifted over cubicles. She turned away just as her friend Rochelle shot her a look that warned, *Girl, you're going to get fired.*

She tucked her chin to her chest and squeaked, "Lou is on the phone."

There was a pause, then an eruption. "It's your job to get it through Lou's thick-skulled brain that I'm in a very important meeting."

"I explained that. But he wouldn't take no for an answer—" Her voice cracked as she lost her confidence.

"I don't care what he said!"

Aspen shrank from the door, her back to the cubicles as her face burned. The entire office was hanging on every word of this conversation.

Except for Rochelle, she received little sympathy from her coworkers. They seemed to relish her public humiliation.

Announcing Lou's ultimatum in front of the office was like facing a public firing squad. All ears were leaning toward her, eager to catch every word.

Her voice emerged as a half-strangled whisper. "Lou said he'd send his business elsewhere."

"He what?" She heard Mr. Hartford's chair squeak as he rose. She backed away from the door just in time as it flew open. Mr. Hartford's glasses had slipped down his nose slightly, and his tousled hair appeared in desperate need of a trim.

He leaned out his door and pointed at her. "Then tell Lou he can take his business elsewhere!" He slammed the door shut, causing a stack of papers to fly off a desk nearby and float to the floor, like birds softly descending to the ground. For a few seconds, nobody moved. Only the sound of the fluttering papers filled the space.

Aspen knelt to gather the papers, hiding her face as she blinked back hot tears. Rochelle edged around her cubicle and joined her on the floor. For a long time, neither said a word.

"It's not your fault," Rochelle whispered. "You were just doing your job."

Rochelle handed her the last paper before Aspen slinked back to her seat, feeling the heat creep up her neck. Not only had he humiliated her in front of the entire staff, she was about to get a verbal beating from a client. There was no way that Lou would take Mr. Hartford's message well. What she hated most was that for every angry client, she became the punching bag.

Mr. Hartford's punching bag. Lou's punching bag. And the butt of every water cooler joke in the office.

Aspen stared at the red light blinking on her phone where Lou sat on hold.

This demeaning job was not only causing her significant stress, it had effectively held her back from reaching her actual goal: pursuing her love of photography. Ever since she'd graduated with an art degree, she'd wanted to pursue photography, but a huge student loan had held her back along with a growing insecurity that she could never make enough money. Working at a marketing agency had given her hope that perhaps if they saw her photography talents, they'd use her in the art department. But all they'd done was steal a few pictures from her—*by accident,* they said—for one of their marketing campaigns. The incident still stung.

Clicking on the email for the five-thousand-dollar photography prize, a surge of courage pulsed through Aspen. Like a hit of adrenaline, it snaked through her body, coiling in the pit of her stomach.

What if the contest could be the seed money she used to pursue photography? Never mind that she didn't have a clue how she'd make real money chasing gigs. Her only thought was getting out. *Now.*

Her gaze flicked from the email to the red blinking light and then back again. If she walked out now, she'd no longer have to put up with clients like Lou or bosses like Vincent Hartford.

She'd become her own boss. Do things on her terms. Soak her depleted spongelike soul in the waters of creativity.

An email labeled *Matt's memes* had landed in her inbox too late, but his name sent a surge of warmth through her middle. Matt despised the way Mr. Hartford treated her, and she knew he'd support her decision to quit even if she didn't have a backup plan.

With a calm flick of her fingers, she deleted a few personal files from her computer, then unloaded her desk into a box representing the last five years of her life. Buried deep in one drawer, she pulled out the gaudy plaque she'd received for five years of service, which she promptly tossed in the trash as her final goodbye to the Hartford Marketing Agency.

With her arms full, she stood and cleared her throat. "Excuse me, everyone."

Heads darted around cubicle walls.

"As of today, I'll no longer be working here," she announced. "Five years is my limit, and I'm ready to try something new. Please let Mr. Hartford know."

Spinning on her heel, she started for the door, then stopped. "Oh, and Lou's still holding on line one if anyone wants to break the news to him."

Her coworkers sank behind their cubicles again, afraid of facing the red blinking light. Only Rochelle remained standing, pumping her silent fist in a show of solidarity.

Aspen walked through the door into the warm breeze of summer and took a deep breath. Her great-aunt Lizzie had been right. *Never say never.*

As she stepped out of the agency, her chin held high, she promptly tripped over a pothole in the sidewalk. Her box pitched forward as she stumbled to the ground.

Her knees screamed in pain as her personal items clattered to the curb. Staring at the pitted cement with a sinking feeling, she realized she'd broken one of the *never* rules: *Never quit your job without having a clue what to do next.*

She'd just made the best—or worst—decision of her life. Either way, there was no turning back now.

As she approached her apartment, the gash in her knee throbbed painfully. The scrape from her fall caused her to limp with every knee bend like a rabid dog had mauled her. If she hadn't rushed out the glass door of the agency, she might have made an unforgettable dramatic exit. Instead, she'd tripped in front of the entire office. At least she would avoid the snickering that had likely followed at her expense. She didn't need a door to hit her on her way out. She was perfectly capable of making a fool of herself.

She fumbled for her keys in her purse while balancing her box of office items in one arm. Pulling out a metal key chain with a tiny hot-air balloon dangling from the bottom, she rubbed her thumb over it, remembering how Matt had given it to her at last summer's carnival when he'd dared her to go for a ride in the balloon with him. Her reply? *Never ever.*

It was an ongoing joke between the two of them—all the things she'd *never* do. She didn't enjoy flying. Or heights. The decision was a no-brainer.

As she slipped her key into the door, the bolt was already unlatched.

"That's weird," she mumbled, tucking her chin on the edge of the box and turning the key again. *Definitely* unlocked.

As she pushed the door open with the toe of her shoe, a loud thump from the back of the apartment startled her, like someone had dropped a heavy object on the floor.

Aspen's stomach jolted at the sound as she lowered her box and grabbed the nearest object, a heavy green vase her mom had given her.

A dresser drawer slammed shut followed by the slow scoot of someone dragging an object.

Aspen hid next to the closed bedroom door with the vase in the air, her heart pounding wildly like an out-of-control ping-pong ball. Her already defective heart didn't need any more stress. She said the only prayer she could think of—a silent shriek for help—and then played out the scene in her head. Should she smash the vase on the intruder's head as he opened the door? Or stay hidden and attempt to get a clear view of his face?

The door clicked open, giving her no time to decide. A heavy object that looked like a mattress balancing on one end slid out the door first. Someone was stealing Megan's furniture.

Unsure what to do, Aspen bolted around the door, her vase held high, ready for attack. "Don't move or I'll call the police!"

Adrenaline surging, she threw the vase at the man, whose face was fuzzy in the darkened room. He ducked as the container crashed against the wood floor, splintering into a thousand pieces.

She hadn't expected to miss her target with the vase. The thought of a plan B had never occurred to her.

"Aspen?" The man straightened from his crouched position. "What are you trying to do, kill me?" He glanced at the shattered vase.

Aspen's mouth dropped open. She'd know that voice anywhere. Even under pressure, his tone was husky and deep, like rich caramel.

"Matt, I thought you were—" She clamped her mouth shut. She didn't need any more humiliation today.

"You thought I was what?"

"An intruder," she admitted.

He threw his head back and let out a laugh that roiled Aspen's blood.

"Seriously?" He ran his hands through his hair. "You almost took me out while moving my sister's mattress. I'm glad your aim is terrible."

"What was I supposed to do?" she shot back. "Stand here, like an idiot?"

"It would have been better than throwing a vase."

"Then what would you recommend, Mr. Know-It-All? Call you?" She gave him a smug smile before grabbing the broom to clean up the shards.

"Careful, Little Bit." He only used her nickname when he was trying to annoy her. "You know I hate my nickname."

"As do I," she agreed, sweeping harder.

He'd started calling her Little Bit back in elementary school. With four years between them, she'd always been smaller, while he'd developed into a tall, ripped Hollywood hunk. It wasn't even fair.

"If this was a real home invasion, you'd be in trouble," he advised her. "Civilians constantly make things worse."

She couldn't stand when he used the term *civilian* with her, as if she were some random stranger. Growing up, her family had only lived a few streets over from Matt's. Since her parents often worked late, she ended up at his house more evenings than her own, and Matt had treated her like a fourth sister in his family, something she both relished and hated.

It was only when she reached her teen years that her heart fluttered oddly whenever he was around. This time, the problem wasn't her arrhythmia. The fluttering was the soft whisper of butterfly wings pulsating against her ribs, the first signal of blossoming love, though she'd never admitted it and still wouldn't. Now that she was an adult, she attempted to rid herself of any silly teenage fantasies.

Plus, Matt was way out of her league. Like miles away. Her chance of winning him over was one in a zillion. It wasn't rocket science: If she were a family sedan, he was a Lamborghini.

As he balanced the mattress against his body, his T-shirt clung to his sculpted shoulders. Instead of packing on the pounds in his twenties, he'd packed on extra muscles, competing in triathlons while he worked as a firefighter. Every single girl in town fell over themselves to catch his eye.

"You could have warned me you were here," she added, dumping the pieces of vase into the trash and returning the broom.

"I did, when I sent the memes. Did you get them?"

"Oh." She wasn't ready to confess that she'd quit her job yet.

Even if losing her position was a relief, she mourned the loss of the memes. "Yes, of course."

"And did you enjoy them?" He seemed genuinely interested in her response. Like he actually cared about whether they brought her joy.

"They're the best thing about my Mondays," she admitted with a goofy grin.

"Do you want to help me move this bed, or are you going to stand there and block my way?" His lips curled into a mischievous smile as he steadied the mattress.

"Like you need my help," Aspen mumbled as she grabbed the front of the mattress and pulled. It only budged an inch.

Matt balanced the mattress with one arm as she tugged again. "You're not getting very far."

Aspen gave him a look. "Oh, be quiet or I'll find something else to throw at you."

"With your aim, I'm not too worried." She dropped her end, catching him off guard while he stumbled to corral the mattress before it fell.

"I don't have to help," she countered. "I could just stand here and watch you do all the work." She crossed her arms and smiled.

"What's new? You always liked watching me work." His smile stretched a little wider as heat burned up Aspen's neck.

How did he know that she'd secretly enjoyed watching him work? Had her teenage crush been that obvious?

Hiding her flushed face, she grabbed the end of the mattress and yanked it toward the door. She wasn't about to let him see the way he'd made her feel since middle school. It embarrassed her to think he might have known about her crush all those years ago.

"If you will steer it, I'll push from behind," Matt instructed as he slid the mattress forward.

As they inched closer to the front door, Aspen pulled it open.

"Don't push too—" she tried to say, but Matt shoved it out the door before she had time to steer it, sending the mattress down the front porch stairs like a slide.

As she attempted to catch the bed, the momentum pulled her forward so violently that she lost control and fell against the padding as it toppled over, rolling onto the mattress as it landed on the sidewalk.

Scrambling to recover, she propped herself up on her knees and hoped that Matt hadn't noticed her epic fall.

The smile on his face revealed everything she needed to know. He not only had seen it, he was thoroughly amused by it.

"Don't you dare make fun of me," she warned with a glare. "I didn't realize you were ready to launch it out the door."

"Why did you attempt to catch it?" he asked through a stifled laugh. "You're so tiny, the mattress could have squashed you like a bug." His gaze flicked across her body like he was imagining how easily a large object could crush her.

She climbed off the mattress and straightened her black pencil skirt, which had twisted uncomfortably across her legs. Matt never failed to taunt her about her size, as if she were still twelve and he was sixteen. Next to his massive body, she looked downright ridiculous. Like a gnat next to Goliath. No wonder he'd always treated her like his fourth little sister.

Aspen stretched her spine to its full height and threw back her shoulders, even though she knew it didn't help. "I was trying to be helpful."

She brushed past him toward the house. Her day had been humiliating enough. She didn't need Matt making it worse.

As she rushed through the door, Matt's steps echoed behind her. "Aspen . . . wait."

She flopped onto the couch and propped her legs on the coffee table, pretending to read a magazine so he'd leave her alone.

He sat on the arm of the couch, peering down at her. "I shouldn't have laughed."

She looked up from her magazine. "Then why did you?"

"You were just so . . ." A corner of his mouth turned up.

"Funny. I know, my clumsiness is *hilarious* to you." She flipped a page, hoping he'd go away.

"I was going to say *cute*," he confessed.

On another day, she might have been flattered, but after her blunder, she sensed he was trying to make up for hurt feelings.

His eyes drifted out the window. "You did this little roll onto the mattress that was—I don't know how to say it—graceful, actually."

She squinted, trying to decide if he was being serious. His expression was soft and kind with no hint of teasing, and her heart jumped in her chest. "Graceful? That's a stretch. Even so, a little assistance would have been nice."

He glanced at the wood floor and folded his hands as he measured his words. "You're right. But I know you better than anyone, and I knew you wouldn't accept my help."

She stared at him for a moment. Matt rarely showed his emotions. He was stalwart and logical, the type of person you wanted in an emergency. It's what made him a good fireman, but as a friend, he was hard to decipher. Other than laughter, his facial expressions were so consistently the same that she'd once accused him of being a robot and not human. But over the years, she'd learned the nuances of his looks—what the tilt of his mouth meant, how his eyes glittered or darkened depending on his mood. Only she could see these things, and the understanding of those nuances felt like a secret the two of them shared.

"What happened to your knee?" He glanced down at the gash still raw from her fall earlier in the day. His brow knitted with concern.

"I fell on the sidewalk after quitting my job today." She

closed the magazine and dropped it on the coffee table. "This was my second fall. I've had enough humiliation for one day." She didn't dare look at him. What would he think of her quitting with no plan other than the ridiculous hope that she could win a photography contest?

"It's about time," Matt assured her. "You were always too talented for the Hartford Agency."

She turned to him, her mouth falling open. "But I don't have another job," she stammered. "Not even a backup plan."

He shrugged. "I wouldn't be surprised if someone snatched you up by tomorrow." His confidence in her lit a warmth in her chest. She'd love to be snatched up in more ways than one.

"Tomorrow, huh?" she marveled. "You have way more faith than me."

"Maybe." He stood and glanced down at her knee again, his gaze lingering there longer than normal. "Let's get you a bandage for that scrape."

He started toward the bathroom as she leaned her head back and closed her eyes.

Under Matt's brick-wall exterior, his soft side would occasionally show. For years, she had wanted to imagine that softness was just for her, but she knew it was only a matter of time before he found someone else and gave that same tender affection to another woman.

He came out of the bathroom holding the bandage in his fingers like a winning lottery ticket.

"Success." He shook the bandage, then dropped it in her lap. "Did you clean up your knee yet?" His eyes flicked back down to her leg.

"I just came from work. It's fine."

He stole the bandage from her fingers. "It could get infected. Let me grab a washcloth."

"It's really unnecessary," she called as he rushed to the bathroom.

Matt had worked as a firefighter continually since college, and now he treated everything like an emergency. Seeing the worst in life had made him extra protective of his entire family, including her. Ever since she'd received a heart arrhythmia diagnosis as a child, he'd always harbored more concern for her. She could tell by the way his eyes narrowed whenever she was in pain. Her health had become his personal responsibility, even though he had no control over whether her heart kept beating.

"I'm okay. It's just a scrape," she argued as he approached her with a wet washcloth and gently laid it on her knee. She swallowed hard as the warm water stung her skin. Her heart ricocheted off her rib cage from the pain and pleasure of his touch.

"Sorry, that probably hurts." He left his hand lingering on top so she wouldn't pull the cloth off.

If the wound hadn't throbbed, she might have enjoyed the warmth of his touch more. But as her bossy big brother, he was ensuring she didn't go against his wishes.

She pulled at his hand. "This is kind, but it's not like a little dirt is going to hurt me. Ryder tells me that all the time."

"Well, Ryder's wrong," Matt replied abruptly. His brow furrowed as he gently wiped her knee.

She hadn't meant to bring up her on-again-off-again boyfriend, who was more recently on-again.

Ryder and Matt had butted heads ever since they'd worked together at the fire department years ago. Matt had helped to enforce very specific processes at the station and couldn't stand when tasks were left incomplete, or worse, performed shoddily. Ryder, on the other hand, bucked authority and accomplished his responsibilities on his terms, not Matt's, which only added to the tension. After a year of a strained working relationship, Ryder quit his job, but Matt had never let go of his old grudge against the former fireman. He'd never spoken a bad word about him, but his annoyance was pushing a deeper wedge between them.

"Thank you for your concern." She pulled the washcloth away. "But I can bandage my own wounds now."

"Suit yourself." He backed off. "But someone needs to ensure you take care of yourself now that Megan is moving out."

Megan's wedding was still months away, but she was already transferring her furniture into the new home she and Finn had bought for after they were married.

As thrilled as Aspen was for her best friend, the thought of living alone was as depressing as working for the Hartford Agency. Not only would she have to deal with a new loneliness, she'd need to shoulder the full rent. With no income, there was no way she could afford it.

"Do you think your job is to rescue me?" she probed, uncertain she wanted to hear the answer. The more he cared about her welfare, the more she struggled not to care for him. It didn't matter if his feelings were platonic, hers most definitely *weren't*. Dating Ryder was supposed to have been the solution, but so far, it had only created more internal conflict.

"Correction. Not rescue, but look out for," he explained. "You're like one of the family."

A little sister. Of course. She gave him a tight smile before she slipped on the bandage and hopped off the couch. "I don't need taken care of. Not by you. Or Ryder. Or anyone."

Something flickered across his face. The tiniest of emotions settling in the tension of his jaw "Fine by me." He stood to leave. "I should deliver a mattress, anyway."

"You need help? Not that I'm much of one, but I can at least provide the entertainment."

Part of her knew this was a bad idea. Too many opportunities to let her feelings get tangled up even more.

"I've got this. You stay home and look for a new job. Or a vase-throwing class."

She gave a tiny snort-laugh. "Just what I want. Beg someone to take pity on me. Are you hiring at the fire station?"

"Nope. But I could use a personal chef."

"What about Aunt Lizzie?" Since Matt had moved into the inn that Great-Aunt Lizzie owned, she'd made him dinner every night in exchange for his handyman and landscaping skills. "Too many salads. She thinks I'm a rabbit," Matt complained.

"But maybe she'd hire you."

His cell phone beeped loudly with a message. His eyebrows furrowed as he read it. "I should head to the fire station."

"An emergency?"

He gave a quick nod, his eyes concealing his emotions like the close of a zipper.

"Be safe out there," she reminded him. "I can't have anything else go wrong today."

He stopped in the door. "Aspen, I don't want to alarm you, but I think you should come with me."

Her stomach bottomed out as her voice faltered. "Is everything okay?"

His eyes turned dead serious. "Get in my truck, now."

CHAPTER TWO

MATT

Matt pulled up next to The Red Poppy Inn on Lakeside Drive after the ambulance had already arrived. Judging by the faces of the EMTs, he suspected the news about Aunt Lizzie wasn't good. He'd worked long enough in crisis situations to interpret the status based on body language. Their solemn faces told him what he didn't want to know.

"I need to check on Aunt Lizzie." Aspen was climbing out of the car when Matt grabbed her arm.

"Let me find out what's going on first." He didn't want to be overly harsh with her in an emergency, but he needed to protect her from the worst. He'd seen far too many families traumatized by death to understand she shouldn't go rushing into a crisis.

An urgency settled into her gaze. "But Aunt Lizzie needs me. I'm the only family she has in Wild Harbor since my sister left."

He gave her arm a reassuring squeeze. "I'll get the information as fast as I can. Promise."

As he crossed the lawn of the sprawling inn, he waved down one of the EMTs.

"Hey, Bruce, what's going on? Is Lizzie okay?" A bad feeling settled in his stomach.

Bruce shook his head. "Afraid not. Appears Lizzie died in her sleep. Looks as peaceful as ever, though. Everyone was surprised you weren't here, given you're Lizzie's right-hand man."

It was no secret that when Lizzie turned eighty-five, she'd finally advertised for a part-time groundskeeper and handyman. Until then, she'd maintained the inn herself, but the job had grown into too much, and her stubborn spirit had been overruled by a body that had slowed with age.

Matt had jumped at the part-time opportunity when he'd found out it included free rent. He could usually accomplish the minor tasks on his days off from the fire department. In the last few months, she'd become like a grandmother to him.

"Who called the ambulance?" Matt asked.

"One of her friends stopped by, and Lizzie didn't answer the door." Bruce ran a palm over his whiskered face and shook his head.

"When I didn't hear her this morning, I figured she was tired from the guests she'd hosted over the weekend. Now I feel awful I didn't check on her."

"It wouldn't have made a difference," Bruce assured him with a pat on the shoulder. "Most likely it happened while she was asleep. If I ever die, that's how I want to go." Bruce peered at Matt's truck. "Is Aspen with you?"

"She is. Should I break the news?" Matt asked reluctantly.

"Is she the closest relative?"

"Other than Aspen's parents, yes. They live in Florida now, and her sister moved after she got married last year. Aspen is the only family nearby."

Bruce nodded before Matt slowly made his way to the car. Aspen watched him approach, her eyes wide, still clinging to hope. She jumped out before he could reach the truck, unable to wait any longer.

"What did he say? Is Aunt Lizzie okay? Can I see her?"

The way she pleaded with him was like a punch to the gut. He didn't want to tell her. Even though he was a man of few emotions, he hated to witness her hurt.

"Aspen," he said, steadying his voice. "Aunt Lizzie passed away last night."

Aspen's mouth dropped open as she shook her head. "What?"

He rested his hands on her shoulders. "She passed away while she was sleeping. Bruce said it was peaceful."

"That can't be true. She probably just needs a doctor. Someone would have known if she were dying. *You* would have known." Her eyes were wild with desperation as she tried to brush past him.

He grabbed her arm and spun her around. "Aspen, I know it's difficult to believe that she's gone. But there was nothing they could do for her."

Aspen tried to blink away the tears, but they pooled and slid down her cheeks. "Please let me say goodbye to her. I want to see for myself."

Matt eased his grip on her arms. "We'll go together, and if it's too hard, say the word, and I'll take you home."

She nodded, a mixture of fear and grief mingling behind her eyes.

As they walked across the spacious lawn, Matt replayed all the times he'd given bad news to a family after a tragedy. It was always horrible, but his relationship with Aspen made it doubly worse. She was someone he cared deeply about, and it tortured him to realize he couldn't fix her pain.

He knew Aspen's relationship with Aunt Lizzie had filled a deep hole left when her own mother had been mostly absent, building a successful law career instead. Her great-aunt's death, on top of everything else today, would shake Aspen's world.

Even though her life was toppling by the minute, if he insisted on helping her, she'd likely push him away. They'd always had this complex relationship of push-and-pull. One second she'd be staring at him with those eyes that made him crazy, and the next, she'd reject any help he offered.

Aspen stopped before she opened the door. "This is going to change everything," she murmured in a low voice.

"You mean for you or the inn?"

"Both. Aunt Lizzie already said she was giving it to me and Jessica. My mother had no interest in the inn, so Aunt Lizzie hoped that one of us would take it over. But now that Jessica's living in Atlanta, I doubt she'll want to move back, especially since her recent divorce."

"Do you want to run it?"

"I've never dreamed of running an inn, if that's what you mean." She paused to consider. "But Aunt Lizzie told me once that I'm like her in more ways than I realize. An old lady in a young woman's body. That doesn't bode well for my dating life."

"Not at all. It means you value things that older people do," he corrected. "Aunt Lizzie enjoyed inviting people into her home, making them breakfast, and treating them like family. It's a lost art that our grandparents valued, and she saw it in you."

"But I don't want the inn right now." Aspen covered her face as if blocking out the world would help her problems to disappear. "How can I manage a bed-and-breakfast if I'm not living in Wild Harbor?"

"Where are you planning on going?" he asked, confused by her sudden change of plans.

She pulled her hands down, her shoulders rounding with exhaustion. "I had this crazy idea that I could travel the world and do photography full-time. Stupid, huh?" Her gaze shifted to the lake. "For the longest time, I've wanted to see the world. Now that my parents have retired to Florida, I don't know where I belong. I thought Aunt Lizzie would live for another decade, but it's just my luck that on the day I quit my job, she'd leave me the keys. It's like she *knew*, and was trying to stop me."

As the lake wind picked up, Matt tucked a curl behind Aspen's ear. "Aunt Lizzie didn't know last night. She said the same thing to me she always did at bedtime. She didn't concoct any plans to ruin your future."

"Then what am I going to do?" Aspen rubbed her forehead. "I don't want the inn."

"You could always sell it and split the profits with your family. That would provide the money for traveling." Even as he suggested it, the idea of her leaving felt wrong. But guilting her into staying wasn't right either.

"Aunt Lizzie would hate that. It would be like betraying her memory."

"There's no rush," he reminded her. "Take some time to think it over. You don't have to decide anything today."

Or ever. If she stayed, he could help her pursue photography from here. But only if she had enough clients. Wild Harbor didn't have a bustling art scene like the big city. She'd have far better odds if she settled in a metropolitan area, and that meant once she left, she'd likely never come back.

"You're right. I need to find an apartment while I get the inn ready to sell." Her eyes grew wide. "If I'm inheriting the inn, I could live here until I attract a buyer." The words sunk in before she realized what she was suggesting. "There's plenty of room, and I'd have the whole place to myself, except for . . ."

Her eyes met his for a brief second as her face flashed with realization. "Oh wait, you live here."

He shook his head. "I could move out. If you're going to sell, I'd have to find a new place, anyway."

"Why move? As long as you don't mind us living in the same house temporarily."

The idea made his head swirl. He'd see her every day. And night. This wouldn't help his current state of conflicted feelings for her. She was his friend, an attractive one, but nothing more. If he tried to initiate something more between them, Megan would kill him. That was, if Ryder didn't first.

"Oh, no," he stammered. "The house is enormous, and I live on the east side where Lizzie's room was. You could take a guest room upstairs. We would hardly see each other."

"Are you sure you don't care?"

"Aspen, it's your inn now. You get to make the call."

She blinked a few times as the idea sank in. "I can't afford my rental without Megan, and I don't have any other place to go. Does it bother you to say we're roommates?"

"You're actually my boss now," he corrected. "But please don't rub it in."

"I'm not sure I could think of myself that way," she responded.

"If you're running the inn, you might as well get used to it, *boss*."

"That's *Boss Little Bit* to you," she shot back with a pleased grin before surveying the exterior. "The outside looks great. You've done a beautiful job with the landscaping. The poppies that Aunt Lizzie planted look the best I've ever seen."

"Lizzie had some very specific requests. Only red poppies in the bed around the signpost."

"The vibrant color reminds me of her. She was—how shall I say it? Anything but subtle."

Matt laughed. "Even at eighty-five, that woman was feisty."

"I suppose she wouldn't mind if I added some small touches." Aspen glanced at the cement pad that doubled as a patio. "Stringing lights there, adding some outdoor furniture and changing the decor. Aunt Lizzie's wallpaper choices might have been popular thirty years ago, but today?" She gagged like it was revolting. "If I updated the interior, it would sell for even more money."

"Now you're thinking like a boss. What's your timeline?"

"A couple of months, at most. What else do I have to do now that I've quit my job? This is my new project until I can sell the inn. I just need to hire someone."

"There's no way Jessica is going to volunteer," he told her.

"I wasn't referring to my sister." She gave him a pointed look. "I'm talking about *you*—my convenient, live-in handyman. You're going to help me get this inn ready to sell."

"I don't know, Aspen." He rubbed his hands through his hair. "This was only a part-time gig when Aunt Lizzie hired me. Mowing the grass. Weeding the beds. Fixing things. It was pretty minimal, to be honest."

Lizzie hadn't worked him too hard, especially since he enjoyed breaking a sweat in the yard. But things were quickly getting more complicated now that Aspen was in charge. Not only was he going to be sharing a house with her, but she wanted his assistance on projects, which meant more time alone with her. He had to draw a line somewhere.

"Don't worry about it," she interrupted, as if she'd already settled the matter. "I'll ask Ryder."

He wasn't about to let that tool Ryder hang around the inn. He'd more likely mess up her plans than help her sell the inn.

"No way," he responded. "I'll lend a hand. It's what Aunt Lizzie would want."

If he could keep his feelings in check for her—and that was a big *if*—it was a nearly perfect plan.

"Are you ready?" he asked. Even though he didn't want to go inside and face the truth, it was time to say goodbye to Aunt Lizzie.

She gave a hesitant nod and began walking toward the house.

He understood why she was reluctant to move forward. It was the same reason he was. With Lizzie gone, everything was about to change.

CHAPTER THREE

ASPEN

It had only been a week and a half since her great-aunt had passed, but Aspen still hadn't found time to pack her former apartment. With all the arrangements for the funeral, she'd totally forgotten about moving her own things. She slid off her shoes at the door and flopped down on the couch, rubbing her forehead with one hand while she held her cell phone in the other.

"Mom, I can handle this," she explained over the phone. "It's only a temporary arrangement, and I want to fix it up."

As the only family member left in town, she felt the weight of her great-aunt's estate more heavily than she had expected, especially since her parents and sister had basically given her free rein to do whatever she wanted with Aunt Lizzie's affairs.

"That funny-looking house?" her mom argued. "Not even sinking major money into that building would help it."

"It doesn't look bad on the outside." Aspen didn't sound convincing.

"But it doesn't look good, either. That handyman improved

the exterior, but the inside is a whole other matter. Your great-aunt's eccentric taste, combined with three decades of decay, has not done any favors for the place."

This wasn't a pleasant conversation to have with her mom, who'd never liked the inn to begin with. "Aunt Lizzie's outdated decorating is why sprucing it up with fresh paint would be the perfect low-cost option before selling."

"If she had left it to me, I wouldn't even bother," her mother admitted. Letting Aspen handle the estate meant she had more time to lie on the beach. "Its lakeside location makes that property top dollar. I say get rid of it as soon as possible, and you'll have a nice nest egg for your own house."

For quite some time, her mother had known that she would not be inheriting the inn from Aunt Lizzie. The two women had never seen eye to eye on things and often clashed whenever they were together. It was only when Aspen and Jessica were little that Aunt Lizzie had taken an interest in the family, treating the two young girls as her own daughters. Mother had come to terms with the decision and had been quite pleased to send the girls over to Aunt Lizzie's for free babysitting.

"I'm not planning on staying in Wild Harbor forever." Aspen stood and moved to her bedroom, surveying the huge mess she'd yet to pack. "Until the inn sells, I need a place to live temporarily."

"And then what?" Concern filled her mother's voice. "Honey, you can't live with us. In a few weeks, we're planning on touring Spain after our stop in Italy. We won't step foot in Florida for another two months. We rented our house until then."

Her mother prided herself on the fact that they were making money by renting their home to travelers. That meant Aspen would be essentially homeless once the inn sold.

"I wasn't planning on mooching off of you," Aspen said. "Once I have money again, I can live where I choose."

"It all sounds so unrealistic. It's giving me a migraine."

She imagined her mother rubbing circles on her temples.

"My plan is to travel the world like you and Dad. I'm brimming over with hopes and dreams. It's exhilarating, actually." Despite her mother's criticism, the anticipation bubbled over into her tone. "I want to do something crazy, for once."

"Oh, honey." She could hear ice clinking in the background. The need for more liquids was a sure sign of disapproval. "Before you go hog wild, get a decent job. Not some hobby business shooting baby pictures and senior portraits. I can check with some of your dad's old business friends and see if anyone needs a temp."

Aspen rolled her eyes. "Please, no."

Her mother had never considered photography a *real* job, which was precisely how Aspen had ended up at the Hartford Agency. Even more frustrating, she'd ignored the reality that Aspen was dating Ryder. Her mother lived in denial of anything she disliked. It was her coping mechanism for unpleasant circumstances.

"I'll be fine, Mother." She'd always been fine, just like the time her parents had left her alone when she was ten. It was the first time her heart went haywire, a wild racehorse pounding in her chest. At that age, she hadn't understood what was happening, only that she was scared, and her sister had bolted out the door to find Bill and Becky Woods.

It was Matt who'd raced to her side initially, hovering over her tiny face, whispering that she'd be okay. Even at fourteen, he'd been a first responder in the making. From then on, whenever he was near, she knew she'd always be okay—even if her heart wasn't.

"I need to go. I'm still not packed, and we're having a party since it's our last night in the apartment."

"Let me know if you find anything interesting of Aunt Lizzie's."

Not going to happen. Her mother would probably list Aunt Lizzie's valuables on eBay first. "I'll call you next week."

"If we're available!" Mother chirped before hanging up. Considering her parents had worked extremely long hours through her childhood, they were more than taking advantage of their freedom now by shunning schedules and living according to their whims.

Megan entered the room with a stack of boxes in her arms. "Is your mom giving you grief over the inn again?"

"Only because she thinks I should sell it as quickly as possible."

Megan lowered the boxes to the floor. "Doesn't she understand that it's an investment until your plans are in place?"

It was a relief to have one person agree with her.

"It's not worth the effort, in her opinion."

"When do your first visitors arrive?"

"Funny you should ask." Aspen paused as she unloaded a drawer. "I wanted to repaint the guest rooms before any more people arrived, but Aunt Lizzie's system of reservations is nearly indecipherable. She kept notes on index cards that are hopelessly out of order. It makes it next to impossible to notify guests of our temporary closing while we redecorate."

"Post a sign on the door," Megan suggested as she helped Aspen pack. "Or better yet, let Matt deal with it."

"It feels wrong to turn people away." Aspen tossed another shirt in her box. "You know how I am with stray pets, right?"

"But this is different. She didn't expect you to keep the inn open indefinitely."

"Her wish was for me to take it over, but the timing is bad." Aspen rubbed the back of her neck. "I barely have enough money to pay the inn's electric bill. You know what that place costs to run?"

"Did Aunt Lizzie have much cash in the bank?"

"According to her lawyer, her savings account was minimal.

That's why Matt was a lifesaver. From what we know, she couldn't afford to pay someone to help. Free rent was all she could offer."

"Well, at least you still have my brother. Dependable to the end. Maybe you can liven up his boring life." Megan lifted her eyebrows.

"Even if I could, Matt would never let me." Not that she hadn't tried. Over time, Matt's zest for life had slowly morphed into a regimented series of tasks to tick off a list. Even his triathlon training followed a strict workout schedule. Every once in a while, Aspen could make him burst into a full throaty laugh that reminded her of the boy he used to be, but most days, his emotions were bottlenecked behind a steely glare.

"What am I going to do?" Aspen asked, sinking onto her bed.

Megan shrugged. "What would Aunt Lizzie do? That's where I'd start."

Her great-aunt had seemed to exist on a shoestring budget, but it had never restricted her childlike wonder. Aunt Lizzie had loved life, and she'd never cared what people thought of her eccentricities. Her zest filled the inn with a contagious joy that brightened even the most dour guests. Whenever Aspen and Jessica came to stay, Aunt Lizzie would hide riddles in their rooms, sending them on wild treasure hunts and driving them mad with anticipation.

But now that the inn had lost the magic of her presence, it was up to Aspen to bring that same enthusiasm, at least for a few weeks.

Chin up, my dear, her great-aunt's voice echoed. *Onward.*

Over the next hour, the apartment quickly turned into a jungle of cardboard boxes alongside the chaos of too many bodies in a small space. Finn dove into packing kitchen utensils while Lily and Alex tackled the furniture.

"Well, well. Look who just walked in." Megan's gaze swung across the room to where Matt had entered.

"Can you grab the other side?" Alex picked up one end of the couch as Matt hoisted the other end in an effortless swoop. Through her open bedroom door, Aspen snuck glances at Matt, memorizing the way he looked for her next charcoal sketch.

In high school, she had taken a figure drawing class, which had taught her to see the world in interconnected shapes. Her brain had latched on to the concept intensely, mentally tracing everything she saw in distinct, dark lines. Ryder was more like an oval than the hard edges of a rectangle. His shape was indistinct, blurry almost.

But tracing Matt was a satisfying game, the lines of his body snaking through her mind like the confident sketch of an artist's pencil. To say she knew him like the back of her hand wasn't an understatement. She'd memorized every part of him, even though everything in her told her not to.

Megan stuck her head in Aspen's door. "Finn almost packed your phone. Good thing I found it, because there's a message from Ryder. He's coming over. Maybe you should warn Matt?"

Aspen shrugged. "They're grown men. They can work it out."

"That's exactly it." Megan's eyes flicked back to Matt. "They don't want to work it out. Especially now that you're moving into the same house. You think Ryder is happy about that?"

A tiny prickle of heat slipped down Aspen's neck. "Our arrangement is temporary. Ryder understands why I have to do it. He knows there's nothing between Matt and me."

Megan lifted her eyebrows. "There doesn't have to be. Matt's always treated you like the rest of us—ferociously protective."

Aspen wrinkled her nose. "I don't understand him."

"It's Matt's *thing*. To protect and defend is his default," Megan explained.

"He's like a dog that way," Aspen joked, slamming her dresser drawer shut.

"What's that, Little Bit?"

Aspen spun around, heat rising in her cheeks as Matt leaned against the doorway. "How long have you been there?"

Matt's mouth twitched, even while his eyes held steady. "Long enough to hear you talking about me."

"Just singing your praises." Megan winked at Aspen as she brushed past her brother.

"You need any help?" Matt picked up an expensive camera lens from Aspen's bed. "I had no idea you owned so much photography equipment."

"The amount is ridiculously embarrassing. I'm considering selling it to make ends meet. It's not like I need all this." Her collection filled the entire bed.

"Some people collect cars, you collect cameras." He picked up one of four cameras on the bed.

"It's a weakness," she admitted.

"I didn't realize you had any." He turned his attention to her. His gaze was disconcerting. "What other ones should I know about before you move in?"

She wasn't about to admit her habit of mentally sketching him. "Like you don't have any?"

"Nope," he said flatly. "Well, maybe one or two. And you still didn't answer my question." His eyes wouldn't let her go.

"I won't tell, no matter how hard you stare me down." She fixed her gaze back on her cameras.

Matt held up the camera she'd had since college, turning it over in his giant hands like it was a toy.

She nodded toward it. "In the tech world, that one's a dinosaur. Now everyone uses their phones for pictures. But cameras are still my thing. I like the way they feel in my hands. There's a weight to them that phones can't duplicate."

He lifted the camera and snapped her picture without warning.

Her hand shielded her face too late. "You're supposed to

warn someone before taking a shot." She grabbed for the device as he pulled it away.

He dangled the camera too high for her reach.

"It actually turned out well," he said, twisting his neck to view the picture. Then he flipped it around so she could see it.

"Delete that," she ordered, reaching for the camera.

"Not a chance," he shot back.

"It's terrible. I look too serious."

"You always look serious. It's not a bad thing, Aspen." Matt snapped another picture, likely just to annoy her.

She swiped at the camera as he yanked it over her head.

"Okay, now you're in trouble." She lunged. He dodged.

Grabbing another camera off the bed, she pulled it out like a pistol, ready to duel.

"You can't get a decent photograph of me," he challenged, weaving through the room. They were acting like middle schoolers, each trying to one-up the other in their little game of *who can snap the worst shot.*

"Is that a challenge?" She climbed onto the bed, zigzagging over photography equipment, playing cat and mouse.

He lunged for her camera. She shrank back, stumbled over a tripod, and tottered on the edge of the mattress. Instinctually, he grabbed her arm to steady her.

When their eyes met, concern had replaced his playfulness.

"Careful, Little Bit." Matt's fingers lingered there, and she wondered if he sensed the energy between them.

His expression grew dark. "Hand me the camera, and no one gets hurt."

She knew he wouldn't hurt her in a million years, but there's no way he'd let her get away with stealing pictures of him. If he noticed the spark between them, it was carefully hidden behind his ultimatum.

"Only if it's an equal trade," she countered, offering him the camera for the one he was holding.

"Is that how this game works?" His eyes sparked with interest. "Because I need to know the house rules before you move in."

"I only play fair," she explained. "No taking advantage of short people."

"Oh, really, Little Bit?"

"Yes, really, Know-It-All."

His lips turned up at the corners as he dropped the camera in her hand before taking the one from her.

"How do you delete things?" He pushed a button, and his face appeared on the screen.

She glanced at the image. "See how the light catches the side of your profile?" Her mind traced the lines of his jaw and cheekbones.

"It's an excellent shot. Better than mine," he admitted. "Not that I know anything about photography except—" His finger pushed a random button that erased the image just as Aspen lunged at him.

"No, that's not fair!" She jumped off the bed and nearly tackled him trying to grab the camera as Megan walked in.

"What's going on in here?" Megan glanced at the two of them.

"Matt erased a perfectly acceptable picture." Aspen searched the memory card, confirming what she already suspected. It was gone.

"That's good. Now he owes you. Did you ask him for your favor?" Megan looked almost gleeful over the fact that she knew something Matt did not.

"Not yet," Aspen confessed, a surge of panic racing through her mind. She had told Megan not to say anything.

Only a few days before, she'd decided that Matt would be the perfect subject for the *Hometown Heroes* contest.

"Ask me what?" Matt set down her camera, curious.

Aspen shrugged. "It's nothing."

"It's *not* nothing." Megan turned to Matt, ignoring Aspen's *I'm gonna kill you* glare. "Aspen needs to win five thousand dollars. Until the inn is sold, she's broke and needs your help."

"I don't need help," Aspen argued. "I can ask someone else."

"Matt's perfect," Megan explained like her brother wasn't standing next to her. "He's the picture of a community leader. The choice is obvious."

"Uh, no, thank you." Matt backed away. "Not my thing. Some other guy can do it."

Aspen began packing her camera. "I told you he wouldn't go for it."

His rejection stung, even if she'd expected it.

Matt started to leave, but Megan blocked his way. "You don't have to do anything but let her snap a few shots in uniform."

"I'm not the one," Matt insisted. "Find someone else."

Megan jabbed him in the arm as if to make a point. "Fine, then she'll ask Ryder."

"He isn't a fireman."

"*Former* fireman," Megan countered. "The rules don't say they have to be serving now."

Matt's jaw clenched for a second as he locked eyes with his sister. "Then why don't you ask him? He'd probably do anything for Aspen."

Megan stared at her brother as the front door slammed and a visitor entered.

"Well, speak of the devil." Megan grinned triumphantly. "Look who just walked in."

CHAPTER FOUR

MATT

Matt finagled the last box into the back of his truck, like the final piece to an intricate puzzle. Figuring out how all the moving boxes fit together was far easier than forcing himself to work alongside Ryder. Out here, he could breathe again. The rubber band wrapped around his rib cage was no longer constricting him.

As he pulled out his phone, Aspen stepped out of the house.

"Hey, is the back of the truck full?" she asked, waving a small box in his direction.

"I'll put it in the cab with me." He took the box from her.

She paused, watching him expectantly.

"Is there something else you need?" He suspected she hadn't approached him for one thing.

"Since you asked," she said nervously, "could you help Ryder with a box of books? It's massively heavy."

He shifted uncomfortably. "Isn't there another guy? Alex? Finn?"

"Megan has Finn sorting old magazines, and Alex had to run

to the store. Please?" She pressed her hands together and gave him the sweetest, pleading look.

Matt ran his fingers through his hair. "Fine. But this is my last box."

"The final one, I swear!" She lifted an arm as if she were making an oath. "But you don't have to be grumpy about it."

"I'm *not* grumpy." Okay, so he was grumpy. Ryder probably felt the same way about him.

Matt followed Aspen inside, where Ryder stooped over an enormous box. He straightened, surveyed Matt, and gave him a curt nod.

Aspen approached Ryder with a tense smile. "I asked Matt to help you carry it to your vehicle."

Ryder tossed a roll of packing tape to Aspen, who fumbled to catch it.

"Said I don't need help." His eyes flitted to Matt. "No offense or anything."

"No offense taken." Matt sniffed and lifted his chin. "Are all these boxes yours, Aspen?"

A half dozen more moving boxes had made their way into the living room since he'd last been inside.

Aspen shifted the one on top. "The label is missing from this box. Ryder, have you been stacking my things with Megan's?"

Visibly distracted by his phone, Ryder glanced up, startled. "You told me to put them there."

"I didn't mean *here*." Aspen pointed to the floor. "Never mind. I'll figure it out."

Matt could see the growing frustration on Aspen's face. All the same reasons Ryder irritated Matt to his core. Cutting corners. Following his own rules. Ignoring those in charge. Ryder could have been a dynamic fireman, but he'd refused to correct his mistakes. His laziness risked the safety of the entire team.

"Let me take that." Matt stole the box from Aspen's arms and organized another pile across the room.

Aspen followed him. "You're supposed to carry the books," she instructed. "I can fix this."

"He doesn't want my help."

"Just go," she urged. "And be nice." She gave him a gentle shove toward Ryder.

Matt approached Ryder with his hands deep in his pockets. He was doing this for Aspen.

Ryder avoided making eye contact. "I got this. You go back to whatever it is you were doing."

"Seriously, man. There's no reason to hurt your back." Matt bent to pick up the box at the same time that Ryder tried to lift it. As both men fought for control, it became an unspoken tug-of-war match. Matt finally released it, causing Ryder to stumble before he steadied himself. He hadn't meant to throw him off-balance, but it proved a point. They couldn't even move a stupid box together, let alone work out their personal differences.

Ryder hurried to the car while Aspen approached with a frown. "What was that about?"

"Ryder just being Ryder," Matt snapped.

"Or Matt just being Matt?" Aspen questioned. "Just because you didn't get along at the fire station doesn't mean you can't now."

He couldn't tell her that there was way more to his clash with the man. Ryder had been a wild young buck when he'd worked on the crew, highly unpredictable, with a smart mouth and a reputation for breaking hearts. Supposedly, he'd changed for the better. But Matt still questioned if it was enough.

When Aspen had started seeing Ryder a few months ago, he'd made a promise to himself not to intervene, no matter how much he disliked the guy.

After a few minutes, Ryder returned, beads of sweat sprinkling his brow. A triumphant look proved he had managed the box on his own.

Ryder, one point. Matt, zero.

"It looks like you have things under control," Matt said, brushing by Aspen on his way out.

MATT HAD JUST UNLOADED the last box from his truck when Aspen arrived at the inn, holding a pizza box alongside an apologetic smile. "You missed the pizza delivery, so I thought I'd bring this over while it's still hot."

The scent of salty meat made him salivate like a hungry dog. "You didn't have to do this. I have food."

"I checked your fridge," she said, shoving the pizza into his hands. "Unless you're planning on existing on air, I don't know what food you're referring to."

He bit into a slice of supreme pizza loaded with Italian sausage, bacon, and colorful peppers and leaned against the hood of her car. "Delicious," he mumbled with a full mouth. "Before I forget, a guest left a message about their reservation."

"What?" Her eyes bulged as she hurried into the house.

When he found her, she was staring at Aunt Lizzie's old-fashioned answering machine, jotting a phone number onto a sticky note.

"Anything wrong?" he asked.

"I thought I cancelled everyone's reservations, but apparently a few slipped through." She held up the sticky note. "They're supposed to arrive next week."

"Call them and tell them you're renovating right now," Matt said matter-of-factly. "No room at the inn."

"That's the problem. They mentioned on the message that everything is booked then. If I cancel their reservation, they won't be able to find another place."

"That's their problem. Not yours." Matt took another bite of pizza as he balanced a packing box in his free arm.

"As the new owner, it's my fault. Aunt Lizzie's reservation system is so archaic. I'm sure I missed a few people." She tapped a pen against her forehead. "I *could* make it work. If I only renovate one room at a time upstairs, there will still be three guest rooms open. Hosting a few guests would give me some cash flow for the renovations. Because right now, I don't even have money for paint."

"I can loan you the money if that's what you need," Matt offered between bites of pizza. He hated to watch her struggle when he had more than enough for paint.

"I'm not taking handouts," she said, her eyes stubborn. "You're already doing so much for me."

"Are you sleeping upstairs? That's where I stacked your boxes."

Her gaze flicked between the stairs leading to the four guest rooms and the back hall where his and Aunt Lizzie's old bedroom was located.

"I really need every room possible for guests," she said.

"You're going to make me move those boxes, aren't you?" he asked, even though he already knew the answer.

"Don't hate me," she pleaded. "But Aunt Lizzie's room is empty. It only makes sense for me to take her room."

The wing where two bedrooms were tucked away had a private entrance and a shared bath in the hallway. The location gave them perfect access to the kitchen and dining area, where Aunt Lizzie would mingle with visitors and make breakfast. The only problem was that they'd be living close to each other.

Matt tried to read her expression. "You sure you want to do this?" He shifted uncomfortably. "You won't feel weird about using my bathroom?"

"It's temporary, right?" Aspen seemed unfazed by this change, while Matt was still processing how he'd handle living next door to Aspen. And by next door, he meant sharing a paper-thin wall and using the same shower. It would require them to abide by a strict schedule so they wouldn't run into each other by accident. Things were quickly getting awkward, and she had just moved in.

"I'll take this to Aunt Lizzie's room," he said, excusing himself.

He needed to clear his mind, think rationally, and not worry about living with a woman who made his thoughts tumble off a cliff before he could stop them.

It's no big deal. I roomed next to Aunt Lizzie, right?

But there was a big difference between living with an eighty-five-year-old grandma versus a gorgeous young woman.

Aspen followed him to the bedroom and did a quick circle to scout out where she wanted things. Aunt Lizzie's massive king-sized bed, oversized armoire, and stately dresser crowded the bedroom. As he squeezed by the mattress to get to the closet, he brushed Aspen's waist with his elbow. A current of energy shot through his arm.

This will not work. He needed to unload the boxes by himself or they'd be bumping into each other the entire time. She was distracting enough as is, but to touch her made his body electric.

"How about you call those people back about their reservations, and I'll move the boxes?" he suggested.

"Sure. Let me know if you need any help." She dashed out of the room as he slowly let the air out of his lungs. As he moved another package, his elbow bumped a small box on the dresser, spilling it upside down on the floor. As he lifted the overturned container, he realized, to his horror, that undergarments filled the box. Satin slips and colorful bra and panty sets littered Aunt Lizzie's Victorian rug. His face immediately heated.

Don't be weird about a bunch of panties. This was no different from living with sisters, right?

Wrong. No matter how hard he tried to reason, this was completely different from having three sisters. These undergarments belonged to Aspen, and the last thing he needed to think about was her in them.

Trying not to look, he dropped to his knees and stuffed the garments in the box as fast as he could. One silky strap captured his attention as he plucked the last bra from the floor.

"What are you doing?" Aspen stood in the doorway, her cheeks flaming, her mouth open as her eyes fell to the bra he was holding on the end of his finger.

Matt stumbled to his feet like a robber caught red-handed. "Your box fell off the dresser, and I was trying . . ."

He glanced at the bra still looped around his finger. It didn't matter how he tried to explain it, his red face made him appear guilty. He held out the bra to her like it was a poisonous snake about to bite him. "I was cleaning up."

With pink splotches spreading across her neck, she glared at him and snatched the bra from his fingers before wadding it in her hands. Judging from her appearance, he wasn't the only one embarrassed by this awkward situation.

"It's not a big deal," he reasoned calmly, attempting the same mental argument that had failed on himself. "I grew up with sisters." His voice cracked on the last word, making him sound like a hormonal thirteen-year-old.

She avoided his gaze as she grabbed the box from his hands. "Why don't you finish your pizza in the kitchen? I'll put this away."

As he left the room, a mixture of dread and embarrassment climbed up his spine. No matter how hard he'd try to forget, he'd probably never live this moment down.

CHAPTER FIVE

ASPEN

"Rochelle! I'm so happy you stopped by." Aspen wrapped her arms around her former coworker's neck and gave her a careful squeeze. With a paintbrush in one hand and a paint-splattered shirt, Aspen looked nothing like the girl who used to work at the Hartford Agency. Although Aspen missed seeing her friend, wild horses couldn't drag her back to the office. No doubt jokes were still going around about her epic fall.

"I brought two things you forgot in your desk." Rochelle held them up like trophies in the summer sun. "Your pink umbrella and your secret stash of chocolates. In case you haven't heard, you're legendary now."

Aspen let out a sarcastic laugh. "A legendary klutz."

"No way. You stood up to Mr. Hartford and that jerk, Lou. There's been talk that you inspired the HR manager to change company policy."

Rochelle handed the candy over to Aspen and gave the inn a

once-over. "This is quite the place your great-aunt left you. She never considered selling, did she?"

Aspen squinted against the sun as she admired the grey shingle siding and rugged stone. The inn was attractive, even if it was dated. *Good bones,* her great-aunt used to say.

That she owned it made her shiver with pleasure.

"Not in a million years," Aspen replied. "The inn was her greatest joy. She loved making guests happy. I'm not sure I'll live up to her standards."

"Wait a minute. I thought you were selling?" Surprise crossed Rochelle's face.

"I am. I'm hosting guests temporarily until the renovations are done."

"Temporarily? You just wait. You're going to fall in love with this place the way your great-aunt did."

"Absolutely not," Aspen said firmly as she invited Rochelle inside. "Just between you and me, I'm broke and need the business. I'm not even sure I have enough in my bank account to pay for the redecorating."

Rochelle stopped in the foyer and gazed at the large floral-print wallpaper that looked like an ode to the eighties. "Your aunt certainly loved flowers."

"She loved a lot of things. Namely, bold prints and carpeted toilet seats."

Rochelle crinkled her nose. "Ew."

The curtains fluttered in the breeze, giving the women some relief from the June heat. Ever since she'd looked at her dwindling bank account, Aspen feared she wouldn't be able to pay the utilities that month, which meant no air-conditioning. As long as there weren't guests, she would do things the old-fashioned way.

Just then, the back screen door slammed and Matt interrupted, wiping his face on his sleeve. The heat made his T-shirt extra clingy, making him the perfect subject for a figure drawing.

Aspen ripped her eyes from Matt and focused on Aunt Lizzie's green cupboards instead. The cabinets were boring and safe. They didn't cause her thoughts to spiral into dangerous territory. If only he wasn't so handsome. And her friend. Why couldn't he be a jerk like Lou?

"Lemonade?" she offered, reaching for an empty glass. Aunt Lizzie's cat brushed against her legs, sniffing for stray crumbs.

"You read my mind." He dragged his hand across his forehead. "It's sweltering out there."

"Says the man who just ran five miles and mowed the grass." Aspen lifted her eyebrows as she handed Matt a glass. "By the way, I have an entire list of jobs now that we have guests coming."

Matt glanced at Rochelle. "Now that this is her inn, she can't wait to be the boss of me."

"There are a lot of women who would like to be the boss of you," Rochelle said with a mischievous smile. "Myself included."

"Rochelle!" Aspen turned to her friend.

"Only speaking the truth," Rochelle confessed.

Matt smirked, like he was enjoying this banter. He bent to scratch the cat under his chin. Now that Aunt Lizzie was gone, Lester had become quite attached to him. "So, how are things at the Hartford Agency without Aspen?"

"You can't ask her that," she responded in mock horror.

Rochelle's ruby lips stretched into a smile, her brown skin glistening from the heat. "Nah, it's fine. Everyone can see that the office is falling apart without you. You were our cheerleader. The glue that held us all together."

"Oh, I don't know about that." Underneath, Aspen secretly smiled. It felt good to be missed, proof she'd actually made a difference, even if she didn't quite believe it.

"Even Mr. Hartford misses you."

"What?" Aspen nearly spilled her lemonade. "He brought up my name?"

"What did I tell you?" Matt argued. "I knew it."

"He walked over to your desk because he forgot you didn't work there anymore. It was priceless."

That's all she was good for in Mr. Hartford's eyes. Being hired help.

"Give him another week, and he'll forget I ever existed."

Rochelle shook her head slowly. "He's going to kick himself when he realizes how much untapped potential you had. If only you'd stood up for yourself when they used your pictures without asking."

"What pictures?" Matt straightened, suddenly concerned.

"Someone in the art department saw her photos over lunch break and thought they'd be perfect for an influential client. He showed them to the team with a promise that he'd give her credit. Turns out, they adored her picture and used it for their next billboard campaign. He never gave Aspen what she deserved."

Aspen walked over to a stack of dishes and started putting them away. "Mike forgot."

"Mike made you promises he didn't keep." Rochelle set her glass down on the counter as if to make a point. "He took all the credit."

Matt leaned his back against the counter, his arms crossed. "They should have given you credit and compensated you. What they did to you was wrong."

"Mike only cares about Mike. I was too trusting." Aspen shrugged. "Lesson learned."

"You should follow up. Tell the HR department. Make things right," Matt demanded.

She shook her head. "Mr. Hartford will eat me alive."

"Mr. Hartford can . . . never mind. I shouldn't say it." Matt held the back door, ready to face off with the Hartford Agency.

"I will not let Mike or your boss take advantage of you like that."

Without warning, Lester noticed the open screen door and shot outside. He'd always been an indoor cat but was constantly seeking opportunities to sneak out. Aunt Lizzie's lazy feline had become the inn's perfect mascot, spending most days lounging in the sunroom window. But when a guest lingered with the door ajar for too long, Lester was only too happy to risk life and limb to escape.

"Lester!" Aspen scolded, dashing past Matt. "Here, kitty, kitty." The last thing she needed was to lose Aunt Lizzie's beloved pet. Aspen roamed the yard, peering under a few bushes, but came up empty-handed. "I can't believe he disappeared."

After searching everywhere for Lester, Matt sank down into a patio chair and peeled off his sweaty shirt. Rochelle openly gawked at the sight while Aspen averted her eyes and tried to crawl under a nearby bush for the cat. If that man was trying to get women to stare at him, he was doing a good job of it.

"It's a lost cause," Matt concluded as he stretched out his legs. "More than likely he'll be back at the door crying for food around nightfall."

Aspen crossed her arms. "What if we lose him?" Even though she hadn't grown that fond of Lester yet, he was Lizzie's cat. She needed to protect him.

"He'll die a happy cat," Matt assured her. "Trust me, cats want to roam. It's their nature."

"Kind of like men," Rochelle added, shaking her head. "Never met a man who wasn't like Lester."

"Not all men are the same," Matt said, his dark eyes defiant.

"You might just make me believe that." Rochelle sighed. "Keep me posted on Lester, okay?"

Aspen tagged alongside Rochelle as she returned to her car.

"Do you think I'm crazy for doing this?" Aspen wanted some assurance that she wasn't making a terrible mistake.

"Rooming with a ridiculously gorgeous man? You're living every girl's dream right now."

"I meant selling the inn and pursuing this photography contest."

"It's not crazy. But like my mama always said, pray about it first. Otherwise, it could be a complete disaster."

Prayer hadn't been a consistent part of Aspen's life recently, but she knew Rochelle was right. She always felt like her conversations with God were mostly one-sided, bouncing off the walls of her bedroom.

"Who are you going to photograph for the contest?" Rochelle asked with a note of mischief. "I know the perfect person."

Aspen rolled her eyes. "If you're thinking of Matt, he already said no."

"You shouldn't give up so easily. He's got a soft spot for you."

"I don't know what you're talking about." Aspen bent over to pull an ugly weed from a nearby flower bed.

Rochelle gave her a pointed look. "It's obvious, isn't it? He's always watching you when you're not looking."

"Like a little sister."

Rochelle threw back her head and laughed. "Girl, he doesn't look at you like a sister. Believe me, I can *guarantee* that."

She couldn't think about Matt like that. Not when she was dating Ryder. "Well, he treats me as if I were one."

"You'll figure it out." Rochelle climbed into her little sports car and slid on her sunglasses. "With your magical photography skills, I bet you could make me look like I belonged on the cover of *Vogue*."

Aspen smiled. "This isn't *Vogue*, but it might be my next paycheck."

In order to have a chance at the competition, she needed a

suitable subject, then she could play with light, shadow, and angle.

"You want a shot at winning?" Rochelle's eyes lingered on something behind Aspen. "Matt's your man." Rochelle gave her a little wink before she pulled out of the drive.

Aspen returned to find Matt under their neighbor's maple tree, studying the branches above. His body was still, inviting her to sketch the curve of his shoulder, the cut of his jaw, the soft lines around his mouth. Her mind worked in line drawings and still figures. Angles and forms. Light and dark.

She could already envision the photograph she'd take of him —black and white, catching the shadows in the hollows of his cheeks, the resolve in his eyes. If she could capture that on camera, it would be priceless.

He turned, and the picture in her mind dissolved.

"I found Lester." Matt pointed up, where Lester perched on a top branch.

"How did he get up there?"

"He climbed. Same thing I'm going to do right now."

Matt hoisted his legs onto the first branch of the tree and hauled his body over it. With smooth agility, he scaled to the next one.

"Wait, have you done this before?" Her stomach lurched at how far he was climbing. "Are you sure you don't want to grab a ladder? Isn't that how firemen are supposed to get cats out of trees?"

He grabbed another limb and, with biceps bulging, pulled himself until he had reached a dizzying height.

"That would be the right way to do it," he strained, muscling over another branch. "But I've done this multiple times, and Lizzie's ladder is a rickety old thing."

A growing anxiety churned in her stomach as he precariously balanced while moving higher. He was athletic, but he wasn't a little kid who could monkey-climb up a tree and expect the branches to hold. As he made his way toward the cat, Lester huddled in a crook, crying furiously.

When Matt finally closed in on the feline, the animal shifted, scampering upwards into the tree. Matt leapt at him, his fingers skirting Lester's body before he wobbled on the branch and lost his balance. As Matt lunged toward another branch to steady himself, the limb snapped under his weight, causing him to slip and ricochet off several branches. His legs and arms scampered to grasp something, but his body fell too fast to catch himself. He crashed to the ground, almost sticking his landing, but then crumpled in pain as he reached for his ankle.

"Are you okay?" Aspen barreled toward him, falling onto her knees.

Matt blinked a few times, then threw his head back with a grimace. "I'm fine. My ankle hurts, but other than that, I'm still alive."

"You just fell out of a tree. I'm calling for help."

"No," Matt insisted. "I twisted my ankle. Better than falling on my head."

"Better than falling on a lot of things," she agreed with a half-smile. At least he hadn't lost his sense of humor.

She glanced to where Lester huddled on a branch, refusing to come down. "Should I call the fire department?"

"The guys at work will never let me live it down if you do. Text Alex and ask him to bring his tallest ladder. After all his years of renovating houses, that man has no fear of heights."

"Are you sure you shouldn't see a doctor?" She couldn't stand seeing him in so much pain.

He shook his head and groaned as he sat up. "Unless you want to carry me in, could you help me up?"

Aspen offered her hand and pulled Matt to a standing position. He leaned on his good foot and attempted an awkward one-legged hop.

"You're never going to make it inside at this rate. Hold on to me. I'll be your crutch."

He obeyed without protest, hooking his arm around her shoulder. Limping to the house, the weight of his body pressed against hers. If it hadn't been an emergency, this might have stirred something inside her, but a distinct feeling expanded in her chest now. *Relief.*

Matt's accident could have been so much worse.

Remarkably, he had landed on his feet, even if his ankle had taken the brunt of the impact. In those few brief seconds, she'd prayed he would be spared, and somehow, he had. Now, all she felt was a flood of gratitude.

"You make a good crutch, Little Bit," Matt mumbled as they stopped at his bedroom. "I'm going to put my leg up." His face had turned pale grey.

"Why don't I stay awhile? Just in case you need something." She glanced around his bedroom, noting the care he took with his space. The bed was neatly made. A clean, uncluttered dresser lined the wall. In his closet, his shirts hung organized by color.

"I can manage," he insisted as he bunny-hopped toward his bed.

"This is ridiculous." She looped his arm around her shoulder until he reached the edge of the mattress. "Don't be a pigheaded man who can't ask for help." She grabbed a pillow to prop up his leg.

"Like I said, I'm fine, even if I am a pigheaded man." He smirked as he sank into the pillow.

"No more climbing trees for you, mister."

With his eyes closed, he muttered, "That's Mister Know-It-All to you."

Even if he passed off his fall as nothing, she knew Matt lived for danger. He endured potential risks every time he walked into the fire station. That was his life as a firefighter. But for once, he didn't look like the powerful man who could fix anything. Now he was the one who needed fixing.

"I really appreciate everything you did," she said softly. "Your attempt to rescue Lester was heroic."

Matt grunt-laughed in response. "More like a circus act gone wrong."

"Aunt Lizzie would be proud," she reminded him, brushing some dirt from his hair. "I bet you never thought you'd need me, huh?"

He cracked his eyes open and gave her a lopsided grin. "You're right, Little Bit. You do come in handy every once in a while."

CHAPTER SIX

MATT

He'd done stupid things in his life, but this one might have been the worst. After countless tree-climbing attempts without injury, he'd pushed his luck trying to save Lester. The guys at the fire station would have a field day with this story. *A fireman who fell out of a tree rescuing a cat.*

But a bigger question also loomed in his mind: how was he going to work now? He already knew the answer. He wasn't. Not until he could bear weight on his ankle.

Aspen peeked through the doorway. "Apparently, Aunt Lizzie wasn't a fan of ice packs. But I found a bag of frozen peas." She dangled it in the air.

"I'll take it." He leaned his head back on the bed and attempted to adjust the pillow under his knee. As he shifted his foot, his ankle throbbed massively. The swelling had swallowed up his bone, leaving an ugly bruised lump behind. As she settled the frozen peas on his ankle, pain seared through his leg. "If I didn't know better, I'd think you were trying to kill me."

"I'm keeping you from killing yourself. Tree climbing? Seriously?" She dropped two pain relievers into his palm. He swallowed the pills with water, then leaned his head back.

Aspen sat on the edge of the bed, her brow wrinkled. "You look like you're in pain."

"I am in pain," he shot back.

She shifted his foot to the left, sending shooting pains up his leg.

"Ow, that hurts," he complained.

"Sorry, I wanted to get a better view." She gingerly placed the peas back on top. "It looks . . ."

"Bad, I know." He finished her sentence.

She chewed one fingernail, staring at him, concerned.

If he'd been well, he might have found it distracting, but in his current state, all he could think about was ridding himself of this excruciating pain. Pain had blurred the edge of his focus, leaving him helpless to concentrate on anything else.

"Can I get you something? A magazine? Cookies?" She glanced around the room. "It's so clean. Like no one even lives here."

"I prefer it that way. Everything in its proper place." As uncluttered as his bedroom was, his own life seemed a mess. He didn't have time to be injured. The last thing he wanted was to shorthand the crew if there was an emergency. That could leave them in a precarious situation if there was a terrible fire.

"Could you find my phone?" he asked, pinching the bridge of his nose for relief.

She unzipped his bag and riffled through it. Her eyes flitted across the screen.

"Megan sent you a video of her new place." Aspen looked offended. "I wonder why she didn't send it to me."

"Because I'm her brother."

"But I'm her friend." Aspen couldn't hide her disappointment.

Aspen and Jessica had always been part of the family, ever

since they'd shown up on Matt's doorstep as kids. Living only a few streets over, she and Meg had hit it off fast, and after years of hanging around the house, she'd become a constant for his sisters.

Aspen scooted close to Matt. "I want to see what she's doing with the new place."

Matt tilted the phone so they could watch it together, her shoulder pressing into his arm, like old friends who were comfortable leaning on each other.

They were both so entrenched in watching the video that he didn't hear the front door open or the shuffle of steps in the hallway.

"Aspen, where are you?" a familiar voice called.

Ryder appeared in the doorway, dumbstruck as he looked from Aspen to Matt.

Aspen slid off the bed. "Ryder, what are you doing here?"

His eyebrows lowered in disgust. "I could ask you the same thing."

Matt met his gaze with equal disdain, even though he was in too much pain to explain the situation. It was clear he was in no shape to be a threat.

"Matt injured his ankle pretty badly," Aspen said. "I brought him frozen peas."

"Peas?" Ryder's expression walled up. "In bed?"

Aspen moved toward Ryder, eager to pacify him. "He was just showing me a video on his phone."

He hated the way she walked on eggshells around the guy. Ryder didn't seem convinced.

Aspen grabbed his elbow. "Why don't we talk about this later?" She gently nudged Ryder out of the bedroom.

Before she shut the door, she gave Matt one last look. "You good for now?" Her eyes had lost their usual energy.

"Besides my ankle?" He shrugged. "Nothing you can do about it." That wasn't entirely true. He wished she'd stay and lean into his body like she was doing before Ryder interrupted. At least that would take his mind off the pain.

"We'll probably head out for supper. Can I get you something?"

"Don't worry about me. I'll find some leftovers in the fridge." He tried not to sound pathetic, but she saw through his lame attempt.

Aspen tilted her head with a concerned expression. It was the only time she looked like her mom. "You can't even walk to the kitchen properly. I'll bring you a meal."

"Where are you headed?" he asked, not that it mattered. He'd gnaw on a cardboard box at this point.

She kept her distance. "Probably Brewster's."

"Is it a date?" He didn't mean for it to sound like an accusation, but he was in too much pain to care.

"It's just dinner," she told him, but he knew better.

"Have a nice time," he mumbled, even though he hoped they didn't. He didn't want to prolong her goodbye anymore. As long as she was with Ryder, he had to numb his feelings.

"Are you sure you're okay?" she asked.

"Do I look okay?" His words twisted with sarcasm. The pain was making him grumpy. So was her concern for him.

"You look terrible," she replied.

"What do you expect? I just fell out of a tree." He couldn't figure out why her presence was frustrating him, but it was clear he was in no shape to have a reasonable exchange. More than anything, he wanted to pull her next to him.

"If you need me, send a message." She disappeared down the hall, but he could still hear pieces of their muffled conversation.

Of course he needed her. That was the problem. He grabbed his headphones and turned on some loud music to drown out everything but the wailing guitar in his ears.

Things had always been tense between him and Ryder, but if nothing else, he owed the guy after what Ryder had done for him. When they'd served in the fire department together, Matt had escaped a harrowing house fire thanks to Ryder. The former fireman had discovered Matt overcome with smoke and helped him escape before the situation became dire.

After that, Matt had always felt indebted to the guy. They might not have seen eye to eye on most things, but he'd saved his life, and because of that, there was no way he'd put a hand on Aspen while Ryder was dating her. He owed him this.

Voices rose and fell in the kitchen as the music drowned out the sound of their voices. Matt closed his eyes, the pain reliever and ice finally kicking in. He needed to get her off his mind if they were going to make this temporary living arrangement work.

But could he rid himself of his feelings for her? *Never.*

WHEN HE WOKE LATER, the sunlight was pouring through his window. His stomach rumbled uncomfortably. Was Aspen here? He stepped out of bed, testing weight on his sore ankle.

"Ow," he winced. Definitely not ready to walk yet. A set of crutches sat propped up beside his bed. Someone had left them in his room while he slept.

As Matt hobbled into the kitchen on crutches, he noticed Aspen shooting pictures outside the window. Dressed in a tank top and jean shorts, she stooped low to capture a bed of red poppies. Even when she wasn't trying, she was captivating. Her hair fell over her shoulders before her gaze darted to the glass pane where she caught him staring. Relief and concern spread across her face.

He dropped the curtain, embarrassed that she'd spied him gawking. He hobbled over to the pantry to grab his usual breakfast of dry toast and a protein drink. The screen door creaked open as she dashed into the kitchen, her cheeks flushed with heat.

"You're up. How are you?" Her eyes dropped to the purple, swollen lump on his ankle.

"Not as painful as last night. Who left the crutches?"

"Your mom. They were your dad's."

Matt nodded, a twinge of guilt washing over him. There was a part of him that hadn't wanted his mom to know because she'd worry herself sick.

"Was she mad because I didn't call?" he asked.

"She's your mom. She was concerned about you. I picked up the crutches after dinner."

The mention of food brought back a blurry memory. Aspen's date with Ryder. His stomach soured.

"I'm not sure I'll need them," he said.

Aspen looked at his ankle again. "Oh, you'll need them."

He focused on his toast. If there was anything he'd learned in his years of firefighting, it was mental toughness in all circumstances. Those skills had served him well. Now all he wished was to ride out this injury and get back to work.

"Well, I don't need help." He wanted to send a definite message. Push her away. It was best for them both. As he leaned toward the toaster, he wobbled just enough that it threw him off-balance. He grabbed for his crutches and dropped his toast on the floor.

Aspen retrieved it before he could. "Why don't I make you some new toast?"

"Absolutely not," he said, snatching the bread from her. "I'll just shake off the dirt."

"It's not a big deal." She reached for the bag, but he slammed his hand down on the package, squashing the loaf.

"I don't need more toast," he insisted.

"Okay, Mr. Know-It-All. At least let me get you a plate." She reached for the cupboard.

"You're just getting in my way," he said, holding the door shut.

He grabbed his plate and attempted to balance the toast and crutches at the same time. He'd need a third arm to handle this. Frustrated, he set the plate down and tried to eat while standing on one foot.

Aspen crossed her arms and leaned against the counter. "I would ask if you want me to make your life easier, but obviously, you *don't*."

"I'll stand, thanks," he muttered, swallowing a bite of toast.

"Suit yourself," she replied and started out of the room before she spun around. "You know, it's not weakness to accept help."

"I know, but I don't want *your* help right now. There's a difference."

A hurt look flashed over her face before she crossed her arms.

It was better to enforce the boundary lines now. Make it clear he didn't need her. But something underneath rattled him. It wasn't only about her, was it?

Fresh out of college, he'd learned independence and discipline were highly admired character traits rewarded by the world. As long as he could set his mind to completing a task, he'd finish it without help. Coworkers praised him. Bosses loved him. But now, his own self-reliance tottered on the brink of collapse. He couldn't even eat his breakfast.

She glared at him. "It's clear to me you need somebody's help, so when you're ready to admit it, say the word." Then she turned and left.

He rubbed his hand over his eyes. Hurting her was the last thing he wanted.

A soft, warm animal brushed against his legs. He glanced down to see Lester rubbing against his ankle.

"You're the reason for this whole mess," he mumbled to the

oblivious creature. Irritation bubbled to the surface as he threw his toast down. He needed to get out of the house as quickly as possible.

When he'd agreed to this temporary arrangement, he thought he could handle his feelings. Aspen was his friend. Never mind that she stirred him in ways no other woman had before.

But in the scheme of things, he'd miscalculated one minor detail. He liked to *win*. Letting Ryder date Aspen was like throwing away a big competition. All his instincts told him it was wrong.

CHAPTER SEVEN

ASPEN

Aspen picked up the wooden box from her dresser and ran her fingers over the heart carved in the lid of Lizzie's jewelry box. The one thing she'd yet to open.

As soon as Aspen moved in, she'd cleared Aunt Lizzie's things from her room. Emotionally, she couldn't fathom seeing her great-aunt's belongings without feeling terribly sad. But practically, she needed space for her own clothes, even if she was only living there temporarily.

Until now, the jewelry box had remained untouched. As she slowly opened the lid, she was disappointed to discover only two items: a sapphire ring and a single letter.

Without unfolding the note, she immediately recognized Aunt Lizzie's handwriting, the distinctive cursive looping across the page. A strange feeling of guilt and curiosity washed over her. Why had it never been sent?

My dearest love,

The past few days, I've been agonizing over our fight, so much that I feel I should return the ring you gave me. But my heart told me no, and I've kept it, not for selfish reasons, but because it's the one reminder of your love for me. I see now that our argument was petty and not worth the price of losing you, but I was too stubborn to let you win this fight. It's only my undying love for you that compels me to write and ask for your forgiveness . . .

Aspen quickly folded the note and placed it back in the box. She shouldn't be reading this. It wasn't meant for her, and her great-aunt had never mentioned any sweetheart before. As far as Aspen knew, she had never been in a relationship, but the mention of her dearest love intrigued her.

So, Aunt Lizzie had once had a love interest. Someone who'd bought her a ring and swept her off her feet. But if Aunt Lizzie had been willing to make amends, why was the letter of apology still unsent?

A text from Megan pulled her back to the present. Her friend was waiting at the coffee shop, and she was late.

As she ran out the door, she nearly slammed into Matt. Ever since their last frustrating encounter a few days ago, he'd stayed out of her way, retreating to his bedroom and closing her off. His silence pierced like rejection, and she couldn't take any more hurt. Her body brushed his for a second, and his face expressed visible shock as he recoiled.

She laid her fingers on her chest to slow the drumbeat that knocked against her rib cage.

"Are you in a hurry?" he asked, his surprise settling into a frown.

"Heading to the French Press to meet Meg."

His gaze flicked to her hand, which was still resting on her heart. "You feeling okay?"

She dropped her hand immediately. "Yeah, yeah. I'm fine."

Her heart skipped again. Good thing he couldn't see it or he'd drag her to the hospital. "What's with all the questions?"

"You only touch your heart when it's bothering you."

"I do this all the time." She patted the spot where her ticker was. "Old habit. I'm supposed to get more heart tests this year." Never mind that she couldn't afford it since she lost her health insurance. It gave her another reason to hurry and sell the inn.

"What tests?" Matt frowned. Spending so much time around the house meant he had nothing to do but fret over things.

"Don't worry, it's the norm for me. I'm one of those lucky people who gets monitored for life. The doctor wants to ensure that I'm okay," she said, pausing as she remembered how he'd mentioned "concerning results" and "heart surgery" in the same sentence.

"As long as you don't blow this off," he reminded her. "It's important."

So she'd missed a couple of appointments. The doctor had told her she could live with this arrhythmia her entire life and might never need treatment. He'd only been concerned at her last appointment when she'd complained about her recent symptoms. *Chest pain. Exhaustion. Irregular heartbeat.* The doctor's forehead had wrinkled into deep folds—the same look that Matt was giving her now.

"I find it interesting," she noted, "you're so worried about me taking care of myself, and you won't let anyone take care of you."

Although his ankle was slowly getting better, the fire chief had forced him to take medical leave until he could handle the physical demands of firefighting. Since then, he'd moped around the house, not allowing her to assist him.

"I told you before—"

"You don't need help," she finished for him. "I know, I know."

"Well, if you wanted"—his lips quirked at the corners—"I could use some muffins and a back rub." His smile reminded her of the Matt she remembered from high school, the guy who used to have a sense of humor.

"Yes to the muffins. No to the back rub. But I won't have time until I return."

"For the back rub?" He gave her a sly smile.

"Nice try," she said.

"Don't keep me waiting, Little Bit," he called as she left.

As Aspen entered the cafe, she spotted Meg sitting at a table near the window, her long hair pulled away from her face. Meg had always been a dark-haired beauty with curves that attracted second looks, while Aspen was the exact opposite. As kids, they'd bonded over mac-and-cheese and fruit snacks. Now, it was lattes and mochas.

The French Press Cafe smelled like earthy coffee beans and a dash of velvety hazelnut. She inhaled slowly and savored a bite of the caramel-drenched apple pie that Megan had ordered for her. Getting away from the inn was just the thing she needed.

"How's the inn coming?" Megan asked between sips of her latte.

"Slow. I'm still ripping wallpaper off the second guest room. Two more to go."

"How soon until Matt can help?"

Aspen shrugged. "Not for a while. Although he'd probably enjoy ordering me around like one of his fire crew." In some ways, it was a relief to have him out of her way. There was less tension between them.

The bell on the door jangled as Edna Long, Wild Harbor's unofficial mother hen, strolled in with her friend, Thelma. Edna's face brightened when she spied Meg and Aspen in the cafe. Her Pekingese companion, Peaches, yapped outside where she'd left him.

"How is the new inn owner?" Edna asked, her bright smile an invitation for the latest news.

Edna considered it her job to be the first to know the town gossip, but she also had an uncanny sense for figuring things out.

"I'm doing well, but I can't say the same about Matt."

Thelma clucked her tongue. "I heard about his injury. He should have known better than to climb a tree."

In Wild Harbor, keeping your life private was almost impossible.

Edna nodded in agreement. "He's in his thirties now. Time to stop acting like he's invincible. He always was a terror for his mother."

Edna had been an unofficial grandmother to Matt. In some ways, she still saw him as a wild, daring boy, instead of the logical, dependable man he'd become. Although he still had an edge of daredevil in him, time had softened it.

"At least you're not alone in that big inn," Thelma added. "Nothing worse than an empty house after someone dies."

Having Matt around had made Aspen feel more secure, especially at night. Ever since Aunt Lizzie had given him the unofficial title of inn security guard, Matt circled the house every night, locking all the doors. This was an enormous improvement from Aunt Lizzie's security plan, which was a wooden bat hidden in her closet.

But unlike Aunt Lizzie, Aspen didn't want to spend every night alone until she was in her eighties. Although she couldn't imagine marrying Ryder, she looked forward to the simple things that marriage brought—a hand to hold, a warm bed, someone to guard the door at night.

"Do either of you know if Aunt Lizzie ever had a special man in her life?" Aspen asked the ladies.

Thelma's brow wrinkled. "You mean a gentleman friend?"

"More than that," Aspen explained.

"You mean a beau." Edna clasped her hands together, her bright pink acrylic nails flashing in the light. "She never talked about one. But I always suspected that ring she wore was from someone special."

"The sapphire? It's gorgeous, although I'm trying to avoid becoming attached," Aspen admitted.

Thelma clucked her tongue in dismay. "But you wouldn't sell it, would you? I'd hate to see it leave the family."

"Of course not," Aspen said. "Just don't tell my mother."

"Lizzie wouldn't give me a straight answer about that ring," Edna said. "Her only reply was that it was a gift and none of my business." Edna laughed at the memory. "I wasn't offended. She was my elder, and I respected her privacy."

"But now I'll never know!" Aspen picked at her pie. Why hadn't she asked her great-aunt these questions before?

"Maybe there's a reason." Thelma shrugged.

"Don't worry. The answer will come." Edna's eyes sparkled. "Never say never."

"That's what Aunt Lizzie always said. But she left few clues behind." Her great-aunt had been meticulous about throwing away the past. Except for the letter in her jewelry box, Aspen doubted any other interesting belongings remained.

"What about the travel writers? Are they coming soon?" Edna asked. "Lizzie wanted to treat them like royalty."

"What travel writers?" Aspen glanced at the two women, frustrated that Aunt Lizzie had left her so little to go on.

"The Richardsons," Edna answered. "They're writing a new book about the inns of the Great Lakes, and they plan to include The Red Poppy Inn."

Aspen's eyes widened. "That's who is booked for tomorrow." Aspen scrambled from her seat, offering an apologetic look to Megan. "I'm sorry I can't stay. I didn't know who the Richardsons were."

"Do you want help?" Megan asked. "I can fold towels and do

laundry. Whatever it takes."

"Aren't you headed into work?"

"I am, but if this is important, Finn will give me the day off. I can always finish my stories later." Her engagement to the editor in chief meant that Meg's hours were more flexible now, a nice perk to a once very strict job.

"I could use all the help I can get." Aspen hurried to the door, her mind set on one thing: Making the inn spotless for her guests. "Of all the people, travel writers! I'm totally unprepared for this." She threw up her hands in exasperation.

Edna rushed over. "Honey, it's going to be okay. Lizzie told me once that the best thing you can do is make your guests comfortable. I've always tried to take that advice to heart. Be yourself and you'll charm the socks off them." Edna squeezed her arm in support. "You can do this."

For the rest of the day, Aspen and Megan cleaned and prepped the inn for the Richardsons. They attacked the house with mop buckets, dust rags, and vacuum sweepers. Aspen insisted on hiding any trace of redecorating and closed off the two rooms she had torn apart. Even Matt pitched in, sitting when he could and taking breaks as needed. In a few hours, he'd fixed several small things, including a broken towel holder, a faulty blind, and a door handle that had remained stubbornly stuck. Assigning him tasks had given him a purpose and considerably improved his mood.

By the end of the day, they'd made the place look presentable, leaving Aspen exhausted, but happy. Matt had settled into a kitchen chair, propping his bum ankle on the seat.

"I'm really grateful for all your work today," she said, filling a glass with water. "I can't tell you how much this means to me." She hoped her words cracked the wall between them, even a little.

His eyes caught hers, and a tiny spark flashed in them. "You don't have to thank me."

"You've been quiet lately. Is something wrong?" She filled another glass and set it in front of him, her final token of gratitude.

He shook his head.

If he didn't want to talk to her, fine. But she couldn't bear months of his silence. Ever since she'd moved in, something rumbled under the surface of their relationship, and the tree accident had only exacerbated it. She wanted them to return to that comfortable place where they could tell each other whatever was on their minds and not hold back.

Being with Matt was soothing, like a pair of old jeans that fit just right. But living together had changed everything in their relationship, and she wasn't sure they would ever get back to that place again.

"Nothing is wrong." His words stopped her from leaving.

"Then why are you acting this way?"

"What way?"

"Like you're mad at me," Aspen explained. "Every time I'm around, you're in this funk."

"It's not you," he insisted.

"Then what is it?"

Matt averted his gaze, then took a swig of water.

If he wasn't willing to volunteer the information, she'd have to get it out of him, no matter what.

"Is it Ryder?" His look told her what she needed to know. "Why don't you two get along?"

"It's not just Ryder." His jaw clenched. "But that guy rubs me the wrong way."

"I can tell. You could start a wildfire with the friction between you two."

"Is he treating you well?" Matt's question caught her off guard. "Like how I would treat you?"

Did he think Ryder wouldn't treat her like a lady?

She pulled a curl behind her ear. "Why would you ask that

question? Of course, or I wouldn't be dating him."

Matt nodded. "Good." His face walled off.

"Don't you trust my judgment?" She couldn't let it go. The tension between them rippled.

He looked away. "I do. I just don't trust *him*."

She lowered into a chair across the table, her gaze glued to him. "Why?"

Matt bristled in his seat.

She was making him uncomfortable, but she would not back down until he told her.

He stiffened. "I can't tell you," he responded coolly.

"Why are you more loyal to him than me? If you know something about Ryder, spill it."

"I know how he used to be. Doesn't mean it's true now." Matt played with his glass. "I don't want you dating anyone who doesn't treat you right. You deserve better."

"Like you?"

"I might be biased, but yes."

"Might be?" she huffed. "As if you have any right to tell me who to date."

"Are we friends?"

"Based on the way you've been treating me lately, I'm not sure."

He shrank back in his seat and glared out the window. "I'm sorry if I haven't been Mr. Chipper lately. I've been *adjusting* to the situation." He said the words precisely, his lips wrapping around the words to make a point.

She understood how hard it was to admit his weakness. "I know this wasn't part of the plan," she said carefully.

"What plan?"

"You're a planner, and I essentially moved in and changed everything on you. Am I right?"

"It has been . . . a challenge," he admitted. "Lizzie gave me a sweet deal here. It was more than I deserved."

"That's what she was good at doing," Aspen agreed. "Always giving people more. It's why she was such a fabulous hostess."

"I can see how you're like her."

Aspen laughed. "You mean I have a future as an eccentric senior citizen?"

"How you treat people. You're incredibly generous." Matt smiled, and her stomach did a nervous tilt.

"I always thought that was a weakness." Aspen lowered her eyes and hesitated. "Tell me why you don't get along with Ryder."

"Ask him instead," Matt said.

"I have."

"And?"

"He said you were always on his case. Picking apart the way he worked. Criticizing how he didn't follow instructions."

"He isn't wrong," Matt replied. "Ryder and I had different ways of working. He always did things his own way. I wanted them done right. The two of us were fire and ice."

"He thought you never liked him."

"I didn't," Matt agreed.

"But is there something else?" Aspen asked.

"It's complicated."

She could tell he was hedging. "If you can't be more specific, then you need to stop taking it out on me," she concluded.

He rubbed the back of his neck uncomfortably. "Ryder used to brag about his dating life when he worked at the fire station," Matt finally admitted, not meeting her gaze. "The way he treated women always enraged me. He didn't care about them. It was all about the conquest." He stopped for a second and their eyes met. "Now I have to imagine that's you. The last thing I want is for you to get hurt."

Aspen touched Matt's arm from across the table. "You never have to worry about that. I wouldn't date him if I thought he was using me."

Even while she said it, there was a hesitancy behind her words. What if she didn't see it? What if she was just another pawn in Ryder's game? And how would she know until she lost?

He glanced at her hand on his arm, then slowly removed it. "You shouldn't do that," he whispered.

The way he touched her hand made shivers erupt across her body.

He moved a safe distance away from her. Under the kitchen light, a slight glow caught the high planes of his cheekbones.

"Stay right there," Aspen demanded suddenly. She rushed to grab her camera.

As soon as he saw it, he turned away. "You know how I feel about pictures."

"Just a few shots. Please?" She held up the camera and took a test picture.

He palmed the lens. "If you don't listen, I'm going to take it from you like last time."

He wasn't kidding either. It was hopeless to strong-arm him into it.

"I need to get back into form again for the contest," she begged. "Can you at least be my practice subject? If you hate it, I won't ask again. Promise."

Matt groaned. "If I do this for you, then you owe me. You know that, right?"

"That's fair," Aspen agreed. "What do you want?"

His eyes darkened. "That's a dangerous question."

"I give you one rule," she said. "Don't ask me to stop dating Ryder."

He paused, wet his lips, then gave her one nod. "Deal."

As she lifted the camera, he stiffened. "This isn't my thing." He started to leave, but she grabbed his arm, pulling him back. This time, he didn't resist.

"Give me a chance. I can help you," she pleaded. He dropped his gaze to her touch. She pulled away, suddenly remembering his request from earlier. "I'm helping you get into the same position as before. Let me at least place you where the light is good."

She backed him against the counter and placed his palms on the edges, like he'd been standing earlier. She snapped some pictures, but Matt grew more rigid and uncomfortable with every shot.

"You need to shake out your arms. You're gripping the counter too hard." She eased his hands away and rubbed them between her own. "Loosen up."

His fingers were warm and pliable, like a giant's enveloping her own.

He stared at the ceiling in frustration. "I'm trying, but it's so hard when you're . . ." He ripped his palms away from her.

"When I'm what?" she asked, confused by his sudden outburst.

A look of pent-up emotion swept across him. "Touching me." His voice was low and warm.

As her eyes trailed up his neck, she realized he was focused on her, not in the same angry way as before, but in a passionate one.

Trying to position his body for the practice photo was strangely intimate, but she'd thought it hadn't affected him. His emotional fortress had always appeared impenetrable. Only a strong woman could pull it down. Not someone like her.

What she hadn't expected was that she'd overestimated his defenses. He was standing inches from her, staring into her eyes, a deep-seated longing crumbling the walls between them.

For a moment, his gaze dropped to her lips like he was going to kiss her, and admittedly, it would be hard to resist if he tried.

But she also knew this would ruin everything. Her relationship with Ryder. Her plan to sell the inn. Most of all, her friendship with Matt. She couldn't kiss him and expect things to be the same.

Although everything in her body pulled her toward him, she forced herself away. He wasn't hers. He never would be. That was the painful truth. Her heart squeezed like a tiny match forced out with a quick puff.

"I was trying to pose you for the picture," she stammered, looking at the floor, anywhere but him. "I'm sorry if it came across some other way."

"You shouldn't do that to me," he whispered.

"I didn't know I was doing anything wrong," she admitted.

"That's just it," he replied, his eyes still blazing. "You weren't. With you, everything feels right." He turned to leave.

"Matt, wait." She reached him before he made it to his bedroom, where he'd close her off for good.

She tried to block his way, but the look he gave her told her he wasn't messing around. "I'm going to run over your half-pint frame if you don't get out of the way."

"I just need one more thing," she begged.

"No." He tried to pick her up, but his ankle was still too weak.

She stood her ground even though she dwarfed him considerably. She may not have his strength, but she made up for it with spunk.

"What did you mean by saying it didn't feel wrong?" Her mind spun in confused circles. Through the years, they'd flirted and fought, teased and tormented each other, but she never had believed there could be anything more than friendship.

All she knew was that her body lit up whenever he was near, her heart thrumming happily in response. In their relationship, she was the only one with feelings to hide.

"Tell me," she insisted again.

His eyes traced her face as he lifted his palm and gently caressed her chin. "The only thing you need to know is that as long as you're with Ryder, *never* touch me that way again."

CHAPTER EIGHT

MATT

Matt slid on a pair of shorts and pulled open the blinds, squinting as the early morning light reflected across the lake. The waves rolled in like a furling carpet, but he wouldn't have time to swim. Although his ankle still twinged painfully, he was determined to work on the landscaping, tackling a mass of weeds to make it presentable for the travel writers arriving today.

Lost in his mental to-do list, he crept to the bathroom and nudged open the door. Aspen was leaning over the sink, dressed in a knee-length fuzzy bathrobe, balancing a toothbrush in her mouth. She squealed and nearly lost it while he backed away apologizing profusely. "I didn't know you were in there."

Aspen peeked around the doorway, her cheeks glowing like a neon sign. The toothbrush was gone, but there was still a smear of blue toothpaste on her lips. "Next time, could you at least knock?"

"Next time, could you lock the door?" he asked.

"Didn't you hear the water?"

"I didn't hear anything." His eyes dropped to her mouth. "You have something right here." He pointed to the corner of her lips. With one smooth stroke, she brushed the toothpaste away, then slammed the door shut. "Give me one more minute," she called from inside, embarrassment coloring her tone.

He trudged back to his bedroom and flopped onto the bed. If this was going to work—and he desperately wanted it to—they needed to set more ground rules. Locking the bathroom door for one. And two, no more traipsing around in that bathrobe. Or better yet, she needed a new robe, preferably one that covered her ankles.

Most important of all, she could never touch him like she had last night. The mere brush of her fingers was overwhelming. Even worse, a weakness of his. More than anything, he hated feeling weak.

There had to be another way, one that didn't involve his body reacting like Fourth of July fireworks. If he kept his distance, it would keep them apart temporarily. She was dating Ryder, and he believed in honoring her wishes, even if that meant hiding his feelings.

Wandering to the kitchen, he downed some coffee and attempted to devise a plan that didn't make things more awkward between them.

When Aspen entered fully dressed, her hair still damp from the shower, he cleared his throat.

"Sorry about walking in on you like that." He tried not to sound weird, even though he felt like an idiot.

She poured coffee and held the mug to her lips. "It's not your fault. My mind is on the Richardsons' arrival. I'm a complete mess today." She downed the drink in one long gulp.

"Tell me what we need to do first," he offered.

She cocked her head. "Wow, this is a switch from last night's failed photo shoot. Why aren't you this cooperative when I take your picture?"

"Pictures are different." He avoided an argument. "Do you have a list for today?"

"Preparing food and finishing last-minute touches on their guest room. I feel like Aunt Lizzie would have baked something homemade for breakfast."

"Muffins," Matt answered. "That was her go-to. She made dozens of them every week."

"I'm not the baker Aunt Lizzie was, but I can make a decent blueberry muffin." Aspen opened the pantry and grabbed a bag of flour. "I'll have you prep the tins and I'll get the ingredients."

Matt froze, his eyes flitting across the cupboards. "And where are those?"

"You mean you don't know?" She gave him a wry smile and then opened a few doors.

"I may have lived here, but Lizzie never allowed me to go riffling through her drawers. She didn't want her system messed up."

"Like her inn reservation system that I'm too dumb to figure out? If I have any more surprise guests show up this summer, I'm going to kick myself for not selling this place like my mom instructed."

Matt searched a cupboard by the stove. "You said you wanted a few guests so you could pay for the redecorating. Look at it as a blessing."

"But I'm not good with spontaneity like Aunt Lizzie."

"You don't have to be Aunt Lizzie," Matt told her. "Just say no."

"That feels *very* anti-Lizzie." Aspen opened a narrow drawer and pulled out two tins, waving them over her head. "Look!"

As she handed Matt the items, a blue gem sparkled on her left hand. He clenched his jaw, anticipating her answer.

"Where did you get that?" He nodded toward the ring.

She fingered it self-consciously. "I found it in Aunt Lizzie's jewelry box. It fits perfectly." She held her hand out for him.

"Did you ever see her wear this? I'm wondering who gave it to her."

As long as it wasn't a gift from Ryder, he didn't care.

"A fancy ring like that?" He shook his head. "She was way too practical for jewelry."

"The ring was next to an unsent letter." A guilty look passed over Aspen's face, like he'd caught her spying. "Did she ever mention anyone who could have given her this?"

Matt shrugged. "Not that I know of."

"The letter mentioned a fight and how she wanted to give back the gift. She apologized but never sent it. After reading it, I had this strange feeling that there's more to the story."

Matt gazed at the blue stone on Aspen's finger. He wasn't really the jewelry type, but he had to admit it looked good on her. "How so?"

"Like I need to do something. Perhaps return it to the man she loved." She spun the ring around her finger. "I don't know how long I'll keep it, but until I find him, I'll enjoy it."

"Why would you give it away? It's yours now."

"Half of it is mine," Aspen corrected, as she measured flour into a cup. "Technically, I split everything with my sister. But if I can't pay my bills on the inn, I might have to sell it."

Matt shook his head. "Not if I can help it. That ring fits you perfectly. You should keep it." His voice was firm.

Aspen shrugged. "I don't know if Jessica will let me. She has expensive taste, and Chase used to indulge her. Perhaps there's something else she'd want, and we can make an even trade."

"When is she coming?"

"Not until we're accepting an offer," Aspen said as she added more dry ingredients. "It's better if she's not involved."

"Why's that?" Matt didn't know Jessica as well as Aspen, but he always sensed that Jessica was the boss.

"I love my sister, but she makes everything more difficult.

With her recent divorce, I'd rather she stay in Atlanta until we're ready to sign papers."

"But you told me she doesn't want the inn."

"She doesn't." Aspen spooned some baking powder into the bowl. "But she complicates things. It's her superpower."

He gave the wooden spoon a hard stir and flour flew out of the bowl, dotting his shirt with white. He tried to wipe it with his hand, but that only made the flour smear across his dark clothes even more.

"I'm making a mess." He wiped his hands on his shorts.

As she glanced at his flour-splattered shirt, her lips curled into a smile. "An apron might have saved your shirt, but not your face."

He rubbed a hand across his left cheek.

She shook her head. "Let me help." She hesitated. "If you're okay with it?"

At least she had acknowledged his request from last night. He nodded and her hand quickly stroked his jaw.

"The flour was stuck in your whiskers." When she was this close, it was easy for him to forget that he was supposed to be staying away from her.

As the warmth of her hand moved across his cheek, he caught the curl of her eyelashes forming a half-moon shape. Her lips were so close now, he wanted to trace them with his finger.

"Excuse me." An unfamiliar voice caused Aspen to pull away with a jerk.

A man and woman stood in the entrance, their faces a mixture of weariness and relief. The man wore a navy polo shirt and khaki shorts, while the woman dressed in a vibrant sea-blue flowing skirt with a yellow flowered blouse and a stunning wide belt. They seemed like the type of affluent people her parents would brunch with. An awkward pause punctuated the silence before the woman's face melted into a smile.

"We didn't mean to scare you. Long trip. We're just glad to

be here." The woman put her hand out. Her stacked metal bracelets jangled. "I'm Lisa Richardson. Are you the new owner?"

"Yes, yes." Aspen attempted a polished front. "I'm Aspen." She shook Lisa's hand, and the bracelets clanged together like silverware. "This is Matt."

Lisa nodded at Matt, then turned to the man next to her. "My husband, Ted. We have reservations for tonight, but we arrived a little early. I hope that's okay."

"Oh, it's fine!" Aspen exclaimed, her voice lilting higher with nervousness.

Given that it was only eight in the morning, they were a lot earlier than expected. They hadn't even made the muffins yet.

Aspen straightened her shirt, trying to maintain a polished facade. Matt was relieved that she had at least changed out of her bathrobe.

"Unfortunately, your room isn't quite ready yet," Aspen said.

"Oh, we expected that," Ted explained. "We made good time on the road this morning and thought we'd drop off our luggage early so we could spend the day exploring Wild Harbor."

"Leave your luggage with me," Matt interrupted as Ted examined the crown molding. "I'll make sure it gets taken to your room."

"Wow," Lisa said, admiring Aspen's hand. "That's a beautiful ring." Then she glanced at Matt. "You have very good taste."

Matt shot Aspen a look. "Actually . . ."

Lisa interrupted him with a hand on his arm. "Don't be embarrassed. It's wonderful to see a young couple in love. I'm sorry if we walked in on you."

"Oh." Aspen's face heated. "Um, well, we're not—" Her voice wobbled. She looked over at Matt for help.

He lifted his eyebrows. *Tell them the truth. NOW.*

"No explanation required." Lisa patted Aspen's shoulder. "I can see it in your eyes."

Matt stared hard at Aspen, but Lisa seemed unfazed. "You're the first young couple I've met on our inn research tour. Management companies run most of the places these days. No more family-run establishments. I have a feeling this inn is special."

"It is special," Aspen agreed. "But just to set the record straight, we're . . . um . . . not married." The confession unfurled like she was guilty as charged.

Lisa laughed and waved her hand. "Oh, I see. An engagement ring, then?"

"No," Matt corrected her quickly.

The woman tilted her head, studying Matt with a gleam in her eyes. "Oh, of course. Young couples don't always feel the need to make it official. It's obvious you two are madly in love. Don't you think, Ted?"

Ted absently nodded, scanning the home's architectural details.

Matt's shoulders tensed as he stared at Aspen. *Do something.*

She responded with a tiny, helpless shrug.

"This will add so much to our book. A young couple running an inn together. How very *romantic.*" Her lips slid over the word like she was rolling it around in her mouth like wine. "I daresay this idea is perfect for some travel magazines I have connections with. I can get you national exposure." Lisa clapped her hands together with a flourish. "Thank you for letting us impose on you early. What time are afternoon snacks?"

"Excuse me?" A flicker of panic flashed across Aspen's face.

"When we reserved, the lady mentioned snacks."

Aspen glanced at Matt, her eyes wide with alarm. Matt had forgotten to mention Lizzie's midafternoon charcuterie board.

"Four," Aspen responded as Matt said, "Three."

Aspen frowned at him.

"We'll come at three thirty, then." Lisa winked. "Don't go to too much trouble for us, you lovebirds." Lisa wiggled her fingers in a cutesy wave before she grabbed Ted's arm to leave.

Aspen turned to Matt, her cheeks still flushed. "What are we going to do? She thinks we're . . . together."

A laugh escaped his lips. "You got yourself into this mess by not explaining the truth."

"Me? What about you?"

"You let her assume we were a couple."

Aspen covered her eyes. "I felt cornered once she fell in love with the idea of presenting our inn with a romantic backstory."

"Then set her straight this afternoon," he insisted.

"Or . . ." Aspen clasped her hands together and placed them against her lips. "What if we don't?"

Matt shook his head, his eyes intense. "Remove that thought from your mind right now. We're not pretending anything."

"I don't mean pretend, exactly. We just don't offer all the details. Tell her we've been friends since childhood and let her think what she wants."

This was a terrible idea, but Aspen seemed set on it. "What happens when this romantic backstory of ours goes public?"

"I'll ask to see it before it goes to print. Right now, we don't have to do anything different from normal. The ring was enough to make her believe you gave it to me."

"Aspen, what's the point?" he challenged her.

"If the inn gets featured in a travel magazine, it will give us more attention regionally. It's possible we could get a better offer from an investor."

"That's a big *if*," he reminded her.

"But what could it hurt?"

Matt rubbed the back of his neck. "Did you forget you have a boyfriend? What if he finds out?"

"He won't. He's working for the next few days. They'll be gone by the time I see him."

"What are the requirements? Nothing like . . ." He circled his hand near his face where she had wiped the flour off his face right before they walked in. "I have a no-touching rule, remember?"

She rolled her eyes. "Just pretend you like me in a friendly way."

Pretend to like her? That wouldn't be hard.

She focused on the muffin batter. "Nothing romantic. Be a gentleman. That's it."

"That's it? It's a tall order to play along with this little charade."

"Can you handle it?" She lifted her eyebrows. Another dangerous question.

"Of course," he promised before escaping outside for some fresh air. He could handle anything. As long as she didn't touch him, he could pretend to be her boyfriend. What could possibly go wrong?

CHAPTER NINE

"I can do this," Aspen whispered as she stopped in front of the polished walnut buffet and placed a cream cheese platter with crackers and vegetables on it. Her heart banged against her rib cage like an erratic pinball. She didn't know if she could pull this off. Her first hosting gig was now complicated by the added pressure of acting like she and Matt were a couple.

She straightened the oatmeal raisin cookies she had whipped up that afternoon. Her great-aunt would be proud of how she'd pulled things together at the last minute.

But the idea of pulling off their romantic charade twisted her stomach into knots. Aspen was a notorious people pleaser. By offering the fake story Lisa wanted to believe instead of the one that really existed, she'd assumed it would boost the couple's review of the inn. The charade was a desperate attempt to erase Aspen's self-doubt while trying to please the two most important guests who'd ever stayed there.

"Have you seen my work gloves?" Matt charged through the

back door, the sweat pouring down his neck from the soaring humidity.

"You can't come in here." She pointed to his mud-caked shoes. "I just cleaned, and you're tracking dirt everywhere."

He backed up reluctantly. "Any chance you know where they might be?" A smudge of dirt stretched across his neck. She wanted to wipe it off, but after his no-touch warning, she wasn't about to break her promise.

"Not a clue. But the Richardsons are returning at any moment, and I just put out food." She bent down to wipe the floor. "How is your ankle holding up?" Black soil spotted his brace.

"My ankle will be fine. It's my hands that are hurting. I have two broken blisters already from trying to dig out landscaping."

"I appreciate your hard work, but do you really want to look like that when the Richardsons return?" She gestured toward his dirty appearance.

"Like what?" He glanced at his clothes. "It's how you're supposed to look when ripping out an oversized bush."

"Can't you take a break? I was hoping you'd connect with Ted while I chat with Lisa. Engage him somehow."

"Ted's more interested in the house than any conversation he might have with me. My job is to maintain the landscaping, not mingle like I'm at a social event."

"But I can't be alone. I need you," she pleaded.

"For what?" His tone was doubtful.

"Moral support?" She shrugged helplessly. "I'm not exactly confident in my hosting abilities. If my first guests weren't reviewing the inn, I wouldn't feel any pressure. But this . . ." She gestured to the tray of food that carried so much importance. "This scares me."

Matt's face softened. "The food looks perfect. All you need to do is be yourself, and when you don't know what to do, ask, *What would Aunt Lizzie do?*"

"And if I don't have a clue what she'd do?" Aspen asked.

Matt wiped the sweat off his forehead with the back of his wrist. "Let me clean up and I'll stay awhile. Just don't expect me to do this every time. Only once."

Aspen clapped her hands together. "Thank you, thank you, thank you," she repeated.

Just then, the front door made its usual squeaky sound. "We're back!" Lisa's voice rang out across the house.

Aspen rushed to greet them, transforming into hostess mode as Matt disappeared to shower and change.

"How was your day?"

"A delight in every way," Lisa chirped, looking windblown and sunburned. "We toured the coastline, shopped downtown, and even discovered the cutest little chocolate shop."

"I'd love some water." Ted dabbed his forehead with a handkerchief while examining the bookshelf in the living room. Lizzie had been an ardent fan of cozy mysteries, and her shelves were filled to the brim.

Lisa sank into a chair at the dining room table and crossed her legs. "Make that two waters. According to my fitness tracker, we walked almost ten thousand steps. My legs are exhausted." She kicked off her sandals and stroked one foot. "Everyone was so friendly. They simply didn't have a bad thing to say about this place. It's like Mayberry with a lake." Then she leaned back to address Ted. "Be sure to write that down for the book."

Aspen handed Lisa and Ted their waters, hoping their guests would keep the conversation rolling. As long as Lisa didn't circle back to her and Matt, they'd be fine.

"If you ever plan a honeymoon, it will be hard to beat this cute little town," Lisa gushed, holding up her glass of water.

"Oh, I've never thought about where I'd go." Aspen glanced at Lisa, who was staring at her peculiarly. "It's tough to leave when you run an inn."

"Oh, honey, everyone needs to get away. Where is that young man of yours?"

Before she could answer, Matt entered the room.

"Ah, there he is," Lisa said. "We were just talking about you." Her eyes flitted across his soft white shirt and dark-wash jeans.

He smiled. "Oh, really? About what?"

"Oh, it's nothing," Aspen interjected, attempting to keep Lisa from answering. "The Richardsons were telling me about their day."

"As I was saying, this place is incredible," Lisa gushed. "I told Aspen that you'll never find a honeymoon spot as wonderful. She claimed she's not even thought about it. Surely, if you get married, you won't let her talk you out of one?"

Matt's smile suddenly vanished. "We haven't talked about it yet." He cleared his throat and recovered his composure. "But when we do, I'm planning on finding the most amazing honeymoon spot ever."

Aspen couldn't bring herself to meet his eyes. To her surprise, his whole hesitation with the arrangement had now turned into a game.

Lisa nodded, satisfied with his answer. "The cream cheese dip looks delicious." She scooped a dollop on her plate. "I'm curious how you two met."

"We grew up in the same neighborhood," Aspen stated. "Their house was a second home."

"After she started coming over, she wouldn't leave," he teased.

"Childhood sweethearts. How darling," Lisa added.

"Not at first," Matt admitted. "She did everything in her power to annoy me."

"That's usually how it begins," Lisa concluded. "Ted and I met on a blind date. It was mostly a disaster until Ted hugged me at the end of the night. That's when I saw what a sweet, kind man he was."

Aspen couldn't imagine Ted hugging anyone. If opposites always attracted, then Ted and Lisa were the perfect example.

"So when did it become apparent there was more between you two?" Lisa asked, nibbling a cracker.

Aspen's heart ping-ponged in response. "I thought we were discussing the inn. Aren't you writing a book?" Aspen wanted to dodge the question to save her from concocting a tale. Or worse, admitting her feelings accidentally.

"Oh, we'll get to the inn. I want the backstory." Lisa turned her attention to Matt. "When did you know you liked her?"

Matt leaned against the wall and sunk his hands into his pockets. "Why don't you ask Aspen first? I want to hear the answer."

His eyes swung to hers, and she suddenly felt forced into the spotlight. He wasn't going to let her slink away from the question.

"Oh, well, it's not that interesting." Aspen waved her hand in the air, hoping Lisa would drop the subject.

"Sure it is," Matt countered, his lips quirking at the corners.

Aspen glared at him. "It was a *really* long time ago. So long ago, I can hardly remember the details."

"Do tell," Matt said, amusement in his voice. He was enjoying this way too much.

Aspen gave him a look. "Matt is four years older, so he was this intimidating eighteen-year-old, all legs and arms from a massive growth spurt. I was invisible to him."

Lisa nodded knowingly. "Ah, yes. Teen crush."

It may have been typical, but it wasn't for Aspen. She'd been looking at him this way for so long, she couldn't recall a time when she didn't adore him.

And that was the problem. She'd always adored him. But he'd never looked at her in the same way. Why would he, when she was your average girl next door?

Lisa turned to Matt. "And you?"

Aspen couldn't bear to look at Matt, so she fiddled with the serving tray on the buffet. The awkward pause spidered down her back.

"I was home on college break," Matt began. "She was getting ready for prom with my sisters. When she came downstairs, I couldn't stop staring. That was before she left with some jerk from the lacrosse team who didn't deserve her."

As she turned around, the heat of his gaze was searing. Was this part of the charade? If not, she'd been clueless to his fierce reaction that night. But now, she couldn't even look him in the eye. Her gaze flitted to the red embroidered flowers on the tablecloth.

"I sat in the living room and waited," he continued. "I knew she'd come home eventually."

She remembered that first dance. The pinkish-red spaghetti-strap dress. The sparkly choker necklace she'd borrowed. She'd twirled in circles in front of the full-length mirror, her blonde curls carefully pinned back, cascading over her shoulders. A little girl playing dress-up in a teenager's body.

She hadn't known her date all that well when he'd asked her to the prom. *Rookie mistake.* As soon as they'd arrived, he'd quickly dumped her for a tall brunette. Megan and Lily had been lifesavers, linking arms and dragging her to a corner of the dance floor they claimed as their own. They hooted, shimmied, and shook their curls, the way only high school girls can and not look like fools. She walked away that night learning that friendship was so much better than love at this age. Twice the fun and none of the heartbreak.

When the girls had burst through the door at midnight, Matt had still been waiting, a sulky look on his face. His gaze had washed over her in disapproval. That was the first time she'd noticed it: he had on this weird expression that she'd dubbed his *bodyguard eyes.*

Megan and Lily had rushed upstairs to change, leaving

Aspen in a circle of lamplight, watching for her dad's pickup to rumble into their drive.

Matt brooded in silence as she stared out the window.

"How was your date?" he finally asked.

"It was fine." She didn't want to confess that her date had abandoned her.

"Fine, huh? You don't sound impressed," he concluded.

She shrugged. "I can stand anyone for a night." Never mind that her date hadn't lasted the evening.

"You deserve better," he blurted out.

The memory rippled like an icy wave through her body, sending a shiver down her arms.

Matt looked at Lisa. "I didn't like that guy who took her to prom. After that, I didn't want her dating anyone else."

Lisa nodded, fully enraptured, as Aspen turned his words over to see if there was any grain of truth in them.

He was good at embellishing his memories and letting Lisa believe what she wanted.

"Now that's a love story right there." Lisa tapped the table for emphasis, then turned to Aspen. "What did you think of him saying you deserved better?" Lisa rested her chin on her hand. She was eating up this story.

Aspen shook her head. "You don't really want to know."

"Oh, I do." Matt responded so quickly she didn't even have time to think.

"I was mad," she answered. "What right did you have to decide who I went out with?" Whenever she had a date, Aspen had sensed this weird vibe. It was like he couldn't turn off his protective instincts.

Something flickered in Matt's expression, and Aspen wondered if he'd sensed her conflicting emotions back then.

"But the other part of me was relieved," she admitted. "Because after every bad date, he'd be there waiting to make sure I was alright."

Neither of them said anything while Lisa sipped her water. "And?"

"And what?" Aspen lowered into a chair. "The rest is history."

Lisa laughed. "You're skipping the best part. The moment someone finally admitted the truth about their feelings."

How could she explain to Lisa that the story was over? The grand gesture never transpired. After all these years, nothing had happened between them worth retelling. Aspen had kept her feelings tucked away like a carefully guarded secret.

Matt cleared his throat. "I confessed last year after asking her to the town festival." His voice was wooden, punctuated by false notes.

Even though they'd attended the summer festival together, Matt had made it clear it was not a date. He'd played carnival games most of the night, ignoring her to shoot off a gun and compete for cheap stuffed animals. There hadn't been one thing remotely romantic about the night.

"You jumped from high school to last year," Lisa noted. "What happened in between? Did you date other people? There's a sizable gap in the story."

Neither Aspen nor Matt responded. More than a decade had passed, and what could Aspen say? Matt had become her litmus test. Her standard for every date. Every potential candidate had to line up to him, an impossible gauge. Hands down, he outshone everyone, including Ryder.

But Ryder's qualities were strong—traits similarly matched to Matt's, which made him a close contender. In some ways, he was like her *substitute Matt*. Almost as good, but not quite. But was she okay with second best? She had to be. Matt had never loved her that way.

"Only when it was the right time," Matt told Lisa. "We had to get everyone else out of our system to finally realize there was no one else."

Aspen shifted in her chair as he leaned back, hands still deep in his pockets, his gaze meeting hers. *Bodyguard eyes again.*

Was he thinking of Ryder? Or some other jerk she'd dated years ago? Her mind circled through this short list, and it always ended with Matt.

After every date, he'd ask her the same question: *Is he the one you want to be with forever?*

No wonder she couldn't find a guy that measured up, not when Matt was setting her standards so high. Maybe this was the reason she was still single. He'd taught her to expect better. To expect someone *like him*, even though she couldn't have him. He was the only one off-limits to her.

He'd causally skipped twelve years in his storytelling like there was nothing remotely interesting about their relationship. But did his memory, like hers, pause on the night that had changed everything? It was a story she'd never confess to Lisa or anyone.

A few years after that prom date, Aspen had returned from another dating disaster, lamenting to Megan about her heartache. She was a novice at love, totally unprepared for an unrelenting losing streak of bad boyfriends.

It was Matt who'd found her waiting on her front porch, too sad to go inside. He offered to sit with her and listened in silence as she recounted her problems. When she stood to go, that's when she noticed his eyes had turned dark, the way the lake appeared when black clouds rolled in.

He leaned in to say goodbye, but she'd misinterpreted his hug for something more. In one disastrous moment, she'd closed her eyes and tilted her head to meet his lips.

There were a few seconds of warmth before his hands grabbed her shoulders and pushed her away.

He looked furious and scared. Then he'd given her one ultimatum: *Never ever let that happen again.*

Those were his words. *Never ever.* Like two bullet holes in her heart.

For a glorious moment, she'd made herself believe that he could love her. Then, without a single explanation, he'd crushed the moment for good.

After that, she questioned her chance at love. What was wrong with her? Was she really not girlfriend material? Those doubts chipped away at her heart, scarring it over time so that she doubted whether she could find someone who truly loved her.

Now here they were, forced to replay the messy middle they'd avoided for so many years. He'd kept his word, and neither of them had ever brought up that disastrous kiss again.

Lisa was staring at them now, a smile playing on her lips. "Well, I'm glad you are together now."

"Me, too," Matt added, locking eyes with Aspen until she could feel the heat building in her neck. Even if he was doing this for her, she needed to stop this ridiculous charade before it got out of hand.

"It turned out the way it was supposed to," Aspen said, before turning toward Matt. "Don't you agree?"

"Right," he added. "Meant to be." With a few strides, he closed the gap between them, wrapping himself around her so that she was banded inside his arms. Her head melted against his chest as she buried her nose in his shirt. It smelled so much like him she wanted to roll in the scent. Her body folded naturally into his as her brain lapsed into sketching a still life of this hug. The curve of his arm across her back. The jut of his chin on her head. Angular lines blurred by the merging of two bodies. Pencil smudges softening the hard edges. She had always believed that loving someone meant losing those sharp edges, like a blurry filter on a photograph.

After this hug, she'd wear his scent on her for the rest of the day, a dizzying reminder of his skin on hers. Her heart settled into a contented rhythm. *Pat-pat, pat-pat.*

"Aw, how sweet," Lisa gushed, then lowered her voice. "Ted isn't a hugger."

Aspen pulled away, her still life sketch filed into her memory bank. "Neither is—" She nearly slipped and said Ryder. *Almost.* "My dad," she corrected.

Ted didn't even consider his wife's comment. Poor Lisa.

But Matt had noticed. He was looking at Aspen peculiarly, like he'd filled in the blank before she had changed her answer.

A timer dinged on the stove. "It's been lovely chatting with you." She excused herself and walked into the kitchen to turn off the timer, still reeling from their conversation and the heat of his body. How much of it was true? Did it affect Matt the way it had her? She moved to her bedroom and flopped down on the bed, where a pile of laundry sat unfolded.

A gentle knock sounded at the door. Was Lisa following her now?

She clamped her lips and prayed whoever it was would go away.

"It's Matt. Can I come in?"

She opened the door wide enough for him to enter.

He glanced around her room nervously. "I just wanted to make sure everything is okay."

"Why would it not be okay?"

"I don't know." He shifted anxiously. "I didn't want there to be any misunderstandings."

"Yeah, of course." She leaned against her bed and folded a shirt. She'd never admit that their conversation had stirred old longings. "Thanks for covering." She wanted him to think it was all a charade and that it hadn't affected her.

"I'm sorry about the hug." He looked at her uneasily, as if he'd crossed a boundary line.

If only he knew how much she enjoyed when he wrapped his arms around her. A wave of guilt swept over her. She was dating Ryder now. Not seriously, but they'd gone out enough times that she probably shouldn't be thinking of Matt that way anymore.

"With Lisa, I don't know what to expect," Aspen confessed. "She's really interested in our story. You don't think she'll publish that part, do you?"

"She wasn't taking notes. I think she just likes to hear how couples meet."

"You zipped through twelve years like it was nothing," she remarked.

"What was I supposed to say?"

"I don't know." Aspen shrugged. "If she asks us anything else, we should have a few stories worked out, like our first kiss."

A dark look flashed across his face.

"I don't mean . . ." She was backpedaling now. "I'm not trying to bring up that one time."

He glanced at the floor uncomfortably. "Avoid that story."

"From now on, I'll use Ryder's stories and say it was you. She'll never know the difference."

"No." Matt's tone was firm. "You're not using any stories about you and him."

"But we need something in case she asks."

"Absolutely not," he said, incensed at her request. "I refuse to play along if you mention him."

"Can I ask for one thing?" She didn't need his permission, but wanted him to hear her out. "Stop making me sound like I only dated idiots until I found you."

His mouth curled up at the corners. "But you *have* only dated idiots."

She took a clean sock from the laundry and threw it at him, hitting him in the chest as he caught it.

"So you think you're perfect?"

"I'm not perfect, by any means." Matt opened the door to leave. "But I know you deserve better."

CHAPTER TEN

MATT

"**D**on't wait up for us," Lisa chimed down the stairwell, her brown bob bouncing with every step. "I like to stay out late. Ted, not so much." She wore an emerald-green sheath that made her look ten years younger, while Ted had on a freshly starched white shirt and tie.

"I can't believe they require a suit coat in this sweltering heat," Ted complained, his jacket draped across his arm. They were headed to DeSoto's, a high-end restaurant that never listed prices on its menu.

"They'll have the air-conditioning cranked," she assured him. "It'll be like walking into Antarctica after being in the Sahara." She gave Aspen a wink before they left.

The Richardsons' plans offered Matt and Aspen a break from any more interrogations that evening. After Ted and Lisa waved goodbye, the pair climbed into his truck to meet his sisters at Brewster's, a greasy burger joint.

Pinwheeling through the crowded restaurant, a smile spread across Aspen's face as she scoot-bounced down the bench next to Megan, Lily, and Cassidy. The sisters immediately launched into conversation while Alex and Finn finished a pinball game in the back.

As Matt slid into the booth beside Aspen, their shoulders and legs bumped, shooting a spark through their contact points. With other girls, this wasn't an issue, but she held some sort of magic power over him.

"How are things going with your guests?" Cassidy asked while squeezing a lemon slice into her water.

"Fine, I think. But I feel like they can see right through me. They probably suspect I'm a fraud, but are too kind to say it."

"You underestimate yourself. Your guests are oblivious," Lily countered, stirring the ice in her lemonade.

"Lisa keeps asking so many questions." Aspen leaned her elbows on the table and rested her chin on her hands. "It feels like I'm under interrogation."

"She's a writer," Megan added. "Questions are key to getting a good story."

"A good story? She's asking things I wouldn't dare ask a stranger."

"Like what?" Megan eyed Aspen with curiosity.

Matt couldn't meet Aspen's eyes. He stared at the menu, hoping Aspen wouldn't mention their charade. If she did, he'd be a dead man.

"My first prom. That sort of thing."

Megan crinkled her nose. "Please don't bring up the memory. Our dresses were . . ."

"Like glittery marshmallow puffs?" Lily added.

"Worse," Megan complained.

Aspen shifted in her seat. "When my date came up, Matt couldn't help but offer his opinion." She glared at him, and it looked like daggers were going to shoot from her eyes.

"If you act like a jerk, you get labeled one," Matt concluded about her prom date, keeping his eyes on the menu, even though the list of losers didn't stop there. Aspen had dated her share of blind fools who ignored her calls, ghosted her texts, and dropped her without reason. He couldn't stand that anyone treated her that way. "Despite Lisa's questions, Aspen's got the makings of a great host. Aunt Lizzie would be proud."

Aspen turned to him, the dingy yellow light reflecting off her flushed cheeks. Packed into a booth together, he wasn't sure if she was overheated or embarrassed.

"You really think so?" A trace of doubt colored her tone.

"Yeah, I do," he assured her. "You're a natural host." He stopped himself from saying more. He wasn't trying to guilt her into staying, but Aspen still turned toward him, her gaze lingering with questions.

"Have you agreed to model for the camera yet?" Megan leaned on one elbow and gave Matt an amused smile. She knew he was camera shy and wasn't letting him off the hook.

"He let me take a few test shots," Aspen interrupted.

"You know how I feel about it," Matt argued, lifting his eyebrows. "I'm not refusing to help. I'll do whatever she wants, except for that."

Megan chewed on ice, mischief playing across her face. "Aspen, don't let Matt fool you. He's a fount of confidence. He'd probably pose shirtless if you asked."

The sisters descended into laughter as Matt shot Megan an annoyed look.

"So hilarious." Matt was not amused. "We'll see who's laughing when I become a swimsuit model."

Their amusement exploded as Matt left the hecklers to play pinball with the guys. He didn't deserve this kind of treatment, especially since he had helped Aspen prepare for Ted and Lisa's arrival. Landscaping was no joke, and his ankle throbbed painfully in response.

After losing a few rounds of pinball, Matt made his way back to the booth, where the curly-haired blonde was noticeably missing. "Where's Aspen?"

"She abandoned us for someone else." Megan's eyes slid across the restaurant to the barstool Ryder straddled. "We invited him to the table, but you know how he is." She shoved a fry in her mouth.

Matt scanned the restaurant, his radar landing on Ryder.

Alex and Finn made their way to the booth just as enormous plates stacked with burgers and fries arrived.

"You know, the girl power at this table can be overwhelming," Alex defended, grabbing the ketchup and slathering it on his fries.

"Maybe he didn't see us in the back," Finn added. "Not everyone is man enough to sit with these girls." He scooped up his burger and bit into the loaded patty.

"What does that mean?" Megan held her sandwich midair, a note of offense in her voice.

Finn shrugged. "Not everyone is like Matt, willing to undergo your heckling. You're intimidating when you team up." Finn wasn't trying to start an argument, but Matt could tell it irked Megan.

"We don't heckle," Meg defended. "We cross-examine. There's a difference."

Matt agreed with Finn. What man could face an inquisition of strong women? It was their method for weeding out the weak.

Alex folded his hands. "As someone who's experienced this cross-examination before, I don't blame him for wanting to sit at the counter."

Cass frowned as she stared at Ryder across the room. "I get the feeling he dislikes us. We should try harder to act friendly." Of the three sisters, Cass had always been the one to adopt hurt animals as her pet projects.

Megan frowned. "I invited him to sit with us. It was Aspen who dragged him off."

"It's probably my fault. I'm the one he's not comfortable around," Matt confessed. It wasn't fair that Ryder took all the blame. "Aspen knows we aren't exactly best friends."

His eyes flitted back to her. Perched on a stool, she had shifted her body toward Ryder, her full focus on him. He turned to face her and their knees touched—an almost imperceptible movement that triggered a current of jealousy inside Matt.

Ryder's gaze slid to Matt and a look passed between them. Then he tugged Aspen's stool closer, marking his territory. Aspen kept talking, oblivious to the showdown between the two men or the fact that her burger would be cold if she didn't return to their table.

Before Matt could second-guess what he was doing, he grabbed her food and zigzagged across the restaurant, urged forward by his own adrenaline and a need to prove something.

Aspen turned toward him, a worried look in her eye. "Hey, Matt."

Without comment, he held out her plate.

"Thank you." She took it and let the silence hang between them.

Ryder eyed him suspiciously before turning his attention to the baseball game on TV.

"It was getting cold," Matt said flatly. He didn't even know what he was trying to prove.

She looked over the food. "I didn't realize Ryder was coming. I'll have him drive me back to the inn tonight." She glanced at Ryder to make sure. "If you're okay with that?"

"What about Ted and Lisa?" Matt asked. He didn't want to make a big deal out of it, but they might think it was odd that she was returning with another man.

"Will it be a problem?" She checked the time and then turned to Ryder, who was immersed in a commercial on TV. "I should leave soon."

Ryder pulled his attention away from the screen. "I haven't even gotten my order yet."

"I know, but they're the guests writing a book," she explained. "I need to be there in case they need anything." Aspen's expression was strained. The last thing she wanted was to get caught with Ryder when Ted and Lisa returned.

Ryder ignored her urgency, his gaze focused on the TV. "What does it matter as long as Matt's there?"

"Matt is not the host. I am." Aspen glared at Ryder.

"I can't hurry if I don't have my food." He gestured to the empty spot on the counter where his plate should be. Aspen looked at her cold burger.

Ryder had backed her into a corner.

She glanced at Matt and mouthed, *Sorry.*

"I'll head back early," Matt assured her. "Don't worry about it."

Before she could respond, he returned to the table and asked for a box. He'd eat at home. This view was making him sick.

As he left the restaurant, someone's eyes bored into him, but he didn't bother to look back.

Aspen had chosen Ryder for now, and he had to respect that choice, whether or not he liked it. His only job was to make sure Ted and Lisa didn't find out.

A TRUCK RUMBLING in the drive alerted Matt to Aspen's return. It idled briefly before he heard the creak of the front door. Ted and Lisa hadn't appeared, which eliminated the possibility of an unexpected meeting between them and Ryder.

Matt tidied the bed, where he'd eaten his carryout while watching sports.

Aspen nudged the door open, heaving a slow breath in relief. "Looks like our guests haven't shown up. I had to convince Ryder not to come in, giving him some excuse about how tired I was."

"Your dinner was cold, wasn't it?" he asked.

"Well, yes," she admitted. "But not inedible, thanks to you." She smiled.

"Aspen? Matt?" Lisa called as the click of her heels echoed across the foyer.

"Just in time," Aspen whispered. "You ready for this?"

Aspen rushed ahead of Matt to greet their guests.

Lisa's cheeks were glowing as she set down her clutch. "I'm so glad you're still up. Ted and I had a wonderful evening." She turned to her husband. "Didn't we?"

Ted opened his mouth to respond, but Lisa didn't give him the chance. "We even met some new friends! Edna somebody. She told us so much about you."

"Oh, really?" Aspen folded her hands, concern wrinkling her brow. "Was it Edna Long?"

Lisa pointed at Aspen. "Yes, that was her name."

Aspen glanced at Matt, her lips tight. He hadn't anticipated that Ted and Lisa would run into Wild Harbor's chattiest lady.

"What did she say?" Matt tried to act casual.

"Oh, only good things," Lisa responded vaguely. "She's quite fond of your family."

Whether or not Lisa knew the truth, he couldn't tell, but so far she gave no indication. If he'd known their scheme would become this complex, he wouldn't have agreed to it. His only saving grace was that they were leaving soon.

"Well, I'm sure you would like some time alone instead of listening to me blabber on." Lisa said, pulling her phone from the clutch.

"Sounds good," Ted encouraged. "We should head to bed." He pulled on his wife's elbow, nudging her to leave.

"One more question." Lisa stopped on the steps. "Do you mind if I get a picture of you two? I'm afraid I'll forget in the morning."

"Lisa, dear," Ted protested. He'd been so close to convincing her to follow him.

"Every time we visit an inn, I take a picture to remember the hosts. You don't mind, do you?"

"Of course not," Aspen answered.

"I'll head to our room." Ted shuffled up the steps, abandoning his attempt to persuade Lisa.

"Could you move together? I can't get you both in the shot."

Aspen inched toward Matt as his arm brushed hers.

Lisa squinted her eyes, dissatisfied with something. "No offense, but you look a little stiff. Could you pose like a happy couple?"

Aspen leaned awkwardly toward Matt, but Lisa still wasn't pleased.

Matt lifted his arm over Aspen's shoulders and pulled her closer. It's not like he didn't want to touch her, but he could sense her discomfort. Aspen followed Matt's lead and wrapped one arm around his waist.

"That's better," Lisa proclaimed.

The familiar floral scent of Aspen's perfume tortured him as he waited for Lisa to figure out her phone. She smelled so delicious, he wanted to bury his nose in her hair. Her pheromones were driving him crazy.

"Okay, smile!" Lisa chirped, holding up her phone.

They froze for what seemed like an eternity. When Lisa finally lowered her phone, they slowly untangled from each other.

"One more picture," Lisa requested.

"I thought we were done." Aspen straightened her shirt, flustered from their pose.

"Oh, give each other a quick kiss and we'll call it a night."

"Excuse me?" Aspen asked, panic crossing her face.

"Just for fun!" Lisa added.

Even though he'd made a vow never to kiss Aspen again, he didn't count this request as breaking that promise. A quick, fake kiss for the camera would be nothing like the real thing.

"Let's do what she says," Matt muttered. He might regret this, but at least it would rid them of Lisa.

"What?" Aspen's mouth dropped open. "But I thought—"

Matt's gaze steadily held hers. "Just hold still."

Aspen gave a tiny nod, then she closed her eyes and tipped her head back.

As many times as Matt had imagined this, he never once thought of the moment quite like this. As her arms threaded through his, he closed his eyes and leaned in. Their warm breath mingled as they came together, not in some passionate display, but in a slightly awkward, first-kiss encounter. The warmth of her body pressed against his chest, her soft lips slowly melting into his. They pulled apart reluctantly before Aspen dropped her gaze to the floor.

"How sweet," Lisa murmured. She stared at the photo on her phone before she slipped it into her pocket. "Reminds me of when I met Ted," she remarked with a twinge of sadness.

How could love go from intense attraction to lackluster companionship? Lisa offered no clues. All Matt knew was that if he ever got married, it would be to someone who continued to nurture their love long after the initial sparks faded.

"Well, goodnight," Lisa said. "I hope Ted isn't already snoring when I return to the room." Then she looked at Aspen. "See what you have to look forward to?" Her lips pursed into a knowing smile, but behind the smile was a truth that Matt didn't want to face. Even if you're madly in love with someone, it required effort to love that person when the moments turned mundane.

As Lisa slipped up the stairs, Aspen and Matt drifted separately to their rooms.

"I'm sorry if I put you in an uncomfortable situation," Matt blurted out when they were alone outside their bedrooms. "I wanted Lisa to leave."

"I dragged you into this mess." She shook her head. "At least tomorrow they'll be gone, and we can go back to how things were."

"And that was?" He let the question hang between them.

Aspen managed a small smile. "Handyman, landscaper, security guard. Basically, my Swiss army knife. The one who does everything I can't."

"Your list of expectations keeps growing," he pointed out.

"But you were my friend first." She leaned against the doorframe of her bedroom, her face suddenly serious. "I hope we haven't ruined that part."

"Who said it was ruined?" he assured her.

He'd never let it come to that. Though their relationship was no longer black and white since she'd moved in, his logical mind had tried to keep a line between friendship and love in place. But the longer they shared a house, the harder it was becoming with her around all the time. Everything between them had turned fuzzy, including the boundary lines.

"Remember that night you found me on the front porch, upset after my disastrous date?" she said softly.

Like he could ever forget the hug that had turned into the most awkward kiss ever. It's not that he hadn't wanted to kiss her. But back then, he'd resolved to always hold the line between love and friendship. Because once he stepped over, he knew he could never go back.

"You said that would *never ever* happen again," she reminded him.

So that's what was bothering her. He'd broken his promise.

How could he explain that kissing her was a fool's game?

They'd both been young and directionless back then. The way he'd pushed her away had been cruel, even if his reasons were valid. It was for *her* sake.

"What happened tonight was part of the charade, right?" Aspen hesitated, like she needed his reassurance.

He nodded slowly. "You'd know if it were a real kiss." He didn't let himself look away. "Because if it were real, then we could never go back to how things were."

He slipped into his room and leaned his head against the door, the only thing between him and her.

Like it or not, he'd stepped over the line.

CHAPTER ELEVEN

ASPEN

Aspen balanced a basket of dirty sheets in one arm and a trash bag in the other as she descended the stairs like a circus act. She didn't know how Aunt Lizzie had managed everything without help for so many years. Since Aspen's parents had spent most of their time working, they'd probably never thought about assisting her.

During the summer, when the girls were off from school, Aspen and Jessica would get dropped off at Lizzie's doorstep like stray cats. Aunt Lizzie had welcomed them with hugs and fresh-baked goods—the scent of orange-cranberry muffins or cinnamon-drenched banana bread inviting them in.

Aunt Lizzie required daily chores as their repayment, but she also made it a game, clocking how many towels they could fold or who could polish the dining room chairs until they gleamed. At the end of the week, she'd drop handfuls of loose change into their pockets, letting the girls raid the candy machines outside of the drugstore, much to her mom's dismay.

It was Aunt Lizzie's way of injecting life into their dull summers, but for Aspen, it was so much more. Her great-aunt didn't see her as an interruption. She folded the girls into the chaos of her day, like flour into bread.

And how did Aspen repay Aunt Lizzie? She had chosen the Woods family over her great-aunt, opting for summer adventures with Matt's sisters rather than a matronly relative.

Only now did she think of how much Aunt Lizzie must have missed the girls' presence, her only faithful companions other than Lester. Back then, Aspen had been too young and selfish to consider her great-aunt's feelings; instead, she'd wanted the chaos of a lively and loud home to fill that need for belonging.

Now that she was an adult, owning an inn carried that same sort of appeal. Having a place where laughter filled the space around tables and she could make a humongous pot of coffee that was drained in twenty minutes—all of that sounded like a piece of heaven.

So why was she considering the exact opposite: running from the thing that made her feel rooted?

Aspen nudged open the laundry room door with her foot. As she stuffed the sheets into the washer, a voice made her jump.

"I can take that for you." Matt grabbed the garbage bag from her hands. "I'm leaving for work now that Ted and Lisa are gone."

Aspen closed the lid to the washer and looked at his foot. "You're approved to go back?" His ankle couldn't possibly be better yet.

"It was supposed to be a few more days, but my ankle feels strong enough, and the firehouse is desperate for help."

She flicked the power button, and the washer clicked to life. "It's Lisa's fault, isn't it? You'd rather risk fighting fires than face another couple like the Richardsons."

"I can't blame Lisa," Matt said. "The fire chief called and

requested my help. Lisa and Ted were more than agreeable this morning."

As nerve-wracking as their charade had been yesterday, this morning's final interview had been nothing like the previous ones. Lisa asked specific questions about the inn while Ted jotted down notes and verified information on the history. When they left, Ted took pictures of the inn and told them they'd be in touch in a few months.

To her surprise, it had been the least demanding part of the visit. But how could anything be more stressful than their fake kiss last night? Even thinking of it made Aspen's heart clang in her chest.

As the washer sputtered to life, Aspen leaned against the machine. "So you're not going to quit on me? Because I thought for sure after Lisa left, you'd be moving out of here as quickly as possible."

"Now that we're over this hurdle, any other visitors will seem easy." Matt was trying his best not to make her feel guilty.

"If it helps, when Lisa calls back, I'm going to tell her the truth," Aspen told him. "Just so she doesn't get carried away."

She tore her eyes away from his T-shirt, a visual reminder of yesterday, when Lisa had forced them to snuggle closer for the picture. In that moment, Aspen had discovered how perfectly she fit into his arms, and how his scent had lingered long after the shot.

She needed to imagine Ryder's shirt that way now. But unexpectedly, her mind went blank.

"Don't worry, I won't force you to act like my boyfriend again," she clarified. "From now on, I'm going to explain that you're employed by the inn. Nothing else."

"From boyfriend to employee? I think you've demoted me."

"Not a demotion. Just safer." Even as she said it, she didn't believe it. There was nothing safe about her feelings. "Good friends."

He repeated it softly. "Friends, huh? If you say so."

His eyes seemed to rip through her, exposing her as a fraud. Friendship was only a coverup. She wanted more, but Matt had made his feelings clear years ago. Her whole life now revolved around selling the inn and pursuing her photography dream.

"You're a great hostess," he added.

Aspen shrugged. "My imposter syndrome has been raging. I can't wait to get back to photography. Finn and Megan agreed to let me take some engagement photos today."

"I thought my sister wasn't into engagement pictures."

"Finn volunteered them, much to Meg's dismay. When I told them I loathe cheesy photos, she reluctantly agreed. It seems you've rubbed off on them."

"Just for the record, being self-conscious is not the same as being stubborn."

"I can't believe I'm hearing this. You're the most confident person I know, other than Megan." She hopped on top of the washer.

"I'm only confident about certain things," Matt admitted. "Posing for the camera is not one of them."

"Really? Then what's the other thing you're not confident about?"

He paused before leaning into her on the washer. His eyes grew dark as he brushed her chin with his finger. "You don't want to know, Little Bit." He smiled and she glimpsed something sparking in his eyes.

"At least tell me before you go." She jumped off the washer, following him as he lifted his backpack. "It's not fair. I tell you everything."

"Everything?" he questioned. His look demanded a confession from her.

"Okay, not *everything*. But almost," she clarified, before glancing at his pack. "Are you staying overnight at the station tonight?"

"Probably." He unlocked the back door. "Why?"

"I just haven't stayed overnight at the inn by myself yet." She hesitated. "Even though Aunt Lizzie did it all the time."

He studied her, attempting to read her expression. "Are you sure you're okay tonight?"

"Why wouldn't I be? I'm not twelve." If she was being honest, she still felt like an awkward teenager some days, but she had to get over her fears. Her parents' frequent absence during her childhood made it difficult to live alone. She craved company, chaos, and constant noise. Now that Matt had been home after his accident, his presence had brought her the thing she longed for most—companionship.

"Call me if you need anything," he said.

She gave him what she hoped passed for a confident smile. "I'm also going to stop by Joshua's salvage shop and see if he can answer some questions about Aunt Lizzie."

Matt stopped in the doorway. "What would he know about Aunt Lizzie?"

She shrugged. "His expertise is old things—furniture, homes, restoration projects. I thought he might have a lead for me."

"He's pretty private. He can tell you all about the antiques in his shop, but with anything else, he's a man of few words."

Matt caught sight of the cat trying to sneak out the door. "Not this time, Les." He propped his foot up to prevent Lester from escaping. "No more tree climbing for you or me."

"When will you be home?" Aspen asked, trying not to make a big deal out of him leaving. "Not that I need you but—"

"You hate being alone, don't you, Aspen?" Matt said, grinning.

"I do not," she exclaimed.

He didn't seem convinced.

"Okay, maybe just a little."

"Lester is here for you," he teased as he brushed his hand

across the cat's back. "And I'm only a phone call away. If you need anything, I'll be here."

～

ASPEN KNOCKED on the door of Joshua's salvage shop and waited as a summer breeze tossed a curl into her face.

The sign on the door read *hours by appointment only*, but everyone in town knew that Joshua spent most of his time here, even if he didn't keep regular store hours.

"Joshua?" she called, stepping into the dimly lit room. Despite it being a cloudless day, the shop only let in light from a few windows. She crept forward, her eyes adjusting to the darkness.

"Is there anyone here?" Windows and mantels perched on the floor like missing puzzle pieces. Glass trinkets collected dust on shelves. It was like someone had dismantled an old home and dropped all the parts here, unassembled.

A muffled voice came from a room in the back. "Who's there?"

Aspen found Joshua hunched over an antique music box.

Joshua adjusted his bifocals. "Well, I'll be. Haven't seen you in a while." He gave her a familiar smile that wrinkled his face into a thousand lines.

"My visit is long overdue," she apologized. "I hope I'm still invited."

"Of course." He motioned toward a rickety wood stool. "Have a seat." He rotated the handle on the box slowly and music tinkled from the inside. "Are you looking for something special?"

"Perhaps when I redecorate." She paused, wanting to ask about her great-aunt. "When did you hear about Lizzie?"

Joshua's face grew solemn. "Right away. I'm very sorry for

your loss. She was a wonderful lady, and she'd be so proud of you taking over her inn."

"You knew her well, then?" Aspen perked up. She hadn't seen Joshua at the viewing or funeral, but then again, everything from those early weeks was a blur.

"When you've been here long enough, you know everyone in town."

"I guess that's a perk to staying in one place."

"Certainly," Joshua agreed. "But it's difficult to see friends leave this life and head on to the next without you."

Aspen didn't want to imagine being left behind with only your memories of someone you loved. That was a different kind of hard.

"Did you know my great-aunt long?"

"Knew her since she was a girl," Joshua said, his mouth turning up at the corners. "We were in the same class at school, and she always beat me in the spelling bee." His eyes glazed over with the memory. "Funny how some things stay with you."

"Then you might know the answer to something." Aspen leaned forward.

"My memory isn't as good as it used to be," he admitted. "I'll try, though."

"Do you remember if Aunt Lizzie dated anyone? Or even fell in love?"

Joshua turned his head to her quickly and frowned. "Why?"

"I found this ring." She held up her hand to show him the sapphire stone set in a gold band. "Do you have any idea who this was from?"

Joshua glanced at the ring. "Pretty piece of jewelry. But how do you know it was from a man?"

She shrugged. "Just a hunch." Aspen avoided mentioning the letter. It would only stir up more questions.

"Perhaps Lizzie didn't want anyone to know about the ring."

Joshua turned to his music box and fiddled with the handle. Light reflected off his glasses as he bent over the contraption and tightened a screw. "She was always good at being mysterious. Sometimes you have to trust that you don't need to have all the answers."

Aspen played with her aunt's ring, spinning it in circles. "I was only curious."

"Anything else I can help you with?" Joshua looked at her oddly, like the case was closed.

Aspen shook her head and slid off the stool. "Thanks, anyway."

She didn't like being left with unanswered questions, but unless she found another clue to her great-aunt's past, the secret was likely gone for good.

ASPEN GLANCED AT THE SKY, surveying the light for her photo session. Too sunny for a decent shot.

"I hate to change our plans, but the park won't work for photographs today," Aspen explained to Finn and Megan. "You'll end up squinting and washed out."

"Like every childhood vacation photo Dad took," Megan retorted, before slumping onto a park bench. "My face already hurts thinking about all that smiling. Where are you forcing us to go now?"

"It's not *forcing*. It's fun," Finn reminded Megan.

"Do you remember that adorable porch swing at Joshua's cabin?" Aspen asked. The swing had played an integral part in their romance, and she hoped that would be enough to convince her friend.

"Any place else would be a hard pass," Megan warned.

Aspen pulled Meg to standing, like when they were kids.

"And if it had been anyone but your best friend asking, you would have said no. But it's me, so pretty please, be cooperative."

"You're impossible," Megan replied with a grin.

"Me?" Aspen laughed as she packed her camera. "You're every photographer's worst nightmare."

"As if anyone could squelch your optimism," Megan said, handing her the tripod. "It's ridiculously contagious. I even see it worming its way into Matt."

"Really?" She didn't want to sound too interested in Megan's hypothesis. "He'll probably be glad when I go."

"You'd be surprised what's going on in that over-analytical mind of his," Megan said, pulling her friend aside. "You're his tipping point."

"For his sanity, maybe," Aspen remarked.

"Matt's always been a tidy thinker." Megan loaded Aspen's photography equipment into the car. "An organizational genius. He once *alphabetized* my pantry."

"So you're saying I'm ruining him?"

"Not ruining," Megan explained. "Upsetting the apple cart."

"That's not any better."

"His whole life has become so routine that he shuts out all emotion," Megan explained. "He's a machine, not a man. You flip over his emotional apple cart, and who knows what's going to happen?"

Oh, she knew alright. He'd already warned her. *Don't you ever touch me again like that.* It was all the *never evers* he'd been so fond of repeating to her. At some point, he was going to go all terminator on her and shut her out for good. When that happened, it wasn't his apple cart that was in danger. It was hers.

As they drove to Joshua's cabin on the other side of town, Aspen thought about what Megan had told her. Megan had meant it as a compliment, but to Aspen it felt like a warning. Perhaps this arrangement was only going to leave her with an empty life and a hard goodbye. When it was time to leave, did she really want to go through that?

As their car slowly approached Joshua's place, another car pulled into the cabin.

"Who invited my entire family?" Megan said, as Lily and Cassidy waved from the front seats, while her parents sat in the back.

"Don't look at me." Aspen put her hands in the air.

"It was me," Finn admitted sheepishly. "I texted them where we were going."

"Great," Megan said. "The peanut gallery just arrived. I'll be heckled mercilessly."

Finn realized his mistake. "Should I tell them to go home?"

"No," Aspen insisted, a strong emotion rising inside her. "These people love you. Do you realize how rare and special that is? If I had engagement photos, my family wouldn't even bother asking, let alone show up. This is their way of supporting you one thousand percent."

Megan's clenched jaw softened. "What'd I tell you?" She looked at Aspen and screwed her eyes shut, trying to hold back tears. "Apple cart flipper."

Bill and Becky slowly made their way toward Aspen as Megan's sisters crowded around her.

"Well, isn't this a lovely spot for a picture?" Becky smiled and admired the trees that formed a perfect canopy over their heads, giving them a break from the sweltering summer day.

"How's my bonus daughter?" Bill squeezed Aspen's arm, using the term of endearment he'd given her years ago, then rested on the porch step. As long as she could remember, Bill Woods had been a pillar of strength, but since his stroke, even small things wearied him. "I hope my son is keeping up that inn of yours."

Aspen kicked a stone with her foot, wondering what Matt had told them. He was too private to mention their disastrous first encounter with Ted and Lisa.

"The job has been a huge learning curve," Aspen admitted. "Who knew my next career move would be as an innkeeper?"

"Matt told me it's temporary. Is that still the case?" Bill asked.

"Until I sell it," Aspen stated as she set up her tripod. "In a weird twist of fate, Aunt Lizzie is funding my photography dreams. She just didn't realize it."

"I hope you won't stay away for long." Becky wrung her hands, a brief flash of sadness crossing her face.

Like most dramatic life changes, it hurt too much for Aspen to think about leaving them. In order to pull it off, she'd need to approach it like the removal of a bandage. One swift rip.

"I'm sure there will be opportunities to visit," Aspen said, trying to ease the pain. "Weddings. Babies."

The thought of Matt marrying someone else made her stomach clench. She didn't know how she would survive his wedding. She clicked through some settings on her camera, trying to erase the nightmarish scene. "Would you be my test shots for a minute?"

"This saggy old hen?" Becky laughed as she climbed the porch steps.

"Beck, you're still my beautiful bride," Bill gushed as he helped his wife to the swing. "Even prettier than the day I met you." After all these years, he was completely smitten with Becky.

The older woman lowered onto the creaky swing, letting the motion rock them gently. Aspen adjusted her camera and snapped a few shots. Scrolling through the photos, she stopped on a lovely photo of Bill kissing Becky's cheek.

Bill pinched Becky's leg and snuck her a mischievous look.

Becky swatted at his hand. "Stop that, Bill."

Aspen hid a smile. She could tell Becky didn't really mean it.

Megan leaned over her shoulder, eyeing the shot. "Wow. That one is gorgeous. How did you persuade my parents into an impromptu photo session?"

Aspen shrugged. "I didn't do anything. Their affection for each other is just natural."

Lily and Cassidy were now crowding around Aspen, trying to capture the view.

"Those are incredible," Lily gushed. "Maybe we should plan family shots before—"

Cassidy's eyes swung over to her sister to silence her. "Don't even say it or I might cry."

Bill's stroke had taught them that no one lives a life untouched by grief. They already knew what the future would eventually hold and were resolved to enjoy every minute with their parents while they could.

"Megan," Aspen whispered. "It's your turn."

This time, Megan didn't protest. She took Finn's hand and walked to the swing, ready to let Aspen capture something beautiful.

After spending the rest of the day with the Woods family, Aspen finally returned to the empty inn after dark. As she stood at the back door, she fumbled for her keys in the bottom of her purse. When she attempted to turn the key, the bolt stuck hard.

"Piece of dirt," she mumbled under her breath, pushing her body against the door while twisting the key. She grunted and strained on the lock, then kicked the door in frustration, but the deadbolt wouldn't budge.

"Ow!" she howled, her foot throbbing.

She already knew about the next project for Matt. *This stupid deadbolt.*

As she made one last attempt, the lock finally gave way, causing the door to fly open so that she nearly fell into the back hall.

Shaking off her clumsiness, she was immediately overcome by loneliness. Gloomy darkness cloaked the interior of the home, like a gothic mansion from one of Aunt Lizzie's mystery books. Even the back hall had taken on a decidedly creepy feeling now that the house was empty. A soft warm animal grazed her shin bone and she jumped into an umbrella stand.

"Lester," she howled at the innocent creature, who'd skittered away when she crashed into the metal bucket. It wasn't Lester's fault he was so ridiculously friendly, but she still wasn't used to the tickle of his fur in the pitch black. Spending tonight by herself might persuade her not to travel the world by herself anytime soon. Or ever. Wasn't it her sister who had confessed that neither of them were good at being alone?

Jessica's confession might have been spot-on, but her solution had been a terrible one: latch on to the first guy who proposed. Aspen suspected it was mostly because she was afraid of being alone. The unfortunate outcome was that Jessica and Chase had ended up separated after six months of marriage and only recently finalized their divorce.

She drew a deep breath, attempting to soothe her nervous heartbeat which catapulted against her chest. A creak shuddered from somewhere inside, followed by a click. More than likely, her overexaggerated fears were stirring up her imagination.

Aspen fumbled for the lights to search for Lester while the cuckoo clock ticked in the darkness. Dropping her bag, Aspen checked the front hall and living room, then dashed up the steps. Everything appeared normal, but there was a hollowness to the place without any company.

It was only when she descended the stairs that she noticed the dizzying scent of fragrant flowers wafting through the house. *Lilacs.* How was it possible when the only lilac bush was outside her bedroom window?

Her heart slid into her stomach as she prayed she was

wrong. The smell grew stronger as she dashed down the hallway toward her room and nudged open the door. Stepping inside, a warm breeze filled her nostrils, exploding with the perfume of blooming lilacs.

She stared at the opposite end of the room, where her curtains danced in the night wind. Her bedroom window was open. Not just a crack either, but a gaping hole, large enough for a human to fit through. Goose bumps shot up Aspen's arms. She hadn't left her window open.

Her curtains flapped lazily as her mind circled through potential scenarios. If she hadn't opened it, who had? The only other possibility was Matt. Perhaps he had returned home to pick up something, but that didn't seem consistent with his obsessive behavior. He didn't forget to close windows. Unless . . .

She backed away and leaned against the wall, fumbling for her phone, her fingers shaking as she punched each letter to Matt.

Aspen: Did you open my bedroom window?

She hit send and waited for his text bubble to appear. If she called the police now, Matt would find out. As first responders, they always received news about emergency calls. His reply was almost immediate.

Matt: No, why?

If she told him about the open window, he'd probably call the police himself and ask them to send an officer over. The last thing she wanted was for him to make a fuss over what was likely a mistake.

Matt: Aspen, what's the matter?

Aspen: Nothing is wrong.

At least, not yet. Her heart hammered in her chest as she fought to regain control of her emotions. Her first night alone and she was already failing. The fluttering curtains drew her eye across the room, where Aunt Lizzie's jewelry box sat open. A slip of paper flickered in the breeze.

She darted across the room and opened the note, which wasn't the same size as the letter she had found before, nor the same paper. The words were identical to Aunt Lizzie's cursive, but this was not the letter she'd read before.

Dear Aspen,
It only seemed appropriate to leave you a note with one final riddle after my death. As a child, you always loved solving riddles more than anyone. Should you figure out the solution, you will be most delighted at the end. It is my treasure for you, the daughter of my heart.
Love,
Lizzie

The Key to Everything (A Riddle)
To find the key, look under the sea.
Only then will you be free.
The answer lies under three clocks
in the shape of a box.
Love opens the door to answers and more.

Aspen stared at the words hard. How did this riddle end up here? She was sure she'd searched the jewelry box before and all she'd found were a ring and the apology letter to a mystery man. Now the letter was gone, replaced by this riddle.

Was this a joke? If so, it was a cruel one.

But then another thought stuck in her mind. *What if her aunt had orchestrated this by asking someone to leave it for her?*

Her phone vibrated in her pocket, shaking her back to reality.

Matt: Do you need my help?

Ignoring his text, she moved swiftly to Matt's room to check if anything appeared out of place. At any moment, she expected someone to jump in front of her. What would she do then? Her only weapon was a semi-lame roundhouse kick she'd practiced on the school playground. She wasn't even sure her leg stretched that far anymore.

It's not as if there were many crimes in Wild Harbor. The mayor's bribery scandal had been the biggest thing in decades, but most of the broken laws were minor traffic violations, not breaking and entering. Murders were nearly unheard of.

There's always a first time, a voice in her head warned.

"Oh, shut up," she muttered to herself.

Like usual, Matt's bedroom was immaculate. She swung around and locked his door, suddenly feeling safe inside the peaceful cocoon of his room.

She slumped on his bed, still trembling, and nestled her head on his pillow, pushing her nose into the soft cotton case. She hated that fear could make her sick. Her heart was racing, careening like a car without brakes, and no amount of deep breathing could slow it down. As the scent of his skin washed over her, it slowed the anxiety that pulsated through her slushy, cold veins.

Pulling back the covers, she slipped under his blankets. Matt's sheets were a luxurious soft grey, inviting her to stretch her legs out. Without thinking, her body folded into the warm center of his mattress until her blood heated and the fear settled.

The next thing she knew, the sound of a fist pounding on the door jolted her awake.

"Aspen, are you in there?" Matt's voice called urgently.

Her eyelids snapped open as she rubbed the heel of her hand in her eye and sat up. Was it the middle of the night? Her mind was hazy, like dense fog on a humid morning.

"Is everything okay?" Matt persisted.

She bolted to the door, her bleary vision adjusting to the dark. This wasn't her bedroom. Or her bed. Turning the lock, it flung open, nearly smacking her in the face.

Matt flipped on the light and glanced at her disheveled state before his eyes swung to the rumpled bed.

"Were you sleeping in my bed?" His incredulous tone made Aspen want to cower under his covers. She'd messed up his flawless comforter.

"I don't know," she stammered. "I guess I fell asleep."

She rubbed her forehead as the memory slowly unfurled. *Curtains rippling. Window open. Riddle found.*

"It felt safer in here," she confessed. She swept the covers up, a sorry attempt to remake his bed.

Matt raised his eyebrows. "Is that it, *princess?* You're scared of the dark?" The way he said it wasn't a compliment.

She might as well tell him the truth. "When I returned home, my window was open and someone had been in my room—"

Before she could even finish, he was gone, bolting down the hall in a few strides. She followed him, her legs sprinting to keep up.

His fingers checked the latch twice before he yanked on the window and checked for the missing screen. "These screens are so easy to pop out, a kid could do it."

"But why would someone want to break in?" she asked, still confused by the incident. The riddle spun in her mind like a car circling on ice.

"Don't have a clue what they wanted." Matt inspected the

window closely, his hand sliding across the frame. "Did you call the police?"

She figured he already knew the answer.

"No," she mumbled, certain he was about to launch into a lecture about safety.

"So you ignored common sense and fell asleep in my bedroom without telling me what was going on?" His usual controlled tone grew sharp with accusations.

"I didn't mean to. I came to see if anything was out of place."

"You thought you'd check for intruders instead of calling for help?" His lips tightened into a tight line. "Aspen, how naïve could you be?"

"I am not," Aspen shot back. "How am I going to travel the world if I can't survive an open window? It was probably some stupid kid trying to prank me."

"Kid or not, you should have told me." Matt's eyes were black now, like the lake before a storm. *Bodyguard eyes.*

"You can't protect me all the time." The words spilled out before she could stop them.

For a moment, an emotion crossed his face that she couldn't read. "I can't help you unless you let me."

Just then, a knock at the front door interrupted their conversation.

"Are you expecting someone?" Matt asked, before rushing toward the sound.

"No." She sprinted after him. "Who would stop in the middle of the night?"

He turned to her, hand on the knob. "This conversation isn't over."

As Matt swung the door open, he blocked Aspen from viewing their midnight caller.

"Hello, stranger. Is Aspen here?"

Aspen knew the woman's voice before she even glimpsed her.

"Jessica?" Aspen pushed by Matt, her arms reaching for her sister. "What in the world?"

Aspen's sister held a suitcase and a wide smile as her eyes swung from Aspen to Matt. "This might be a little last minute. But do you have room for a guest?"

CHAPTER TWELVE

MATT

"Why didn't you tell me you were coming?" Aspen couldn't hide her shock at seeing her newly divorced sister from Atlanta.

"I was in the neighborhood," Jessica joked. "Now that the divorce is final, a vacation sounded like just what the doctor ordered."

Jess was dazzling for a late-night visit. Leopard heels, drop-dead skirt and silky blouse, topped by a slick ponytail. Three years older than Aspen, Jessica could hardly look more different from her sister. Jessica had inherited the height and the curves in the family, which meant she'd always drawn attention without even trying. Aspen's thick, blonde curls were a stark contrast against Jessica's dark straight locks, pulled so tightly back her forehead was given a natural lift from the tension. They were yin and yang. Oil and water. Spicy and sweet.

"Aren't you going to greet your only sibling with a proper welcome?" Jessica opened her arms for a hug.

Aspen stepped into them, still dazed and confused. "Why didn't you say something? A text, a call?"

"I thought you'd be happy. I didn't know my visit needed a forewarning."

Jessica's eyes swung across the living room. "So many memories. I wanted to see it again."

"See what?" Aspen followed her sister across the room.

"Our inn," Jessica replied matter-of-factly.

"I figured you weren't interested. You said the divorce was enough to handle right now and gave me permission to do as I pleased." Aspen's tone had lost its normal zest. Matt knew her sister's visit would not speed up the redecorating project.

"I changed my mind." Jessica shrugged. "This is a pleasant diversion from—" She couldn't bring herself to say the word *divorce*. "Life. Can't I enjoy Aunt Lizzie's inn one more time before it's gone for good?" Her heels clicked on the floor as she ran a finger across the mantel.

"Is that really why you're here?" Aspen questioned. "Or were you afraid I might mess things up?"

"I'm not afraid of anything." She turned to Aspen. "You're just a people pleaser to a fault. That's why I came. To make sure you don't give away the inn."

Aspen clenched her jaw. "You came to complicate things."

"Not complicate. Smooth over. Make sure all of this"—she gave an elegant turn of her hand across the room, like a game-show model—"gets top dollar for us."

She smiled like she'd given her sister a million dollars, then pinned her attention on Matt. "It's good to see you." Her hug was a little too eager, a quick diversion from a tense conversation. Jessica had always been a flirt, and her arrival at the inn was going to throw a monkey wrench into an already complicated arrangement. "How did Aspen rope you into staying?"

"She didn't. I wanted to." There was no way he'd let Aspen carry the workload of the inn on her own.

"Aunt Lizzie was a lucky lady," Jessica added. "I'm surprised some lonely widow hasn't snapped you up for yard work." Her smile was almost wicked.

"Aspen needs help around here," Matt explained. "She can't do it all."

"Well, pity," Jessica teased. "You'd make great eye candy for some spinster."

"Jess, stop." Aspen pulled her sister away and grabbed her suitcase, ready to haul it up to the second floor.

"I'm only joking." Jessica held up her hands and widened her eyes, trying to appear innocent. Matt knew that her flirting drove Aspen crazy, especially when it was him.

"If you act like that in town"—Aspen frowned—"people in Wild Harbor will get ideas."

Jessica's mouth twitched at the corner as her ultra-confident mask slipped a little. "Well, somebody's grumpy tonight."

Aspen ignored her sister and dragged Jessica's gigantic suitcase up the first two steps.

"Aspen," Matt called, racing to stop her. Their hands brushed as he took the suitcase from her. "Let me help." For a second, their eyes met. She looked weary after the window incident. "I'll show her to one of the guest rooms."

"You don't have to—" She tugged on the luggage handle, their fingers touching again, like sparks flaming.

"I want to. You grab clean towels for her room."

Aspen's shoulders relaxed as she mouthed the words *thank you* and darted down the stairs.

Then he turned to Jessica and nodded toward the second floor. "Follow me."

He could handle Jessica for one night. But her presence for the duration of the project was bound to shake things up, and not for the better.

~

THE NEXT MORNING, the sound of ripping wallpaper filled the inn. Apparently, this was how Aspen took out her stress. As Matt stirred creamer into his coffee, the clinking of his spoon against the cup was punctuated by her fervent efforts.

Scrape, scrape, tear, scrape, scrape, scrape, tear.

Jessica slinked down the stairs in a black satin robe and a sleepy yawn. Matt's eyes flicked up to catch the sun glinting off the silky tie around her waist.

"You up, too?" She rubbed a tired eye and searched the cupboards for a mug.

"Mugs are here." He handed her a spotless white coffee cup, avoiding the urge to stare at her robe. "You know you can't dress like that around here."

Her eyes dropped to the space where the robe folded over, covering her chest. "I'm fully dressed underneath, if that's what you mean."

Her bare legs stuck out from the bottom.

"You don't appear fully dressed. This is a bed-and-breakfast with a mostly retired clientele."

"Then they'll appreciate my morning attire even more." She blew on the coffee and gave him a look that dared him to challenge her. "Besides, there's no one here. I already checked."

"I'm here, and I'm not related to you. That's reason enough to come downstairs fully dressed."

"You haven't changed much, Matthew Woods." She sipped her coffee and looked him over. "Still playing the hero."

He wished people would stop calling him that. He wasn't a hero, especially after last year's accident when his simple mistake had threatened the lives of his crew. The event had shaken him badly. Now, he'd become even more determined not to make another error. He needed to be in control. On top of his game. He couldn't mess up again.

"If only you knew," he mumbled.

"You mean life hasn't been perfect?" She leaned against the

counter, her robe gently shifting against the curves of her body. Jessica was the type of girl who demanded attention. To her frustration, Matt had never given her any. Not that she wanted him, specifically. It was just a game for her.

"Hardly." He gave a sarcastic huff and looked away. "I love my work as a fireman. But it's not glamorous like they make it on those unrealistic TV shows. Houses burn to the ground. People get hurt, even die. Heroes don't always come home."

How could he respond to the fact that life could wreck people pretty badly? Worst of all, he didn't have any explanation when people asked him how God could allow it. How *could* God let it happen? In the last year, he'd fallen into a deep hole of questions without answers.

"You're sounding cynical," Jessica claimed before sipping her coffee. "Aspen's Pollyanna attitude apparently hasn't rubbed off on you."

"It's starting to. But Aspen has endured her fair share of discouragement this year." He parked his coffee and newspaper at the small breakfast table. "She bounces back like no one else. The most hopeful person I know. That's not Pollyanna; that's resilience."

Jessica shrugged like optimism was old news. "I don't know why she was stupid enough to quit her job. If there's one thing I learned after my divorce, it's to always have a backup plan."

"The inn *is* her backup plan," he replied.

"Join the club." Jessica lifted her chin toward the wallpaper scraping above her. "That noise is driving me crazy. She could have waited until a decent hour to start."

"You're the one who showed up at midnight."

Jessica rolled her eyes. "I intended to arrive earlier, but I made the mistake of stopping at Brewster's on my way. I should know better. You can't get out of that place without seeing at least five people you know."

"So, why are you here? Aspen told me you weren't interested in the inn."

"Not the inn, but the sale. My little sister doesn't know how to drive a hard bargain. I'm here to guarantee it's done right."

"Let me guess. You need money since your divorce." He raised his gaze and was met with her answer.

"Well, aren't you a wise guy?" She finished her coffee. "With the divorce now finalized, I need to make sure I'm set up for the future." She cradled the mug in her hands. "Wild Harbor holds wonderful memories. I'm thinking about moving back." She picked up the carafe to pour more coffee. "In the meantime, the inn goes on the market to the highest buyer. I'm holding Aspen to that promise."

"You think she won't?"

"She's always been the type to get too attached. When we were kids, it was dolls and stuffed animals. She'd absolutely refuse to give them up. Now that the stakes are bigger, I can't afford for her to backpedal."

"She needs the money just as much as you do," he defended.

"That might be true, but I'm here to help close the deal. It's why she couldn't make it at Hartford. She never stood up for herself."

Suddenly, someone cleared their throat from across the room. Aspen stood in the entrance, her hair tied up in a messy bun.

"Just to set the record straight, I chose to quit Hartford." Aspen frowned at her sister. "I was tired of the way I'd been treated there, especially after they used my photographs without asking."

"But did you talk to them about it?" Jessica challenged. "Or in your typical fashion, did you hide your feelings until you couldn't take it anymore?"

Aspen gave her a look. "I'm not answering that."

"See?" Jessica said, proving her point. "You don't fight for what you want."

"I sent a letter outlining my complaints," Aspen defended.

"What did they say in response?"

Aspen avoided her sister's glare. "Nothing."

Jessica sighed. "Oh, Aspen. Haven't you learned anything?"

"I thought you'd be proud of me for dealing with the situation." Aspen pulled a cup from the shelf and slammed the cupboard door a little too hard.

"Hey, I'm on your side. You need to take care of *you*." Jessica crossed to her sister and tucked a stray wisp behind Aspen's ear. For a moment, something shifted between the sisters. Jessica had reverted into a big-sister role. "You should relax. Have some fun. Are you still dating Ryder?"

Aspen glanced toward Matt before her gaze flitted away. "Of course."

Matt sank lower in his seat, staring at the newspaper, his mind blocking out the conversation. He wasn't doing a very good job at it.

"Why don't we plan a double date, then?" Jessica's voice bubbled.

"When?" Aspen questioned.

"Tonight. I'm not looking for a real date," Jessica explained. "Just a friend to have fun with."

Matt felt Jessica's eyes on him before he looked up from the editorial he was supposedly reading. Her laser target had zeroed in on him.

"Um, I need to leave for work." Matt dumped his coffee in the sink and hoped he could escape out the back door before they roped him into a date.

Jessica cut in front of him, blocking his exit with one hand on the doorframe. "Pretty please? Just as friends?" The look in her eyes was a mixture of desperation and danger.

"I think it's a bad idea," Aspen interjected before Matt could respond.

Jessica frowned. "Easy for you to say. You're the one with a boyfriend."

"We're casually dating," Aspen explained. "It's different."

"Knowing you, it'll take years before you can admit he's your boyfriend," Jessica accused.

"That's not true!" Aspen shot back. From the look on her face, the statement had hurt.

"Whatever." Jessica threw up her arms, ready to give up the petty argument. "I thought we might need some fun. Apparently, I was wrong."

Jessica pivoted to leave before Matt stopped her. "I'm game if you are," he said, putting one hand on her elbow.

Surprise and displeasure darted across Aspen's face. "What?"

Jessica slowly turned around, her lips stretching into a smile.

Matt repeated it slowly in order to let it sink in. "I said I'll do it."

He didn't know exactly why he had agreed, other than a chance to prove something to Aspen. If he was honest, it was an opportunity to show Aspen that she could do better. A side-by-side comparison. *Ryder versus Matt.*

Aspen narrowed her gaze. "You want to go out with my sister?"

"Why not?" He shrugged.

Aspen shook her head, questioning his motives. "If you make this some weird testosterone battle, Ryder won't back down."

Matt flashed a confident smile. "I won't either, so I guess we're even."

There were a dozen reasons he should say no to this, but he couldn't backtrack now. Not when so much was at stake. The last thing he wanted was for her to get hurt.

Aspen crossed her arms. "You don't know what you're getting into."

~

MATT TOOK one final look in the mirror, adjusting the collar of his crisp white shirt under his immaculate charcoal suit. Tonight, he looked more like a contestant on *The Bachelorette* than a guy who pulled weeds on the weekend.

A troubling feeling that he'd forgotten something forced him to replay his mental checklist. Cleaned his truck. *Check.* Picked up flowers. *Check.* Made reservations at DeSoto's. *Check.* Even the weather looked gorgeous. The only wild card was Ryder.

The doorbell rang as Aspen's voice floated down the stairs. "Can you get the door, Matt?" Aspen shouted.

The girls had shut themselves in Jessica's room for the last hour. Based on the amount of laughter he heard, it sounded like a girls' slumber party.

Grabbing the flowers he'd bought, he darted to the door.

Ryder was about to get a dating smackdown.

As he flung open the door, Ryder leaned against a porch column dressed in an equally stunning suit, holding an identical bouquet.

Whatever Matt had expected, it wasn't this. He figured Ryder would have to borrow a suit coat just to pass the dress code.

"Let me guess . . ." Ryder's smug smile widened as he eyed Matt's bouquet. "You bought those at the flower shop downtown?"

Matt dropped the bouquet next to his leg. "Good guess."

"Well, you know what they say about great minds." Ryder sounded pleased with himself as he stepped into the house.

"Aspen must have given you strict instructions, huh?" Never once had he seen Ryder look this good for any of his dates.

"She told me we were going to DeSoto's. I figured you had something up your sleeve."

Matt forced a serene smile but didn't respond. It was the way things had always been between them. Friendly competition. But underneath, one thing was obvious: neither would let the other win.

"We're ready," Aspen called as the girls descended the steps.

Jessica's fire-red dress had the kind of attention-getting quality that matched her personality. Bold and hard to ignore. It clung to her figure the same way the robe had.

Between the two women, it was Aspen who stole the show. Her understated peacock-blue dress brought out her eyes and subtly demanded the attention of every man in the room. Matt could hardly take his gaze off her.

"Don't you look nice," Jessica oozed, pulling Matt away from Aspen.

"Oh, thanks. You do too," he mumbled, still distracted by Aspen. He really needed to get his mind off her before he looked like a lovestruck fool.

"Sorry if we kept you waiting." Aspen offered Ryder a smile that made Matt seethe. It wasn't that she didn't have a right to smile. After all, they were dating. But if he was being honest, he wanted that smile all for himself.

Ryder's gaze flitted over her dress. With a satisfied grin, he held up the flowers. "For you."

Aspen's face melted at the lovely gift. "Oh, thank you. These are beautiful."

Matt curled his hands into fists, realizing Ryder had beaten him to the surprise. He'd been so mesmerized by Aspen, he'd lost track of his dating checklist.

Flowers, dummy.

"These are for you." He offered his bouquet to Jessica, trying to recover his confidence.

Jessica eyed the identical gift. "Wow. Did you guys plan this?"

"It appears that way, but no." Matt corrected his irritated expression.

Aspen and Jessica exchanged looks before Aspen looped her

arm through her sister's. "Why don't we put these in a vase before we leave?" She dragged Jessica to the kitchen.

Ryder leaned toward Matt. "What's the deal?"

"What are you talking about?" Matt leaned against the wall, hands in pockets, a picture of calm.

Ryder gave an incredulous half-laugh. "Everything's a competition for you. I remember that from the fire station. You'd try to rope me into playing, but not this time."

Matt didn't have time to respond before the ladies returned, but his entire plan for the night was backfiring already.

"Shall we?" Ryder offered his arm to Aspen. "See you at the restaurant," he called over his shoulder.

Matt watched them leave before Jessica tugged on his elbow, reminding him she was still there. "You ready? Or are you going to keep staring at my sister?"

"What do you mean?" he responded, trying to play dumb. Matt hoped Aspen hadn't noticed him gawking.

All this time with her, he'd pretended not to care, trying to rationalize the reasons he couldn't love her. But there was one thing he hadn't counted on. Love was never logical.

"I think you know what I mean," Jessica claimed. "You're just afraid to admit it."

He shook his head and turned away.

Jessica glanced at Ryder's truck as Aspen climbed in. "If there's one piece of advice I'd give you, it's this—stop being jealous of what they have. She doesn't need you standing in the way of her dreams."

PIANO MUSIC FLOATED across the lavishly decorated restaurant as Matt and Jessica entered behind Ryder and Aspen. Sprays of brilliant flowers embellished every table. Servers rushed silently across the room, oblivious to the gorgeous view of the lake from the massively large windows.

"I forgot how beautiful this place is," Jessica remarked as she lifted her chin at the enormous chandelier in the middle of the foyer.

As a hostess led them to their table, the two couples drew every eye in the room. Their double date was fodder for the gossip mill in this small town, especially since Jessica had only recently returned after getting a divorce.

Sitting at a cozy table tucked near the window, two older women waved to the girls.

"There's no escaping Agnes and Marla," Jessica whispered, returning a less than enthusiastic smile and wave. "They probably can't wait to ask me about my divorce."

Aspen gave a curt nod to the ladies. "Ignore them. It's none of their business. If you need help dealing with them, I've got your back."

"They're coming over here, aren't they?" Jessica mouthed as she opened her menu and tried to hide.

"I'll cover you." Matt lowered his menu and addressed the immaculately dressed women. "Hello, ladies. You both look lovely this evening."

"Oh, this old dress?" Marla blushed, glancing at what appeared to be a brand-new outfit.

Agnes didn't bother responding to Matt's compliment. Her focus was entirely on Jessica. As one of the richest and most gossipy women in town, she seemed to think she had a right to everyone's personal life.

"Jessica, what a surprise," Agnes's voice oozed saccharine. "Is this a family visit, or are you taking care of business?" She looked between the sisters.

Trying to get dirt on people was one of Agnes's specialties.

"You might say both," Jessica replied matter-of-factly. "You heard about my great-aunt's passing?"

"Oh yes, such a loss," Agnes murmured, glancing at Marla, who nodded with forced sympathy. "What are your plans for the inn? Are you still hosting guests for the summer?"

Matt's gaze flitted to Aspen, who snapped her menu shut.

Revealing anything to Agnes was like announcing it over a loudspeaker.

"We're doing some redecorating before we put it up for sale," Aspen replied flatly.

Marla's eyes widened. "So it's true you're selling the inn?"

"Yes." Aspen glanced at Jessica for support.

"Not right away," Jessica replied. "But as soon as it's done."

Agnes patted Aspen's shoulder. "That inn has needed updates for years. Hopefully, you'll get a decent price." Her eyes fell on Jessica.

"Of course we will," Jessica said confidently, staring hard at her menu.

"But it's not just about the money," Aspen defended. "Running an inn is a huge endeavor that neither of us wants to shoulder. Without Matt's help, I couldn't keep up with the never-ending list of repairs."

"Ah, yes. It must be nice having a man like him around." Agnes turned to Matt. "Maybe you'd like to work at the Bellevue estate next? I'm sure we could find a place for you."

The last thing he wanted was to work for a rich socialite. Aunt Lizzie's situation had been drastically different. She couldn't have afforded a grounds crew like the Bellevues. "I'm not for hire."

"The invitation is always open," Agnes reminded him before turning back to Jessica. "So, what are your plans now?"

Jessica froze in her chair, her face draining of color. The silent question of how she was surviving life after divorce hovered over the table uncomfortably.

"I'm not sure yet." Jessica shifted in her seat. "The opportunity to stay in Wild Harbor is still a possibility."

"Especially when the company is so appealing." Agnes's mouth curved as her eyes flitted toward their dates. "Just don't let your ex get wind of it."

Agnes tipped her chin back to examine Jessica's reaction when she brought up Chase.

"Chase is in Atlanta." Jessica waved away the subject, trying to pretend it didn't bother her. "He isn't concerned about me."

"Oh, so you haven't heard?" Agnes turned to Marla, a wicked smile playing on her lips as she paused for dramatic effect. "Chase is back in town. He returned a few nights ago."

Surprise flashed across Jessica's face. "He's *here?*"

Agnes fingered her pearl bracelet. "I saw him at the coffee shop chatting with Lexy Carmichael."

Color drained from Jessica's face, like she'd just endured a horrendous gut punch.

"I thought you knew." Agnes's unsympathetic expression was heartless. More than anything, she delighted in poking the hornet's nest.

Jessica stared at her water glass, trying to hold back her emotions. "I'm sorry. I need a minute," she whispered before rushing to the lobby.

"Jessica, wait up," Matt pleaded, attempting to catch her before she stepped outside. He didn't know how to help, but he wouldn't let Agnes win.

"I just need to be alone," she said through gritted teeth, bolting for the door. "There's nothing you can do."

"I know I can't fix this for you," he pleaded, stopping her in the foyer. "But I can be a listening ear. Take you home. Whatever you want."

She nodded and clamped her lips, trying to hold back the tears that flooded her eyes. "That's the problem. I don't know what I want."

Matt didn't know either, but he'd learned early from his mom that a hug was always a welcomed response.

"Maybe a hug?" he offered, arms out. "Just as friends?"

Before he even moved, she buried her face in his shoulder. Her breath came in deep gulps, like she was trying, and failing, to pull herself together.

He rested his chin on Jessica's head, holding her tightly before his view landed on Aspen standing at the other end of the foyer. Jealousy flashed across her expression.

"Is everything okay?" Aspen asked weakly, stepping forward.

Jessica nodded. "I'll be fine. I don't know why I let that woman bother me so much."

Aspen rubbed circles on her sister's back. "We don't have to stay. If you want to return to the house, say the word."

"We're not canceling the evening." Jessica was resolute. "A few minutes in the bathroom will do the trick. I probably look like a raccoon."

"You're beautiful," Aspen said, pulling tissues from her purse. "Even if you have raccoon eyes."

As Jessica headed to the ladies' room, Matt lowered himself onto a bench. "What is it?" he asked, studying Aspen's worried expression.

"It's nothing." She brushed a curl out of her eyes and hesitated. "I didn't know how awkward this was going to be."

"You mean the situation with Agnes?"

"That and . . ." She sank next to him. "I was a little shocked to see you hugging my sister."

"She needed it," he explained. Of all people, she should understand that he didn't have feelings for Jessica. "We don't have to go through with tonight. I can take Jessica home and let you and Ryder enjoy the evening." He hated admitting defeat, but the night had taken a disastrous turn, and they hadn't even ordered dinner yet.

"I don't think we should let Agnes win." Her eyes flitted past him to see if her sister was out of the bathroom. "Just promise me one thing."

"What's that?"

Aspen fingered her clutch. "Don't allow my sister to do something stupid, okay? She hides her hurt well, but she's not thinking straight since the divorce. When Chase left, it was a blow to her self-esteem. Her natural reaction is to resort to dangerous flirting."

He looked her in the eye. "You don't have to worry about your sister with me."

She glanced at him again. "I don't want to see anyone get hurt."

Just then, Jessica returned from the ladies' room looking completely unruffled. Whatever pep talk and makeup job she'd given herself had been transformational.

"I'm starving, but I've lost my taste for this restaurant," she confessed, grabbing Matt's arm. "Who's up for pizza?"

"Seriously?" Aspen's mouth fell open. "After all this hard work getting ready, you want to head to George's?"

Jessica offered an apologetic look. "We all know Agnes would never set foot in that kind of joint."

"Then it's a done deal," Matt confirmed. "Greasy grub it is." As Jessica looped her arm through his, he glanced over his shoulder one last time.

Before Aspen looked away, he was sure he'd caught her staring, and one thing was certain. She was not happy.

WHEN THEY RETURNED to the inn later that night, Matt could hardly wait to change out of his suit. Even with the rocky start, somehow they'd turned the night around. He'd eaten too much pizza, and they'd reminisced about high school and all the friends who'd moved away from Wild Harbor. Even Ryder had been agreeable.

As he loosened the tie on his shirt, Aspen's soft voice came from the hall. "You still awake?"

He unbuttoned the collar of his shirt. "Come on in."

Aspen opened the door, her eyes landing on the space where his collar was open. "I can come back," she stammered, backing away from him.

"No need." He gave her a wry smile. "You own the place."

"Well, I do, technically. But this room is still yours."

"Depends who's sleeping here," he noted, referring to the night he'd discovered her asleep.

"I'll try not to let it happen again," she assured him. "I know you hate your bed getting messed up."

He hadn't minded his bedding rumpled when she was the cause.

"I wanted to thank you for tonight," she continued, wrapping her arms around herself.

"I'm not sure you need to thank me for anything." The strap of her dress was slipping off her shoulder, distracting him.

"No, I do," she said. "What you did for Jess meant a lot to her."

He reached up and adjusted the strap as her eyes traced his movement.

"And how you and Ryder got along," she continued, her voice softer now, "I know it took some effort on your part."

Matt hung up his suit jacket, avoiding her stare. "Jessica needed a friend tonight, and I decided it was more important to have fun—even with Ryder there."

"I still don't understand the history between you two."

"We don't get along." He turned to face her. "We're both a little stubborn."

"A little?" She raised her eyebrows.

"Okay, a lot." He rolled up his shirtsleeves. He didn't care for the guy, but he wouldn't break them up. For once, it had to be her decision. All he wanted was for Aspen to see the truth about Ryder.

"I've known you long enough to tell when something bothers you," she urged. "And Ryder rubs you the wrong way."

"Why don't you ask Ryder?"

"Truthfully? I trust you more," she said, crossing her arms.

Apparently, he wasn't the only stubborn one. Matt rubbed the back of his neck. His muscles felt like a brick wall. "It's complicated, okay? I don't know what else to say."

How could he explain he wanted her, but could never have her, not as long as she was dating someone else. Ryder had saved his life. There were some lines he wouldn't cross.

"I have something to tell you." She paused. "An investor called today. He's interested in the inn."

"Really? Someone legit?"

"Seems like it. They want to see the place in a few weeks. That doesn't leave me with a lot of time to fix up things, but I hope I can finish it by then." Her tone was upbeat, but underneath there was a current of hesitation.

He narrowed his gaze. "This is what you want, right?"

She slumped onto his bed, folding her hands across her body. "If I'm serious about becoming a photographer, I need some confirmation that this is the path forward."

"Like writing in the sky?" he joked.

"No, like winning this photography contest and selling the inn. Then I'll know for sure."

"You'll never feel one hundred percent confident," he told her. "Winning is not a measure of your talent. It's subjective. The only way you're going to see if you're successful is by trying it."

"Then help me do it." Her eyes pleaded.

"I'm trying to help you sell the inn," he reminded her.

"I meant with the contest. You're my magic bullet." The way she was looking at him now, how could he say no?

"Aspen," he said, shaking his head, "you're the one who's magic. With your skills and talent . . ."

"But without the right subject, it doesn't matter!"

He sighed. "One photo session. That's all I'll give you."

She jumped from her chair, her face glowing. "Tomorrow, then?"

"I'm at the station." There was no way he could fit a photography session into his day.

"That's perfect! I could take pictures while you work."

As much as he didn't like her coming to the fire station, he didn't want her staying here alone. Not until he figured out who was creeping around the inn.

"Thirty minutes," he instructed. "That's it, okay?"

"I owe you for this." Her arms wrapped around his shoulders for a brief hug that sent fire through his body.

Now, more than ever, giving her up was the last thing he wanted. But he couldn't ruin things for her. Not when so much was at stake.

CHAPTER THIRTEEN

ASPEN

Fire Chief Rodney Larson met Aspen at the door with a wide smile under his large mustache. He was a burly guy with hard lines around his eyes and thinning hair that never quite lay down neatly. Although he wasn't overweight, his belly bulged over his waistband from too many years of eating pierogies and sausage.

"Please don't mind the mess," he apologized. "I would have cleaned up more had I known you were coming."

She wondered what he referred to. The place appeared spotless as usual. "Didn't Matt tell you I was stopping by?"

"About five minutes ago," he answered.

"I'm so sorry," she said. "I can come back another time."

His hand landed on her shoulder. "Absolutely not. You're always welcome here." He grabbed her photography equipment even though she was perfectly capable of managing it herself. Rodney Larson was old school, and helping a woman wasn't just a nicety, it was second-nature.

"If I had known, I would have baked some cookies or something," Rodney replied, setting her bag on the table of the fire station's kitchen.

"You bake?" She raised her eyebrows. "Impressive."

"Nah, not really. I get bored sometimes when I'm on duty. The crew likes it, though it's not great for the fireman-bod." He patted his stomach. "Glad you're not taking pictures of me."

"This isn't a modeling contest." She couldn't resist smiling at the mental image of Rodney as a model for a fireman's calendar.

"Matt's the perfect choice for a hometown hero. That guy would risk his life for anyone and not think twice." Rodney looked down at the floor. He'd probably seen countless situations where life and death were held in the balance of seconds. This wasn't pie-in-the-sky heroism; it was the sacrificial nature of firefighting. No wonder Matt couldn't talk about it.

"Your team is so brave. It was an easy yes for me." Aspen glanced around to make sure Matt wasn't listening. "I finally resorted to begging Matt. He's probably hiding from me now."

"I'm glad you're making him do this. Matt doesn't want any recognition. He's always been that way, but last year's fire on Madison Street really messed him up. A kid suffered serious burns and ended up in ICU. Matt blamed himself because he was the one who called the shots on that run. It shook him good."

She set her camera down. "He never mentioned it."

"It wasn't his fault. When a fire is spreading, you're forced to make fast decisions. The kid was scared and hid, making it harder to get him out. Seconds count in a house fire, and there was a cost to losing time. But Matt's never forgiven himself."

It finally made sense why Matt had been so adamantly against this photo shoot. It was forcing him to come to terms with this tragedy.

Aspen turned her camera over in her hands. "Maybe this was a bad idea."

Rodney pointed at her, a firmness in his eyes. "It isn't. All my men need to see themselves as heroes. He's got to get over this mental block, otherwise it becomes something a lot more serious, you know?" He shook his head. "I've seen too many firefighters deal with this. You're the one who can help."

Her stomach twisted uncomfortably. What could she do? For weeks, she'd pressured him, not knowing she was blindly aggravating a raw wound. All the while, he hadn't said a word about the kid in ICU. How could she ask him for a photo after that?

Rodney nodded toward the door where Matt was. "You're doing him a favor."

She hesitated, looking through the window where he stood checking the trucks. If this was a favor, why did it feel like the exact opposite?

She quietly entered the garage where the fire trucks were parked. Matt worked alone, jotting notes onto an iPad. Holding her camera still, she zoomed in and snapped a few shots.

Matt spun around. "How long have you been there?" His expression was a mixture of surprise and displeasure.

"Just stay there. The natural light is perfect. Ignore me and you won't even notice I'm here."

He gave her a look that said *fat chance*. "I always know when you're around, Aspen."

"Do you have some sixth sense?" she asked, clicking the camera while trying to distract him.

"Nope," he replied without meeting her gaze. "It's just you."

"What are you going to do when I'm gone?"

"Other than cry my eyes out?" A wry smile crossed his face. "Learn to live with it."

As he glanced away, she took more shots, orbiting him like a planet. Even if she didn't win the contest, looking at him through the lens was pure pleasure.

Just then, Chief Larson bolted into the garage. "House fire on Oak Street," he stated with a calm urgency.

Before she had time to react, Matt was gone, suiting up for the emergency. Aspen followed, snapping pictures as fast as possible before the crew left. She couldn't tell whether the lighting was adequate, but the opportunity was gold. Nothing could replace capturing men in action.

All the men loaded into the fire trucks, forgetting she was even there.

Matt took one last look at her. "Stay here, okay? I'll return later. Don't head back to the house alone, either."

"Can I take pictures at the fire?" she asked.

"No," he stated firmly before jumping into a truck. "Too dangerous."

With sirens blaring, they disappeared onto the street.

Aspen's heart hammered from the excitement. She touched her chest lightly, as if her fingertips could somehow stop that weird pulsating feeling. *Calm down, little heart.* She pulled up the pictures on her camera to slow the adrenaline in her body. Raw images of intense faces filled her screen. These had potential, but she needed more to work with.

What if she showed up at the house fire and stayed out of sight? Matt couldn't fault her then. She didn't want to put herself at risk, but as long as she remained unseen, no one would have to know.

Her heart gave a tiny flip-flop in her chest, signaling that she'd forgotten to take her medicine. She couldn't afford to lose time now. Capturing them in action was her first priority.

Once she had a few decent shots, she'd head home for her medicine, even though Matt had warned her to stay at the station. If she took the shot of a lifetime and won the contest, how could he fault her for that? Her phone buzzed in her pocket.

Matt: I meant what I said earlier. Don't leave.

Had he read her mind? He knew Jessica was gone today, and he didn't want her returning to the house alone after the break-in. But staying at the station was a waste of time. Nobody had to know where she was going. All that mattered now was getting the perfect shot.

Finding the fire was easy as she followed the smoke to Oak Street. When she arrived at the scene, fire trucks blocked the street as heavy smoke poured from the windows. Fire leapt out of the roof of a two-story home as men scrambled forward with hoses. Neighbors gathered around the perimeter, staying safely distanced, but unable to tear their eyes away from the blaze.

Aspen blended into the group, trying to overhear the neighbors' conversations. Apparently, the house had been vacant for months, and its owner was out of the country. Visible relief settled over her body. Matt didn't need to risk his life to save anyone today.

As the firemen rounded the house, Aspen realized the street view wouldn't give her the best angle. The action was happening behind the house, which meant she needed to sneak into a neighbor's yard. Slinking next to a tree, she located a nearby shed that butted up to the backyard. If she hid behind the shed, she could snap some close-up shots of the firemen without getting in their way. It was a good plan as long as Matt didn't catch her.

With the firemen focused on controlling the burn, she snuck past a neighbor's house and parked her belongings behind the small building. Slowly angling her camera around the corner of the shed, she steadied the lens and zoomed in on Matt's face. Water sprayed like a rooster's tail as the heavy black smoke rushed from the windows. Matt shouted orders while pulling the hose closer. An intense concentration had settled into the lines of his eyes as sweat glistened across his brow.

Her hands shook. All she needed was one shot.

Out of the corner of her viewfinder, a sudden movement

caught her attention. A small white dog darted from the bushes toward the flaming house and then froze in the yard just behind the firefighters.

No one seemed to notice the pet, who appeared dazed from the commotion.

Aspen dropped her camera and stepped forward, determined to keep the dog from getting in the way. She crouched low and softly whistled to the pup. With several hoses spraying water, no one could hear her.

"Come here, little Fido." She reached her hand out, inviting the dog to approach. "I won't hurt you." The dog cocked his head and crept forward cautiously.

Just a few feet more until she could scoop him up and figure out who he belonged to.

"Come here, buddy. You need to stay out of the way so you don't get hurt."

The dog took another step, then paused.

A sudden crash echoed inside the burning house, causing the dog to bolt the opposite direction.

"Come back!" she screamed as she lunged to tackle him, but Fido sensed the danger and darted away as she stumbled to her knees. "Not that way!"

The dog skittered toward the house, stopping short of bolting into an open door. Racing around the perimeter, the pup made a hard right turn. Aspen hid behind a tree, following the dog's path while staying out of Matt's radar. The pet dashed past a row of bushes along the side of the house where it finally crouched under an overgrown azalea. If she could dash to the bush, pick up the dog and race back, she might make it without anyone spotting her. But it was a big *if*, and the fire was still raging out of control. Getting this close to the house was not only foolish, it was dangerous.

One glance at poor Fido, who was shaking with fear, and Aspen no longer cared about her safety anymore. The rescue only required her to cross a space of twenty feet in order to make it to the dog's hiding spot. Her eyes swung between the fire crew and the puppy before she launched forward into a full-scale sprint across the yard.

As soon as she made it to the bush, she dropped to her knees and scooped the dog into her arms before stumbling to her feet. A gust of wind diverted smoke into her face, causing her to choke out a cough. She covered the dog's nose and mouth with her shirt, but struggled to take a decent breath without a mask. She needed to move away from the fire, but a dark cloud had intensified around the side of the house, leaving her with no choice. As she frantically dashed the opposite direction and turned the corner, she nearly slammed into a fireman.

She staggered back and glanced up. It was Matt, and judging by his expression, he was not happy with her.

"What are you doing here?" His brow creased as panic filled his eyes. "You need to get away from this house. Now!" He grabbed her elbow and dragged her toward the street.

As soon as they emerged from the smoke, she yanked her arm from his grasp. "I'm rescuing a dog." Even while her eyes watered and her heart bounced in her chest, she couldn't let him treat her like a child.

She held up the pooch. "The poor thing was trying to run towards the house."

"I told you to stay at the station." He looked furious. "You weren't supposed to come here. This is dangerous."

"I saw him darting toward the fire, and no one even noticed. I couldn't let the dog get hurt."

"*You* could have been hurt," he yelled, an intensity flaming in his eyes. "This dog isn't your responsibility," he hissed.

"Well, someone had to do it," she yelled back.

"Then let me do it. You have no right to be here. I'm sorry," he said, not sounding apologetic in the least.

He was so regimented and logical, she wanted to punch him.

Was he so hard-hearted that he didn't have any feelings for a pet? She bit the inside of her cheek, holding back her rising anger.

"Not until I get my camera equipment. I left it by the shed near the backyard."

"You're not going anywhere near the backyard!" he yelled.

"I'm not leaving until I have it back." She turned on her heel and stormed toward the burning house before he yanked her around by the shoulder.

"Aspen, are you crazy?" Matt shouted at her, his hand still on her collarbone. "There's a house on fire, and all you care about is a stupid picture?"

Aspen tried to think of a fitting comeback, but her thoughts were jumbled. She wanted to scream at him to mind his own business, but her heart was banging like a jackhammer against her rib cage. She dragged her fingers across the neckline of her shirt while a ferocious cough left her gasping for air.

Matt's eyes dropped to her hand, suddenly concerned. "Are you okay?"

As she struggled to catch her breath, her heart did a weird double beat, followed by a single, then a double.

"I'll be fine," she choked, pounding her ribs with a fist.

"You don't look fine." He grabbed her hand and pulled her toward a truck.

Unbeknownst to him, her heart responded to his grasp, flailing in her chest. His touch was making things worse.

As he waved down another fireman, he threw a concerned glance her way again, his jaw clenching. "Don't fight me on this, Aspen. I'm doing what's best for you. You'll be in excellent hands."

"Whose?" Her gaze darted across the yard. She didn't want to be passed around like a hot potato. She wanted to return home, take her meds, and start editing these photographs.

He motioned to the fireman. "Hal, call the ambulance. This woman needs to go to the hospital."

"I don't need an ambulance," Aspen muttered under her breath. "I want to go home."

He spun around to face her, his hand still holding tight to hers. "You can't drive home in this state, and I can't accompany you because I have responsibilities here. I wish I didn't, but I don't have a choice."

"But what about the dog?"

"Give him to me." He pulled the squirming dog from her arms and cradled him like a football. "I'll make sure someone takes care of him until we find the owner. You stay with Hal until the ambulance arrives."

"I told you, I don't need a—"

"Hush." He touched her lips with his hand. "Don't argue with me. It will only make things worse."

"But my camera . . ."

"I'll find it if you cooperate and go in the ambulance."

"Are you serious? Because a few minutes ago, you were giving me a lecture about my *stupid* pictures." Her heart was still knocking against her chest, but she didn't care now. She could be just as stubborn as him. "Promise me or I'm not going."

He paused and narrowed his eyes. "You won't let this go, will you?"

"Nope."

"As long as you get in that emergency vehicle, I'll promise whatever you want." His words were low and pleading.

A siren wailed as an ambulance turned the corner.

He rubbed the lines on his forehead. "I'll check on you as soon as I can." His dark eyes were rippling with concern, focused only on her.

"I'll be fine," she whispered, waving him away. She didn't feel fine. But she needed to make him feel better.

Even as the ambulance pulled away, he was still watching

her, making sure she didn't break their deal. As his silhouette faded from view, she was suddenly aware of how much she wished he was there with her.

If it was this hard to leave him now, what would it be like when she left for good?

◡

SHE HATED HOSPITALS. The poking, the prodding, the incessantly repeated questions by the medical staff. If one more person asked *how she would rate her pain,* she was going to scream.

If Matt hadn't forced her to go to the hospital, she could be relaxing at the inn, eating ice cream straight from the tub.

"You know it's your own fault," Jessica concluded, holding a bag of chips and an overpriced health food bar from the vending machine. "If you'd taken your heart meds on time, you wouldn't be here." Her sister dug in the bottom of her gigantic purse.

"It's a little late for a lecture. They want to run me through a whole batch of tests now. Help me convince the doctor that my body is back to its normal fickle ways."

Aspen's heart machine gave a shrill beep as if it were protesting against her complaints. Her heart had been setting off alarms ever since they hooked her up.

Jessica popped a chip into her mouth. "It's not like you're a heart expert. Do you have any proof your arrhythmia isn't getting worse?"

Proof? Wasn't her own body proof? Her heart problem had existed for as long as she could remember. If she wasn't meant to be alive, then something would have already happened.

Aspen sat up in bed. "Don't tell Mom and Dad this, but I haven't seen a specialist for a few years. Not because I'm lazy. I just wasn't having any problems."

"Until now," Jessica reminded her.

"It's stress-related, not heart-related," Aspen emphasized. "The last few months have been full of change, but I've always been resilient. I'll bounce back."

"You say that because you're a positive person. But positivity won't fix your heart. A cardiologist should review your results." Jessica dangled another chip over her mouth. "Your heart shouldn't flip out just because you missed your medicine."

Aspen glanced at her phone again, searching for some sign of concern from Ryder. She had texted him, *I'm in the hospital because my heart is being stupid.* And then added the laughing emoji face.

An hour later, he still hadn't responded. Didn't he care that she was in the ER? If Ryder was hospitalized, she'd race here as soon as possible.

She dialed his number again, and for the fourth time, it went straight to voicemail. What could he possibly be doing that was so important?

Though she'd never tell him, his lack of concern was irritating, and it wasn't helping her heart to calm down. She needed to take deep breaths. Listen to soft music. Practice her stress-relief exercises which, recently, had seemed pointless. Her whole life was a dumpster fire.

Jessica rubbed her hand across her stomach and cringed. "I shouldn't have eaten those chips." She set the bag on the chair next to her. "Speaking of stress, I haven't felt like myself lately either. I've been nauseous, emotional, and wanting to stress eat for days. Maybe the doctor should check me while I'm here."

Aspen knew her sister put up a good front, even though the divorce had been taxing. The last thing she needed was someone else to worry about.

"You've had a lot on your plate," Aspen reminded her. "The divorce. Chase. And now me. That's too much for you."

"You're never too much, sis." Jessica gave her a reassuring grin. "Chips?"

She offered her the bag, but Aspen waved it away. Her stomach was still roiling with anxiety.

"I know what I need to make things better," Jessica commented. "To get over Chase. And that means finding a new guy."

"You mean a rebound guy?" Aspen asked.

Jessica rolled her eyes. "I hate that term. To be clear, I'm not ready to get serious with anyone. I need a man who will be my friend first."

"You need time to figure things out," Aspen offered, concerned that her sister wanted to date so soon. Whether or not she admitted it, finding a man so quickly after her divorce was a terrible idea.

"Can I ask you something?" Jessica leaned forward and placed her elbows on her knees. "I need you to be one hundred percent honest with me."

"You can ask me anything."

Her sister nervously rubbed her hands on her pants. "Would you have a problem if I dated Matt?"

"What?" Aspen nearly choked on the word. She couldn't believe Jessica would suggest him.

"It's not okay?" Her sister studied her intently.

"No, it's just that I wasn't expecting you to choose him."

Aspen swallowed down a lump in her throat as jealousy rippled under her skin. Matt had never clicked with Jessica the way she had, although her sister had tried. On more than one occasion, Jessica's flirtatious attempts had created a deep wedge between them. It was almost a relief when she married Chase.

Aspen had always considered her relationship with Matt special, and now it felt like Jessica was trying to infringe on their private territory. Even though she knew Matt would make some lucky girl very happy, she couldn't stomach the idea that her sister might be the lucky one.

Two opposing ideas battled inside her head: Matt shouldn't be anyone's rebound guy. But she'd do anything for Jessica.

"I never considered him seriously until now," Jessica went on. "He always struck me as cocky. But now that I'm here, I've been impressed with his loyalty and concern. He's a great catch. I can't imagine how you live with him and don't feel wildly attracted."

If she only knew. Aspen had been in a losing battle against her wild attraction for some time. The only way she'd kept it under control was because he'd made it clear—*never ever.* Anything more than friendship would never be a possibility.

"Are you okay with it?" Her sister wanted some sort of approval.

Her whole body revolted against the idea of Jessica dating Matt. But no matter what her heart felt, she knew Jessica's happiness should be more important than her own. Wasn't that the kind of sacrifice sisters made?

"If that's what you want," Aspen forced out, "then I'll support you."

Even saying the words hurt. She couldn't imagine them cuddling on the couch, or holding hands and gazing at each other with knowing looks. She wanted one hundred percent of his attention, and she'd had it. But now her sister was asking her for something she didn't want to give, leaving her with a lonely pit in her stomach.

"I wanted to make sure before I asked him," Jessica confirmed. "You've always had this odd love-hate vibe. If becoming roommates hasn't led to anything, then a relationship is pretty much off the table." Jessica tossed her chip bag into the wastebasket.

Aspen wrapped her arms around her knees. She needed to cover up the growing wretchedness she felt. Suddenly, losing Matt felt like hot sauce rubbed into a paper cut.

But if it bothered her so much, why couldn't she say so? The answer was something she didn't want to admit. Throughout their friendship, he'd never once confessed any feelings for her. Never asked her to be more. Even their kiss had been a mistake. They were friends, nothing more, and she was too afraid of ever ruining that.

"Are you trying to scare us all to death?" Megan appeared in the doorway, her brow furrowed in concern.

"I texted you ten minutes ago that I was alive and fine." Aspen held up her phone.

Megan narrowed her eyes, peering closely at her friend as she approached. "I had to see for myself." As the two girls embraced, cords from the machines tangled around Megan's arms.

"Whoa, careful there." Aspen untangled Megan from the labyrinth of wires. "If you pull on these, an obnoxious alarm will sound." Aspen's heart settled into a steady blipping on the monitor.

"I don't exactly have a stellar reputation here since I snuck out after my accident." After nearly drowning in a sailing mishap, Megan had escaped the hospital without an official discharge to stop Finn from leaving town.

"Where is everyone?" Megan turned to Jessica. "I thought you'd have a crowd."

"Matt has an excuse." Aspen rested her head against the pillow. "House fire on the east side of town."

"And Ryder?"

Aspen shrugged. "I've called and texted. He hasn't responded."

Megan frowned. "Doesn't he know the first rule of dating? Always text back in emergencies."

Jessica ripped open her health food bar. "Rule two," she added, using her snack for emphasis. "Always show up when your woman is in the hospital."

Without warning, another visitor appeared in the doorway.

Matt filled the entrance with a commanding presence that startled and calmed her. Streaks of black soot jutted across his jawline, while his eyes were intense and focused, a dark milky way that she could fall into. He hadn't taken off his fireman's jacket, and his hair was a mess from his helmet, but the light reflecting off the hard lines of his face couldn't hide the perfect symmetry of his features. She sketched another mental drawing, capturing the shadowy contours under his eyes and the gentle curve of his chin.

"What are you doing here?" Aspen lifted herself from the bed, shocked to see him appear before her like magic.

"Checking on you, Little Bit." He leaned against the doorframe, hiding his tiredness behind an easy smile, but something sparked in his expression when he said her nickname. "Telling you how glad I am to see you before I give you a lecture."

"I don't need a lecture on firefighting safety now," she replied, crossing her arms. If he was there to make her feel bad, she didn't want to hear it.

Megan turned to Jessica. "Why don't you show me where the vending machine is? I could use a drink."

As the two women left, Aspen's frumpy hospital gown made her aware of how pathetic she must look. She stretched a thin, colorless blanket over her body.

"You're probably going to start by saying I told you so," she huffed, falling back into a thin pillow.

"Not at all. I just couldn't stop thinking of you." He lowered himself onto the bed, observing her carefully. Did he know his presence would ramp up her heart rate? Was this a test to measure whether she was okay?

"You don't need to worry about me." She lifted her chin. "Isn't there a fire you should attend to? A cat you need to rescue?"

"Unless Lester has escaped again, no. The crew has the fire under control now. Chief Larson excused me to come here. I was so distracted after you left, I couldn't even focus. All I wanted to know was how you were doing."

Five minutes ago, she had been calm and itching to go home, but with him here, her thoughts tumbled and her pulse raced. Why did he have to look at her like he was seeing right through her?

His gaze was on the verge of setting off her heart alarm.

"I'm fine," she told him. "You didn't have to come."

"If you were fine, they would have released you by now," he reminded her.

"I'm waiting for the doctor's instructions."

"But is something bothering you?" he asked, concern in his eyes.

You, she wanted to say. *You're making my heart all jumpy.* The heart machine's alarm beeped for a second, confirming her thoughts.

"Slow down there, heart." Matt touched Aspen's hand as his eyes traced the pumping beat on the machine. His touch was making her heart race more, not less.

"There's something I didn't tell you about the night my window was open." What she was about to say was going to sound completely crazy. "I found a riddle from Aunt Lizzie. I think whoever broke into the house left it there for me."

"But why would she do that?"

"When Jess and I were kids, Aunt Lizzie loved to give us riddles to solve. It was something special in our relationship. She delighted in creating mystery."

"But why wouldn't Aunt Lizzie leave the riddle in her will? Or with her lawyer?"

"That's what I don't understand." Aspen pushed a curl behind her ear. "Maybe she was afraid I wouldn't find the riddle on my own. Perhaps she arranged for someone to deliver it instead."

"But why not through the mail? Something less criminal? This doesn't make sense." The furrow in Matt's brow deepened.

"I don't know." She leaned toward a chair where she'd folded her pants before changing into a hospital gown. She pulled out a slip of paper from the pocket. For some reason, she'd started taking the riddle with her everywhere, in case she found a clue.

Matt skimmed the note, his eyes racing over the words again and again. "To find the key, look under the sea. Only then will you be free." He glanced at Aspen. "How could a key be under the sea? Did she drop the key in the lake? I don't understand."

Aspen shook her head, defeated. "I don't even know where to start. None of her previous riddles were this hard."

"If this is real, what do you think her point was?"

Aspen shrugged. "To bring me joy? Maybe one last memory of our time together? Truthfully, it's one more thing to worry about getting done. What if I can't figure this out before I turn the inn over to its new owner? The solution might be gone forever." Aspen crumpled the riddle and sunk it into her pocket.

Just then, a doctor with greying hair and a salt-and-pepper beard entered the room. "Ms. Bradford? We got your results back from the preliminary tests, and my gut feeling was right."

The doctor's face sagged from his long shift in the ER as he squinted at the paper in his hands. "You have some abnormal results that need to be reviewed by a cardiologist. For now, we're releasing you with strict orders not to overexert yourself. Take it easy for a few days. We'll send these results over to the specialist. He'll recommend further treatment."

"Am I going to need surgery?" she asked, hoping he could at least calm the rising worry in her chest.

"I can't say either way," he answered vaguely. "Your cardiologist will determine that."

His response was not what she wanted to hear, but at least she could return home.

"What would you define as overexert?" She sat up.

"Nothing too strenuous on the body," the doctor replied. "Working on your feet all day. Too much stress. That sort of thing."

"So would redecorating a house count?" Matt asked, avoiding her glare.

"Absolutely," the doctor agreed. "You should limit your work until the cardiologist reviews these results. We don't want to place additional stress on the heart. As soon as we have your discharge papers ready, you can go home." The doctor left the room as quickly as he'd arrived.

Matt lifted his eyebrows. "Someone is going to be resting the next few days."

"I can't," she pleaded. "I need to keep working before the investor comes to town."

"Can't you postpone and explain the situation? There's no timeline except the one you place on yourself."

"The investor lives in California and is attending a business meeting in Detroit," Aspen explained. "This is my only shot."

Matt leaned toward her, placing his hand on her arm. "I'll oversee things from here. As long as you let me take care of you."

"I don't need you to. I'm *fine.*" She pulled her arm away and flung her legs over the bed, attempting to stand too quickly, which threw off her balance. "What I really need is to sell this inn." She grabbed the rail for support, setting off a frenzy of beeps.

"From the sound of that machine, I'd say you need to stop worrying." He drew closer and steadied her elbow, turning her toward him.

He looked her in the eyes. "Your great-aunt didn't leave you the inn so you could run yourself ragged. This was her gift to you. An opportunity that could change your life. She would want you to take your time and decide what's best."

Aspen closed her eyes. A delay in her schedule was the last

thing she needed. The longer she remained at the inn, the more confused she became about Matt. She needed to figure out where she belonged and who she belonged with.

Aspen was too much like Aunt Lizzie—unable to stand unsolved mysteries or unfinished business. Her great-aunt's riddle was not only baffling, it taunted her. What did she mean by *only then will you be free*? Free from what? Why did Aspen have the feeling that the answer was going to change everything?

CHAPTER FOURTEEN

ASPEN

"I t's only for a few days," Matt assured Aspen, giving her a look that dared her to challenge him.

She peered at him from a patio chair, an iced tea in hand. Rest may have been the doctor's orders, but every time Matt reminded her, it's like he enjoyed forcing her to take it easy.

To be fair, she didn't like sitting around or thinking about her future. Busyness had been an easy way of escaping hard decisions.

"Don't look at me like that." He pointed at her. "Blame the doc."

Ever since she'd returned home three days ago, Matt had made sure she wasn't trying to sneak a paintbrush or strip wallpaper from the guest rooms. Realizing that she was basically confined to a chair, she'd spent two days editing pictures from the house fire, selecting the perfect one for the *Hometown Heroes* contest.

The first time she viewed it, her reaction was raw emotion, visceral even. The shot was a close-up on Matt's profile. In the blurry distance, billowing smoke highlighted the firefighters. But it was the intensity on his face—the rigid lines, the focus in his eyes, the sweat glistening across his brow—all of it spoke to the sacrifice, courage, and determination of those men. Was it enough to win? She didn't know, but it was enough to move her to tears.

She submitted the photo and whispered a quick prayer, not as a lucky charm like some people used it for, but a prayer of letting go. So much of her own future rode on this wish, but she was slowly realizing that she could do nothing on her own to accomplish it. She only hoped that if her entire dream flopped, she would welcome it with humility and grace. Because that was the hardest part. Learning to accept your life as it was, not as you wanted it to be.

Since the doctor had postponed her plans for the inn, she had little to do but think about her uncertain future. Selling the inn had become top priority now that she knew Jessica's intentions to date Matt. And why wouldn't Matt agree to the arrangement? Her sister was beautiful and bold, the type of woman who would look magnificent on his arm. But Aspen couldn't bear to watch their relationship play out in front of her.

As soon as she could manage, she'd offload this inn to a buyer, even though she knew running away wouldn't solve her problems. Now that she was forced to face her insecurities, they were bubbling to the surface, revealing ugly truths she couldn't ignore. Namely, she didn't want Matt to fall in love with anyone else.

How utterly selfish of her. He had never been hers to begin with. Why wasn't she secure enough to accept that her friend would eventually find someone else? Even if acknowledging that truth tortured her, she needed to discover how to deal with it, especially if that someone was Jessica.

Aspen adjusted her sun hat so that it shaded her face from

Matt's view. The last thing she wanted was for him to notice her low mood. Too much time on her hands was leaving her in a state of pitiful despair. Her phone vibrated in her pocket, a welcome relief from her worrisome thoughts.

Ryder: Sorry I can't stop in today. I was called into work to fix another computer problem, and it's going to take all day. I'll make it up to you with a late dinner tonight.

He'd already explained why he hadn't shown up at the hospital a few days ago. A last-minute work meeting had interrupted his schedule. He'd called as soon as the meeting was over, but ever since, he'd been strangely quiet, texting her less and not listening when they talked.

She had the feeling that Ryder was appalled by the idea of having to take care of her now that she was a semi-invalid. But she tried to reassure him that her health issues weren't permanent. At least, that's what she hoped the cardiologist reviewing her case would say. The doctor's office still hadn't called, and she'd begun to worry about a worst-case scenario.

Distracted by her thoughts, Matt walked by shouldering a ladder, the outline of his muscles clearly apparent under his grey T-shirt. She swore the man could make a burlap sack look good. He set the ladder next to the giant lilac and began whacking away with the hedge clippers now that the blooms were done. Branches and leaves rained down as he pulled something out of the bush.

"What's this?" He studied a yellowed business card as he descended the ladder.

Aspen hurried over, examining the tattered card. She could only decipher part of one line: *appointment only*. Everything else was too faded to read.

"How did this end up there?" Aspen asked.

"Who knows? Probably blew into the bush at some point," Matt guessed.

Aspen turned to go inside, slipping the card into her pocket to throw away.

"By the way, I'm putting a sensor on your window for a new security system," Matt mentioned casually.

"What new security system? I don't have money for that." The thought of paying for an expensive upgrade worried her. She was down to a few hundred dollars in her bank account and had already asked Jessica to cover next month's utility bills.

"Don't worry about the cost. I'm taking care of that," Matt assured her.

"I can't let you do that," she argued. After all, it wasn't his inn. He shouldn't feel responsible to pay for the upkeep.

"I can and I will." His voice was firm. "Don't even try to argue with me."

She knew Aunt Lizzie would've opposed any newfangled technology in her home. The baseball bat Lizzie had kept in the closet made a perfectly good security system.

"Then I'll pay you back as soon as I get the money," she promised.

"You absolutely will not," he challenged her. "It's my gift to you, and I'll take offense if you try to give me money. I don't want anyone coming into this home uninvited again. Especially not when you're alone."

She'd tried to forget about the break-in since nothing had turned up missing other than one letter. Still, she couldn't rid herself of the nagging feeling that someone had left her the riddle on purpose and knew more than they were letting on.

Aspen made her way inside and stood in front of Aunt Lizzie's bookshelf, attempting to find something to assuage her boredom. Her eyes flitted over the titles: *Moby Dick, To Kill a Mockingbird, Pride and Prejudice.*

As a kid, she'd read these novels in between chores at the

inn. Lounging around on the couch, her bare feet propped up on the arm, she'd lost herself in stories of heroes and princesses. Besides the classics, her aunt also had a great love for mysteries and sea-faring tales that involved swashbuckling adventures.

She pulled out a stack of books, their covers decorated with sailing ships and treasure chests overflowing with jewels. As soon as she'd found a comfortable reading spot on the couch and picked up a book, the front door swung open.

"I hoped you'd be home," Megan said as she walked in. "Do you have a few minutes?"

"What else would I be doing? Matt has essentially forced me to submit to complete boredom."

Megan's gaze swung around the room. "Is anyone else here?"

"Only your brother."

Megan settled on the couch next to Aspen, the crease between her brows deepening. "I have some news."

Aspen placed her books on the end table. "The look on your face is sending me some negative vibes." So far her heart was beating steady, thanks to her medication, but worry was rising inside her.

"I don't want to freak you out," Megan tried to assure her.

"Well, you're already freaking me out."

Megan hesitated. "I had an interview for a story in Grand Rapids today. Afterwards, I stopped at a coffee shop when I noticed this couple walking on the sidewalk. They didn't see me, but as the man turned to cross the street, I realized it was Ryder."

"What would he be doing in Grand Rapids? He told me he was tackling computer issues at work today." Aspen shook her head in disbelief.

"I thought it was probably a meeting," Megan added, looking more apprehensive. "But then he put his arm around this woman, and she kissed his cheek." Megan looked as sick as Aspen felt.

"Are you sure it was—?" Her voice faltered, as if she already knew the truth.

"Positive," Megan said softly. "I saw them leave together in his truck. I'm so sorry, Aspen." Aspen closed her eyes, not wanting to believe it was true.

"Are you okay?" Megan asked, touching her friend's arm. "I hope this isn't making you feel worse." Her gaze dropped to Aspen's heart.

Aspen shook her head. Remarkably, the medicine, or maybe her own resolve, was keeping her heart beating steadily. "If your information is correct, can I punch the guy? I can't believe I trusted him. He even promised me dinner tonight." Aspen rolled her hands into fists and covered her eyes.

"What are you going to do?" Megan asked, wrapping an arm around her friend.

Aspen pulled her palms away. "I'm going to confront Ryder over dinner, and it's going to be epic."

"WHAT'S ALL THIS?" Matt glanced over the beautifully set dining room table set for the evening meal. He'd spent the rest of the afternoon priming the walls of a guest room—something Aspen should have been doing, but couldn't. His T-shirt was a grimy mess of sweat, dirt, and splattered paint. He was the one who deserved a special dinner, not Ryder.

"Ryder is bringing over food." She avoided his eyes and placed a cloth napkin on the table. She didn't want to confess the news yet about her boyfriend. Make that *ex-boyfriend*. It would give Matt another chance to rub in that he had been right about Ryder, *again*.

He picked up a shiny knife and narrowed his gaze. "Fancy. Guess you've forgiven him for not showing up at the hospital, huh?"

"We'll see." She turned her attention to the table and straightened a fork. She wasn't sure she could ever forgive Ryder for cheating on her.

The doorbell rang, relieving Aspen from answering more questions.

She frowned. "You're not going to hang out in the kitchen, are you?" She didn't need Matt to witness their conversation. Her nerves were already frayed at the thought of confronting Ryder. An audience would only make it worse.

Matt grabbed an apple and tossed it in one hand. "Not at all, Little Bit." He sunk his teeth into the fruit. "Enjoy your dinner," he said with an edge that hinted he didn't want her to enjoy it at all.

To be fair, he didn't deserve to be treated this way, especially after all he'd done for her today.

Aspen ran her fingers over the neckline of her shirt where her heart lurched like a rocking horse. She tapped her fingers along the skin, hoping to soothe her bucking heartbeat. If Matt knew how anxious she was, he'd refuse to let Ryder in. She prayed her heart could handle it—in more ways than one.

Ryder stepped into the foyer with several carryout boxes. "You ready to eat?" he asked, giving her a quick peck on the cheek. "I'm starving after working all day."

Liar, liar. She pressed her fingernails into her palms until they hurt.

"How was your day?" she forced out with fake cheerfulness. She wasn't ready to confront him yet, even though her anger bubbled below the surface of her rib cage.

"Same as usual. Busy." He carried the boxes to the kitchen.

"I thought we'd eat in the dining room tonight." She nodded toward the table.

His eyes swept over the gleaming silverware and folded napkins. "What's the occasion?"

"I wanted to talk." She glanced at his expression. Not even a flicker of guilt.

She'd come up with this plan after Megan had left. Give him one last date to remember. A picture of what could have been.

Ryder sank down into a chair and began assembling his steak fajita. "I love the smell of steak and peppers," he remarked, licking his lips, hardly noticing the way she folded her hands and stared at him.

Before he took his first bite, she cleared her throat. "So, what were you doing in Grand Rapids today?"

He paused, holding the fajita midair. "Excuse me?"

Red blotches crept up his neck before he sputtered, "I told you I was working today."

"Then why did Megan see you there?" She said it in such an ordinary way that he was forced to do a double take. "She saw you with another woman," she added in the same calm voice.

He lowered his uneaten fajita to his plate, looking disappointed that he couldn't devour it. "She was just a coworker. That's all."

Aspen slowly nodded, but underneath, she was seething. How dare he lie to her.

"I'm giving you a chance to confess, Ryder. To tell the truth and save what we have." She wanted to believe that he had changed, even though she didn't know how she'd trust him again.

A weird guttural sound escaped his lips. "How could you believe Megan over me? That woman has never liked me. Nobody from their family ever has."

"Megan has never spoken against you," she shot back. "Or the rest of their family."

"What about Matt?" he challenged, radiating an angry gleam. "He poisoned this relationship from the start."

"That's not true," she argued. "He told me how you saved him, and because of that, he *refused* to say anything that might hurt us."

She couldn't stand that he was accusing Matt of betraying him when he'd been so loyal.

Ryder slammed his fist on the table. "Then you either need to pick them or me. It's one or the other."

Matt's words hollowly echoed, *Is he the one you want to be with forever?*

If this is what it came down to, there was no choice.

She lowered her voice. "I'm sorry, but I can't date someone who makes me choose between my friends and himself. No one who loved me would ask me to do that." She stood and motioned toward the door. "I'd like you to leave. *Now.*"

"Aspen, we can work this out." Ryder still sat at the table, desperation knitted deep into his face. "You haven't been well," he said softly. "Your heart problems." He vaguely waved his hand in her direction.

"Actually, that's the surprising part. My heart doesn't feel anything at all."

He shook his head and dumped his fajita back into the box, taking it with him. Ryder muttered something under his breath before storming out of the house.

She sank onto the couch, pulling her knees up, wrapping her arms around them. Until recently, everything in her life had been exquisitely good. She'd had a plan for the future, one that she'd been sure was the answer to all her problems. But in a matter of weeks, her house of cards had fallen, each carefully crafted piece tumbling to the floor.

Her heart was numb from so many disappointments, and she longed to rest her head on Aunt Lizzie's shoulder and pour out all her troubles. But her great-aunt wasn't here, and the one man who was her best friend could never be hers. She wanted to beat her fists against the wall. Cry about how unfair life was. But she knew, more than anything, that if she gave up hope, then what else would she have to hang on to?

As she stood to clean up from their failed date, the book

she'd abandoned earlier caught her eye. She'd left it on the end table when Megan stopped by to give her the news. But now the gold lettering glinted in the sunlight, causing her to squint at the title. *Under the Sea.* Suddenly, the words fell into place from her memory. *To find the key, look under the sea.*

She rushed over and studied the spine, then tore it apart. The pages in the center of the book fell open. Someone had manipulated it, revealing a perfect hollow square cut into the middle of the paper, like a tiny container. An unadorned key was nestled inside. She plucked it from the book and examined it in the light.

She had found part one of Lizzie's mystery, but little good it did her. She hadn't discovered any secret compartments or keyholes. Until she could find a lock, the key was useless.

As the back door slammed shut, she dropped the key into her pocket.

She needed to tell Jessica about the discovery, but her breakup with Ryder was first priority.

Jessica bolted into the room, tears streaming down her face, her eyes red from crying.

"I just got the worst news ever," she sobbed, wiping tears with the heel of her palm.

"What in the world is the matter?" Aspen asked, approaching her sister.

"I finally went to see the doctor because I thought I was stressed." Her sister's lips quivered. "But I'm not stressed. I'm pregnant."

"Pregnant?" Aspen's voice nearly choked on the word. This news would change everything for Jessica. "But how?"

Behind her mascara-smeared eyes, her sister gave her a look. "I think you know *how.*"

"But you separated from Chase a while ago, so who is the—"

"Chase is the father," Jessica answered, sniffling as Aspen stared at her sister. "Three months ago we tried to get back together in a last-ditch attempt to reconcile. I moved in with him for a week, then things fell apart again. I never dreamed this would happen. It wasn't until the divorce was finalized that I knew it was over for good, but I never thought I'd end up pregnant."

Aspen didn't want to ask, but she needed to know. "There hasn't been anyone else, right?"

"Of course not. I haven't dated any guy seriously since the divorce." She sank onto the couch and buried her face in her hands. "You know what this means, don't you? It means I'm going to be a single mom, and I don't even have a job. What in the world am I going to live on? How will I take care of a baby?"

Aspen lowered herself onto the couch and wrapped one arm around her sister. "We're going to sell the inn. Aunt Lizzie's estate will help until you can find a job."

Jessica turned to her sister. "So you're not having second thoughts about the inn? You'll sell it for sure?"

Even though a hard lump rose in her throat, Aspen nodded. Images floated across her mind of summers baking tea cakes with Aunt Lizzie, reading books in the window seat, and running along the white sand beach at the edge of the property. Despite how painful it would be, she needed to let it go.

"Yes, I'm selling," Aspen assured her. "You need to take care of this baby and yourself. Once we settle the deal, the inn will provide you with some money to live on for a while." She reached over to tuck a strand of hair behind Jessica's ear. "Have you told Chase yet?"

She shook her head. "I need to figure out how I'm going to break the news. He may want to move back here for good if I'm . . . I mean, *we* are living here." She rested a hand on her belly, which still hid her secret. From this angle, she didn't look pregnant at all.

"Let me break the news to Mom and Dad," Jessica pleaded. "And please don't tell Matt."

Aspen tried to read her sister's face. She wasn't still considering a relationship with him now that she was pregnant, was she?

"Matt won't tell anyone, if that's what you're concerned about."

"I don't know if Chase will have any interest in this child. Is it foolish of me to believe that maybe Matt would?" Jessica's wide eyes glistened with tears, and Aspen realized the last thing she needed was a naysayer.

Jessica closed her eyes. "I know it sounds absurd, but if a relationship with Matt was possible, maybe he'd be open to being something more to this child too. Even if he was just a friend or father figure?" Her face crumpled into tears.

Jessica wanted someone who'd love her child forever. As hard as it was to admit, Aspen could imagine Matt making that kind of sacrifice.

She squeezed her sister's hand. "I think it's worth a try," Aspen assured, though her heart was sinking. "I'll support you no matter what, Jess. You know that, right? I won't leave you or the baby alone."

Her sister wiped a mascara-smudged cheek. "But what about seeing the world and pursuing your dream?"

"We'll figure it out," Aspen whispered, even if she didn't have a clue how. She felt trapped between two gut-wrenching choices. If she stayed, she'd need to give up her dreams and endure Matt falling for someone else—quite possibly, her own sister. But if she left, she'd be abandoning Jessica when she needed her most.

There were no easy answers. Now, more than ever, she needed to leave behind her complicated feelings. Not just for her sister, but for this baby.

CHAPTER FIFTEEN

MATT

"One more picture, then this room is done," Matt said, hanging the last frame on the wall.

Aspen spun around in the newly renovated guest room, scanning the fresh paint, curtains, bedspreads, and wall hangings. They had transformed the space, changing the bold wallpaper into a modern room with all the cozy touches of home. Big, white pillows lay fluffed across the bed. A baby-soft throw was folded neatly on top of a deep blue armchair. Silky curtains pooled on the floor.

Aspen turned to Matt, her eyes bright. "I think Aunt Lizzie would approve, don't you?"

"She'd agree that it was pretty, but not better than her tropical-flowered wallpaper."

A smile spread across Aspen's face. For the first day in two weeks, she wasn't moping around the house, sadness flitting across her face like a storm rolling onto the lake. He tried not to push her for details of what had happened with Ryder, but he knew something was behind her gloomy moods.

"I'm sure Jessica will approve when she gets home." She turned to him, a seriousness settling into her brow. "Did you think any more about what I asked you a few days ago?"

"Going out with your sister?" Matt shoved his hands in his pockets. This was so awkward. He didn't want to date Jessica, he wanted to date *her*. "I don't know, Aspen. Jessica is nice, but . . ."

"I knew there was a *but* coming." Frustration cut through her tone.

Matt rubbed the back of his neck. "I haven't really thought about it."

"It's just one date," she replied, avoiding eye contact with him. "She wants to catch up on life."

He'd known Aspen for years, and he sensed she was hiding something.

"Aspen," he said softly. "She might flirt with me all the time, but the last thing your sister needs is more hurt."

She grabbed his shoulders and leveled her gaze. "You're amazing at treating a woman like she's a queen. Didn't you tell me that once?"

"I was referring to that dork you dated and how he didn't deserve you."

"And you were ninety-nine percent correct." She squeezed his arm.

Her touch made him want more.

She released her grip as if she realized the effect she was having on him. "I won't be mad, if that's what you're worried about."

He looked away. "I don't feel right about this."

"What's holding you back?"

You, he wanted to say, but he couldn't admit it, not when she seemed so concerned about Jessica. He had to try a different approach. Dodging the question wasn't working.

"Truthfully? I can see how much it bothers you when she

flirts with me," he said, leaning against the wall. "I'm afraid of ruining what we have."

Her brow crumpled into a frown. "It's not going to change *us*." She darted across the room and straightened the pillows. Whatever he'd said had clearly annoyed her. Frustration punctuated her sharp robotic motions. "It's fine if she hits on you," she added. "I've put up with it my whole life."

"It's not fine," he insisted, resting a hand on her shoulder so she'd stop moving away from him. "But you're putting me in an awkward situation. Because either way, I can't win."

"What do you mean?" she asked. "I'm giving you my permission."

"But you're obviously not happy about it," he told her.

"Never mind," she said, shrugging him off. He hated when she pushed him away.

He crossed around her, forcing her to face him. "Before you sell this place, I have one favor to ask."

"What is it?"

The question seemed almost ridiculous now that she was frustrated with him, but he had to take a chance. "What would you say to us going out?"

She paused, then shook her head as she circled the bed, putting distance between them. "There's so much to do before the investor comes to look at the inn this weekend. If he makes an offer, things could move pretty fast."

"You can't just sell the inn and leave right away," he told her.

She avoided looking at him, so he cut her off mid-stride. She dodged. He weaved. Finally, he blocked her between the armchair and bed.

"You're not getting out of saying goodbye to everyone," he told her. "You've lived in this town since the day you were born. People have watched you grow up. You need to give them a proper goodbye. That's why I'm putting in my request now for time with you."

He cringed at how formal he sounded, but his plan was a last-ditch attempt to ask, *What if you're the one who was meant for me? What if this is our only shot to find out?*

Her gaze held his as the finality of his words sunk in. She blinked back tears, attempting to stem a flood of emotion.

"You're right about the goodbye," she murmured. "I've been trying to avoid it."

"I know you're busy, but I'd like to celebrate what you're about to do with your life." He placed his hands on her shoulders. "My treat."

Her muscles relaxed under his touch. "If I agree, would you do me a favor?"

"Depends on what it is, Little Bit." His hands remained firmly clasped around her.

"Talk to Jessica." Her face held a trace of sadness. "Then I'll say yes."

A date for a date.

No was on the tip of his tongue, but the way she was staring at him made him unable to resist. He didn't even care anymore as long as he had one shot with her.

"Will you give me the first date?" He wasn't going to let her off easily. If this was the agreement, he wanted the rules clear.

She pulled away from his grip. "I'll check my calendar."

"I already know what's on your calendar. Absolutely nothing."

She propped one hand on her hip. "It's not quite that simple. I've got an inn to finish."

"You have until tomorrow night to give me a date on the calendar."

"Fine." A stubbornness flashed in her eyes as she spun on her heel and left. He knew Aspen was a master of avoidance. This deadline would irk her for sure. But it was the only way of making her fulfill her end of the bargain before time ran out.

Jessica rolled her suitcase to the car before checking her phone once more. "Looks like the plane is on time. I'm dreading this trip, but I need to get the last of my things packed to move here. If only Chase had paid one more month on the lease, I wouldn't be so rushed to clean out the apartment."

Matt hauled Jessica's suitcase into the trunk of the Uber driver's car and tried to give the sisters a moment to say goodbye.

"I wish I were going with you." Aspen pulled her sister into a hug. "Even if only for support."

"I'll only be gone for a few days," Jessica assured her, putting on a brave face. "Chase and I are taking turns cleaning out things. The hardest part will be doing it alone."

"Call me and we'll video chat." Aspen squeezed her sister's hand. "I still have to tackle one last room, so we'll do it together. That way, you won't be alone. Tell me when you talk to Chase."

"I *know*." Jessica shot her sister a look. "I hate that I'm leaving you when you need my help with the inn."

"Don't worry about it." Aspen waved her hand in the air, trying to make her sister feel better. "Matt is a tremendous help when he's not at the fire station."

Jessica's lips twisted into a smile as she lowered her voice. "And not bad to look at either."

Matt smiled and shook his head. Aspen frowned.

Jessica turned to Matt, oblivious to her sister's reaction. "How about when I get back, I'll treat you to dinner?"

Matt swung his gaze from Jessica to her sister. Aspen had backed up a step, peering at him through lowered lids.

"Sure," he answered reluctantly.

"How about Friday? Does that work for you?" Jessica stepped closer to Matt and rubbed her hand on his arm, like she'd staked her claim.

Aspen's expression grew dark, then she turned and headed for the house.

Matt wanted to run after Aspen, but Jessica was blocking his way. "I don't have my calendar in front of me," he muttered, stalling.

The Uber driver sighed.

"Don't forget," Jessica replied, beaming at him as she opened the door. "I'll look forward to it."

Before the driver had even backed out, Aspen had escaped into the house.

Matt hurried after her, trying to stop her on the staircase. "Aspen," he called.

She didn't even bother turning around. "What is it?"

"We need to plan our date."

Her feet plodded up the steps. "I have a lot on my plate today."

He grabbed her arm and spun her toward him. With her a step above, she was almost eye to eye with him.

"Today is the deadline," he explained with a gentle urgency in his voice. "Your sister is gone for three days before I'm supposed to take her out. The agreement was that you'd give me the first one."

Her face flickered with conflicting emotions. "Fine, I'll go tonight," she said before she pulled her arm away and continued up the stairs.

He wasn't letting her leave without an explanation.

"Wait," he called as he reached for her waist so she had to stop. Her narrowed eyes met his. *Shields up.*

All his fears about ruining their friendship came rushing back. He didn't want to taint their final weeks together. "Why are you so annoyed at me? I said yes to your sister. I did what you asked. Now you need to follow through on your end of the bargain."

Her lips tightened. "It's just my sister's behavior whenever she's around you. She has this effect on every male."

"What effect?" Matt defended, the tension rising in his chest. "I don't know what you're talking about."

"That's exactly what I mean," Aspen accused. "You don't even realize it. Why do you even care about my part of the deal?"

He couldn't believe his feelings weren't obvious to her. When she had been dating Ryder, he'd done everything to extinguish his feelings and honor her wishes. But now that she was free, he finally wanted to tell her what she meant to him before time ran out.

"Because I care about you, Aspen," he pleaded. "I care about *us*."

For a moment, something drifted across her face, a soft, animal-like vulnerability. "I'll go out with you tonight." She backed away, a wretched agony in her eyes. "Then my part of the deal is done."

THE REST of the day dragged by. There was a flurry of painting in the final guest room, the unspoken tension hovering over them as they worked.

By the time the hour arrived for their date, Matt waited on the bench in the foyer, impatiently staring at his watch every few seconds. She had avoided him all day, and it had only increased the urgency he felt about tonight. More than anything, he didn't want her to still be mad at him.

Just then, she appeared, her striking beauty causing him to take a quick intake of breath. Her curls were hanging down one shoulder, and she wore a black summer dress that was simple and elegant. Whatever jealousy he had sensed from her before was gone now that her sister had left.

"I had no idea what to wear," she said, running one hand down her dress. "Do you even have a plan for tonight?"

He smiled. "Do I have a plan? Aspen, how long have we known each other? I *always* have a plan. What you're wearing is perfect." He stood and opened the door for her. "Stunning, as usual."

She shook her head. "You don't have to do this."

"Do what?" he asked, grabbing her hand even though he could feel the reluctance in her grip.

"This." She held up their intertwined fingers. "Play the gentleman."

"Remember what you told me?" He rubbed his thumb across her hand. "You said I was good at showing women how they deserve to be treated. That includes you."

He led her out the door, her touch making his heart go crazy.

"Are you telling me where we're going?" she asked as they walked to his truck.

He handed her a piece of paper.

She unfolded it and looked at him. "Not another riddle. I can't even figure out my great-aunt's."

"This one is easy. And just to warn you, I'm terrible with rhymes."

She began reading, *"We're heading here soon. Up, up, and away in my beautiful . . ."* She glanced at him and shrugged. "I don't know."

"Think, Aspen." He gave her an encouraging smile. "It rhymes with *soon*."

"Balloon?" she asked.

"Bingo." He put his foot on the gas as they turned onto the road.

"A hot-air balloon? Seriously?" Her face was white. "I told you I'd never go up in one when you dared me last summer."

"Never say never. Isn't that what Lizzie always said?" He

gave her a look. "Don't worry. You'll be in a basket with me. It's safe."

"Safe?" She let out a doubtful laugh. "This certainly doesn't feel safe."

"What were you expecting?" he asked, curious.

She clasped her hands together nervously. "Just something typical. Dinner at DeSoto's."

"We did that, and you know how it turned out," he said, referring to their encounter with Agnes. "Besides, I don't do *typical*. DeSoto's is nice, but if I'm planning a date for someone I care about, I want it unforgettable."

"You should have saved this for another girl." Aspen stared out the window.

"So now you're the know-it-all?" he said, attempting to lighten her mood. "Can you promise me you'll try to have fun?" He squeezed her hand again.

She couldn't hide her grin. "Promise."

When they arrived at the open field, the hot-air balloon had been prepared for their launch. Its bright rainbow colors filled the sky.

An older man approached them. "I take it you are Matt and Aspen. Ready for your ride?"

Matt nodded. "Can't wait."

The pilot glanced at Aspen. "I notice our co-pilot here isn't answering."

"I'm a little nervous about this." The color drained from her face as she eyed the enormous balloon.

"Once you get up in the sky, you'll feel different," the man assured her with a warm smile. "It's like flying."

"That's what I'm afraid of," she mumbled.

They loaded into the balloon and lifted off the ground, floating higher, until the earth sank away from them.

The balloon moved through the air almost effortlessly,

drifting peacefully over the trees and fields, a patchwork quilt of greens and golds below them.

Aspen clung to the side of the basket, her knuckles white. Matt stepped closer, trying to help her relax as he peered at the sweeping scene beneath them. "So, what do you think?"

"It's extraordinary," she murmured as her grip softened. "Everything looks so peaceful."

Even though her gaze was glued to the stunning view, he couldn't take his eyes off of her. From this perspective, his entire world could burn down and he wouldn't care, as long as she was next to him.

Aspen shivered as goose bumps peppered her arms. There was no way he was going to let the cooler temperature ruin her experience. He took off his jacket and covered her shoulders.

"You don't have to do that," she said, attempting to slip out of the coat. He wrapped his arms around her so she was forced to wear it.

"I want you to have it. I'll stay warm next to you," he whispered in her ear.

He loved tucking her into the warmth of his chest and the way she folded into him so naturally.

As his eyes scanned the orange and pink sunset across the lake, he leaned close to her cheek. "Tell me this isn't fun."

She let out a small sigh. "Maybe, for once, you're right."

"Good, because the last thing I want is for you to be afraid."

"I'll be honest, when the balloon was lifting off the ground, I had second thoughts. Like I seriously considered jumping out. But now that I'm up here, I can't get over how beautiful everything is."

"Me either," he whispered, staring at her.

For the rest of the trip they remained silent, drifting past miniature houses and toy cars. From up here, the world stretched before them, the landscape never-ending, the horizon untouchable.

Their problems drifted away like morning fog burned away by the sun. There was no talk about Aspen leaving or the sale of the inn. From up here, none of their concerns existed.

When their feet finally touched ground, Matt was reluctant to leave. Experiencing that kind of escape was mind-blowing, even slightly addictive.

"So what's next?" Aspen asked as Matt drove them back to the house. "Drag racing? Bull riding?"

He lifted his brow. "You'd go bull riding?"

"Don't even think about it," she warned him. "I don't want any more surprises." But even as she said it, her mouth quirked up at the corners.

Matt parked the truck and led her to the fire pit at the back corner of the property.

"Did you know this was your great-aunt's last wish?" he asked as they approached the raised fire pit he'd built for her. Lizzie had requested it before she passed away. "The sad thing is she never got to use it."

He began stacking wood inside. "In memory of her, I thought we'd fulfill her last wish."

"I didn't know she wanted this." Aspen lowered herself onto a lawn blanket as he lit the brush under the logs. "Do you know why?"

"I don't. But I know she loved sitting outside as the sun set."

Aspen watched as the flames leapt into the air. "Do you think everyone has a last wish?"

"It's human nature." Matt joined Aspen on the blanket. "I bet you have one."

"My last wish is to solve Aunt Lizzie's riddle before I sell the inn, but I'm running out of time." Aspen leaned back on her elbows. "I found the key, but I'm stumped on where the lock is. I'm beginning to think it isn't here." She shifted to her side and propped her head on her hand. "Did my aunt ever have anyone else she confided in? Someone else she trusted?"

Matt took a stick off the ground and poked the fire. "She prided herself on being private. Even Edna and Thelma couldn't get a word out of her."

Aspen shivered and pulled Matt's coat around her. "What about you?" Her voice was quiet as the flames danced in her eyes. "What's your last wish?"

Her floral scent intermingling with the smoke almost made him dizzy. He leaned back on one elbow and looked at her.

"This," his low voice rumbled. "Being with you."

She socked his arm. "Is this your attempt at a guilt trip?"

Her disbelief stung more than her punch.

"It's not," he argued. "Aspen, I mean it. I've been wanting to go out with you ever since prom night." The words slipped out before he could stop them.

She shook her head, frowning. "That was ages ago."

"Ever since you moved in, I've wanted to tell you how I feel. But I couldn't before. I'd convinced myself you put up with me because we were friends. A part of me was afraid you'd be angry, or worse, cut me out of your life."

If he was going to lay it all on the line, now was the time. She could take it or leave it, but he hoped it was enough.

"But why now?" Her voice cracked with emotion. "Why did you wait until it was too late?"

"It's never too late," he argued.

She stumbled to her feet and glared at him. "What about my sister? She's the one staying in Wild Harbor. Not me. Is this some kind of cruel joke?"

"A joke? No." He stood to face her. "I told you because I couldn't let you go without knowing the truth."

"You have the worst timing of anyone I've ever met, Matthew Woods." She turned and stormed away, clearly angry that he'd confessed his feelings.

He chased after her, matching her stride as she crossed the yard. "I don't understand. Did you want me to share my feelings while you were still dating Ryder? That wouldn't have been fair to you or him."

"Fair?" She whirled around to face him. "You want to talk about fair? I've had feelings for you for as long as I can remember, and now that I'm brave enough to move on, you're finally confessing? What am I supposed to do now?"

The tension between them was palpable. "I'm not asking you for anything."

"Don't even try to pull that stunt on me. You just dropped an emotional bomb. Did you think it wouldn't make a difference in whether I stay or go?"

He shook his head, trying to make her understand. His carefully crafted plan to confess his feelings had suddenly turned into a train wreck. "I didn't want you to leave Wild Harbor without knowing how I feel. I'm not suggesting you change your plans."

"That's the problem," she shot back. "This changes *everything.*"

"It doesn't have to." His eyes locked on hers, and in them he could see dark flowers blooming with hunger. Reaching toward her, he gently ran his fingers across her cheek.

"Don't," she whispered, closing her eyes.

As he dropped his hand, she stepped forward, laced her hands behind his neck and pulled him to her. Raising herself on her toes, her lips met his, and the warmth erased every rational thought from his mind.

He threaded his fingers through her hair as her body melted into his, like two magnets drawing together. He kissed her intensely, fiercely, and he wanted more than anything to show her the love he'd held back for so long. As his hands found their way down her back, wrapping around her, she leaned into him, not resisting their pull.

One minute she had been yelling at him, and the next, they

couldn't stay away from each other. His entire plan for the evening had been ripped apart at the seams.

Now, the intensity of her warm lips drinking in his kisses erased every argument about why this couldn't work. As his fingertips stroked across the soft flesh of her shoulders, he gently traced the curve of her neck, trailing kisses along the line of her jaw.

He understood now: she wrecked him in ways he couldn't even express. His jumbled thoughts desperately tried to make sense of what was happening, but he was spiraling too quickly.

"We can't do this," she whispered between kisses, before pulling away and resting her forehead on his.

"If I'm taking it too fast, I'm sorry." His breath was ragged, like he'd just run a marathon.

"No, I meant we can't kiss and pretend everything is right."

"This is more right than any kiss I've ever experienced," he admitted.

A soft smile spread across her lips. "What about the promise you made a long time ago? The vow to *never ever* kiss me again?"

"I was a fool," he laughed softly. "I thought I was protecting you. To be fair, I needed some guardrails to keep away from you or else—" He wanted to kiss the edges of her mouth, to continue where they'd left off.

"Or else what?" Her look nearly undid him.

"Or else more of this would happen." He touched her lips with his again, melting with the softness of them.

"Matt." She pulled away, the crease in her brow deepening. "We shouldn't be doing this. Not when—" She let the words hang in the silence.

He already knew what she was going to say, but he wanted to pretend her plans to leave didn't exist. Their kiss had been too good to ruin now. After tonight, he was determined to find a way to make her stay.

"Sure you can," he assured her. "You're free now, remember?"

"Not really," she said, grabbing his fingers and kissing the tips before stepping back and giving him a look of longing and sadness.

"Take all the time you need," he offered. "I'll be here waiting for you."

She slipped off his jacket and handed it to him. "I hope this doesn't change your plans with Jessica. She needs someone who'll be here for her when I'm gone."

In the aftermath of their kiss, he'd forgotten all about his promise to take out Jessica. It seemed like a strange request, given he'd just revealed his intense attraction for her, but Aspen's face was resolute.

"If that's what you want," he murmured in a low voice. "But just for the record, I don't have feelings for your sister. And I won't kiss her either. That's only for you."

CHAPTER SIXTEEN

ASPEN

Aspen dropped the paintbrush in the can, her arm aching from all the work she'd done on the last guest room. She took a step back from the wall and admired the color. The milky brown was reminiscent of Matt's hair and the way it had threaded through her fingers as she'd kissed him.

She couldn't think about last night anymore.

How would she ever explain to her sister that she'd kissed Matt? The guilt was nearly wrecking her. There was only one way to fix the situation: she needed to do what was best for Jessica, regardless of her feelings. And that meant giving him up.

When she'd brought up the date to Matt at breakfast, he'd seemed uninterested in discussing it.

"How do you feel about your night out with Jessica?" she asked, trying to hide the ugly vine of jealousy that was curling around her heart.

"She's not you," he responded firmly, jaw clenched.

She wanted to capture that face on paper, trace the shape of his lips, sketch his dark hair, smudge the charcoal edges with

189

her thumb. She'd already memorized his face from her photos. His features were so familiar to her that she could trace them from memory.

Last night after their date, she'd lain awake and sketched his image burned into her thoughts. As her weary mind had replayed their kiss, the memory of his lips on hers had been as distinct as his face, and her heart had squeezed in pain.

If she hadn't given her sister permission to pursue Matt, then maybe their story could have had a different ending. But now that she'd promised, the harsh truth seared into her. Removing herself from Wild Harbor was the only path forward. It would help Matt see what was right in front of him, even if he couldn't understand it yet and nudge him toward Jessica. It was the ultimate gift of love—wanting what was best for her sister, even if it broke her heart.

Without telling Matt, she'd scheduled the investor's visit for Sunday, banking on him making an offer. She needed this plan to work. If not for Jessica, then for her baby.

She took off her paint gloves and tossed them in the garbage before grabbing her phone and checking for messages. She had missed a voicemail from an unlisted number.

A strange voice rattled off an official-sounding message:

"Hello, Ms. Bradford. I'm Jeremy from the *Hometown Heroes* photography contest, calling with good news. The competition was exceptional this year, and our judges had a difficult time deciding on the final winners, which is why my call is so last minute. Your photo, *A Firefighter's Sacrifice*, won first place, and we'd like to invite you to the celebration gala this weekend in Las Vegas. We'll hand out prizes Saturday night at the awards ceremony. Once again, we want to congratulate you on the win."

As the man finished, Aspen realized she'd held her breath for the entire message. Letting out a huge puff of air, she tore down the stairs, her body flooding with exhilaration.

"Matt!" She nearly slammed into him at the back door, where he'd just returned from mowing the lawn.

"Slow down, Little Bit," he said as she leapt into his arms and squeezed his neck like a vise. "Easy, girl. You're about to suffocate me."

"I won!" she exclaimed. She dangled her phone in front of him, as if that was the perfect explanation for her lack of details.

"Won what?" He eyed the device in confusion.

"I received a message from the *Hometown Heroes* contest."

"And?"

"The picture I submitted won the contest." Aspen's cheeks hurt from smiling so much.

"What?" He lifted her up and twirled her around. "I knew you could do it. This doesn't surprise me at all." A corner of his mouth quirked up, his boyish grin making her insides turn to jelly.

"They asked me to attend the awards gala this weekend, which means I need to book a flight as soon as possible."

"Jessica will be back, so we can take care of the inn while you're gone."

"Wait a minute, I can't go this weekend." Her brows knitted in concern. "I have plans already."

"You can't cancel them?"

She sighed, realizing she had no choice but to tell him. "Remember that investor who called and was interested in the inn? I arranged for him to see it on Sunday. I'm going to have to miss the awards ceremony."

Matt pulled the phone away. "You'll do no such thing. I'm not letting you miss anything. Jessica and I will take care of the investor. You book your flight."

It wasn't fair that she was leaving such an important meeting in their hands. "But what if he has questions? What if he makes an offer?"

"I can handle the questions. If an offer comes in, you should be home in time to review the details."

She still wasn't sure about rushing off, but she trusted Matt and knew he was more than capable. He'd probably even have a list of questions prepared for the investor.

Pulling out her phone, she scrolled through a list of options for flights. The cheapest one was over five hundred dollars, but would get her home by Sunday. Since she'd maxed out her credit cards on the inn's renovations, there was no way she could afford a last-minute ticket, and she wouldn't receive the prize money until at the event. "Never mind. I can't go anyway."

"Why not?" he questioned, narrowing his eyes.

She moved to the refrigerator to avoid his glare. "I'm not telling you why."

"Then let me guess." Matt pushed the fridge door shut and blocked her way. "Is it money?"

"I said, I'm not telling." She backed away, jutting out her chin.

"Aspen, catch." He tossed his wallet toward her.

She barely had time to catch it before she realized what he was doing.

"Use my card," he insisted.

"I can't let you do this," she protested, handing him back his wallet.

"You can. And you will." He pushed his wallet back to her. "I'm not kidding. If you don't book your flight, I will do it for you."

She hated that she didn't have enough money to even attend her own awards ceremony. But the look on his face dared her to challenge him. "Are you sure?" she asked reluctantly. "I'll pay you back for this as soon as I can."

Matt drew closer as if he sensed her hesitation. He reached up and stroked her cheek, the flecks of gold in his eyes glittering. "You deserve this award. I wouldn't let you miss it for the world."

THE NEXT FEW days were a blur as Aspen finished the final decorating details on the inn. All the guest rooms had new paint that replaced the ugly wallpaper, along with patterned rugs and silky drapes. They'd kept the beautiful hardwood floors, a favorite feature of Aspen's, and some of the furniture, since most of the items were antiques that reminded Aspen of Aunt Lizzie.

In between his hours at the fire station, Matt had tirelessly worked extra hours on the inn's exterior, pulling out overgrown landscaping and replacing it with flowering bushes and blooming perennials. The only thing he hadn't touched was the bed of bright red poppies, a special tribute to Aunt Lizzie and The Red Poppy Inn.

With these minor changes, the inn's appeal had dramatically improved. No longer did the place seem tired and dated. Instead, every corner had become more inviting, beckoning guests to rest their feet and enjoy a glass of iced tea while the lake soothed their spirits.

Unfortunately, all the bills Aspen had racked up were now like a ticking time bomb. Until she could get her check from the photography contest, she could only pay the minimum on her credit card bill. Even worse, the cash prize was supposed to be saved as seed money for her future travel plans, but the inn was draining her account faster than a leaky faucet. She'd need to use her prize money to pay the inn's bills until the place sold. Her current financial state was as precarious as a row of dominoes. One minor mistake would ruin the whole plan.

By Friday, Aspen still hadn't packed her suitcase for her upcoming flight to Vegas that night. She dashed to her bedroom and pulled out her small carry-on suitcase. A layer of dust covered the top.

In the craziness of finishing the inn's redecorating, she'd nearly forgotten that tomorrow she'd receive an award in front of an audience of professional photographers. Nervous energy pulsated through her body.

"Should I wear this black dress or the short grey one?" Jessica stood in the door of her bedroom holding up two gorgeous dresses—one that was a cute but tasteful short black dress, and the other that was a silver flowing number with an off-the-shoulder neckline. Jessica had returned that morning, having moved out of the apartment she shared with Chase. Aspen hadn't even had the chance to talk with her yet.

"For what?" Aspen asked, pulling out a pair of pajamas from her drawer and tossing them into the suitcase. She could barely pull her thoughts away from the gala to focus on her sister.

"For the date with Matt tonight, silly," Jessica said with a grin.

"Oh." Aspen's gaze swung back to her suitcase. She'd totally forgotten. Her stomach lurched uncomfortably.

"I need your help to choose the best one." She shook the dresses on their hangers to refocus Aspen's attention.

"They're both nice." Actually, nice wasn't the right word. They were beautiful. *And sexy.* She almost couldn't stand the thought of Matt staring at Jessica in either one.

"Nice is not helpful, Aspen. Which one will Matt like?" Jessica's honest question irked her.

"How should I know?" Aspen shrugged impatiently, riffling through her closet trying to find something appropriate to wear to the gala.

Her sister's wardrobe was filled with showstopping numbers, thanks to having been married to a very successful financial advisor. In contrast, Aspen's own closet was shockingly small with practical but boring pieces that came in three colors: brown, black, and grey. She'd learned to mix and match these basics with such creativity, it didn't look like she was wearing the same thing. But comparing her dresses with Jessica's prompted nothing but yawns.

"Wear what you like," Aspen concluded. "I can't even figure out what to put on my own body."

Jessica entered her closet and scooted one hanger after another past Aspen.

"Your wardrobe really needs some pizazz." Jessica sniffed as if boring basics were distasteful to her.

"I worked in an office." Aspen touched Jessica's silver dress which hung over her sister's arm. "It's not like I needed a slinky metallic dress."

"You think this is slinky, huh? Then I'll wear it tonight. Maybe I could do a little salsa dancing in it." She clutched the dress to her body and attempted some Latin dance moves.

"Matt doesn't dance. Trust me on this. Where are you going in such a fancy outfit?"

"DeSoto's," Jessica said with relish.

The place Matt had said he wouldn't take her. *If I'm planning a date for someone I care about, I want to make it unforgettable.*

Her date with Matt had definitely been unforgettable. Especially that kiss.

But she couldn't let desire sway her now. She needed to do what was right for her sister.

Jessica held up the silver dress against her body and stared at herself in the mirror. "If I run into Agnes again, I'm going to flaunt it in her face." Her sister jutted out her chin.

"Are you planning on saying anything to Matt?" She sat on the edge of the bed and watched Jessica as she changed out of her clothes, her belly revealing no signs of a baby bump yet. She slid into the dress like it was liquid silver.

"Of course not. Any chance I have with him depends on Matt not knowing." Jessica faced away from Aspen and pointed to the back of the dress. "Zipper, please. You're the only one I've told so far, so keep it quiet. I haven't even broken the news to Chase yet."

"I thought you did that already." Aspen drew the zipper up her spine.

"Chase didn't show. He stayed here while I cleaned out his stuff along with mine."

"How much longer will you keep it secret?" Aspen was so afraid of accidentally mentioning the pregnancy that she couldn't wait for it to be public knowledge. It was one more domino in her perfect setup.

"As long as I can. If this plan is going to work, I need time. That's the one thing I don't have." She touched her belly and then turned, the dress swirling around her ankles. She looked as glamorous as a 1940s movie star.

"Will this work on Matt?" Jessica posed in the mirror as Aspen stood next to her in a plain grey sweatshirt and jeans. The contrast between them couldn't have been more obvious.

As they stared at their reflections, Aspen pasted on a reassuring smile. Jessica was a rose next to a dandelion. Matt would have to be blind not to notice Jess.

"Why wouldn't he choose you?" Aspen whispered. "You're stunning."

"Thanks, sis." Jessica beamed as she left the room.

An hour later, Aspen had settled on an outfit for the gala: a silky black dress that she'd worn to a fancy wedding years ago. A pop of color for her feet would complete the look, so she opted for the red heels she'd stowed away in the back of her closet. The combination wasn't as showy as Jessica's dress, but it fit her sense of style: simple with an understated beauty.

Her goal was to escape to the airport before Matt and Jessica left for their date. As she tiptoed to the front door, Jessica rushed down the stairs, looking like a spectacular Cinderella on her way to the ball.

"You're not leaving now, are you?" Jessica semi-scolded. She had pinned her hair in a fancy updo that framed her face. The makeup on her eyes, accentuated by faux eyelashes, was dazzling, and her lips were glossed to perfection in a perfect red pout.

Dressed in an old jean jacket, Aspen felt like the ugly stepsister. She'd tucked her hair into a ponytail, while stray curls escaped around her face.

"I have a plane to catch," Aspen insisted, a wave of guilt washing over her. So much for sneaking out.

"You can't leave before our date. You're my moral support." Jessica lightly clasped her red fingernails around Aspen's upper arms, holding her hostage.

"You have nothing to worry about." Aspen wrapped her arms around her, leaning close so Jessica wouldn't read her conflicting emotions. "Matt will take great care of you. He's a good man."

There was so much more she wanted to say, but the words stuck in her throat. *I'm doing this for you, sis, because that's how much I love you.*

As Aspen turned to leave, she gave her sister a tremulous smile. "Wish me luck."

She needed it. Not only for this weekend, but for leaving behind the man she loved.

"What for? You already won the award. I'm the one who needs luck," Jessica reminded her.

"But I have to appear in front of an auditorium of strangers. I'll probably trip and fall on my face." Aspen cringed thinking about standing on stage. Although she wanted this award, *needed* it even, she hated the spotlight.

"But it doesn't matter what you do, you already got what you wanted. This is what you've dreamed about, right?"

Aspen gave a weak nod in response. Wasn't this what she had longed for? Somehow, the answer left her empty.

"Then go get your award." Jessica kissed the side of Aspen's head, where the curls tumbled out of her ponytail.

When Aspen pulled away from The Red Poppy Inn, Jessica's words circled in her mind. *You already got what you wanted. This is what you've dreamed about.*

Her wish of becoming a photographer verged on the cusp of reality. But if her dreams were coming true, why did she feel such overwhelming emotion?

She already knew the answer. Somewhere along the way, she'd lost sight of what really mattered. This was her home and Matt was the love of her life.

In the pursuit of her dreams, she'd been so focused on her end goal that she'd ignored every sign showing she was headed down the wrong path. Now that she realized the truth, it was too late. Her line of dominoes was about to fall.

CHAPTER SEVENTEEN

MATT

When Matt found Jessica, she was staring out the window, a hint of sadness shadowing her face.

He cleared his throat. "Are you ready?" he asked hesitantly. His heart thumped nervously in his chest as regret coiled in his stomach. *One date.* That was the bargain he'd made in return for a date with Aspen.

"Oh, you scared me." She spun around, her dress swirling in time with her turn. "Do I look ready?" She gave him a big smile, one hand lingering on her hip, striking the same pose he'd seen on a star's red-carpet picture.

"You look . . . nice." He hoped his compliment didn't seem as strained as it felt.

Her face fell slightly.

"I meant lovely," he corrected. "Perfect for DeSoto's."

Her mouth turned up at the corners. "Let's go, then." She picked up a small clutch and invited him to follow.

"Could you hang on a second?" he stalled. For some unexplainable reason, he wanted Aspen's blessing before he left.

Proof that he was fulfilling his end of the deal. He couldn't put his finger on why, but he needed to know if she was hiding something from him.

He scrambled to find her and discovered her bedroom empty. Her vacant space riddled a hole in his stomach as he realized she'd left without saying goodbye. That was why Jessica had been staring out the window.

Aunt Lizzie's jewelry box hung open, the riddle and business card forgotten. He jammed them into his trousers. As soon as this date was over, there were answers he needed to find.

DURING THE ENTIRE meal at DeSoto's, Jessica seemed preoccupied. She fiddled with her dress and glanced nervously around the restaurant, ignoring Matt as he attempted to make conversation. Her face had taken on a greenish cast, and she kept excusing herself to rush to the restroom.

By the time he finished his chocolate mousse, he set his spoon down. She still hadn't touched her dessert.

"Is everything okay, Jessica?" he asked.

She sighed and slumped in her chair. "To be honest, no." Her eyes dropped to the napkin on her lap. "I've been nauseous and nervous all night, because I know what the right thing to do is, but I didn't want to do it." She rubbed her forehead. "And I thought I'd feel something else tonight, but this feels all wrong." Tears swelled in the corner of her eyes as she dabbed them with her fingertips. "I'm so sorry if I wasted your time."

He reached across the table to assure her he wasn't mad. "Don't be sorry. You just stated what I didn't know how to say. You saved me a lot of agonizing over nothing."

She rested her chin on her hand. "Can I tell you something else? I saw how you looked at Aspen today, and I know you feel more for her than you let on."

He lifted his eyebrows. "Is it that obvious?"

"Only to a sister," she explained. "I was a little jealous at first. I wanted you to look at me that same way. But I realized you never will. So please do me a favor and either chase after her or let her go. You can't have it both ways."

It was a quiet ride back to the house as Matt rolled Jessica's advice around in his head. He knew what he needed to do, but first, he had one more person to see.

As soon as they entered the foyer, Jessica yawned and headed upstairs to her room. Her TV blared from her bedroom, giving him no reason to stick around. As exhausted as she'd looked at the end of their date, she'd probably be asleep in five minutes.

If he wanted to sneak out, it was now or never.

As his feet crunched gravel on the shoulder of the road, the full moon swathed the path ahead in light. If his hunch was wrong, he'd be left with few options to convince Aspen to stay. But if he was right, he knew it could change everything.

He knocked on the door to the salvage shop and held his breath. Except for the breeze rattling in a nearby tree, only silence greeted him.

Joshua always worked late. He'd counted on it tonight. Matt leaned closer to the door, willing it to open somehow.

"Joshua? Are you there?" he whispered.

Behind him, a muffled sound spooked him.

"What in tarnation are you doing here at this hour?" Joshua stood back a few feet, his eyes wild in the moonlight.

"You usually work late," Matt confessed. "What are you doing out here?"

"Same as you, I reckon. Enjoying some night air." Joshua looked at him curiously. "Did you want something?"

"Possibly." Matt hesitated. "I think you have some information I need."

"What would that be?"

He pulled the business card out and flipped it over so that Joshua could read the faded words. "Have you seen this before?"

In the darkness, he couldn't read Joshua's face, but his lips tightened and the wrinkles in his forehead deepened.

"That's my card." Joshua nodded.

"Does this look familiar?" Matt held out the riddle for Joshua to examine.

A pause hung in the air between the two men.

"Come inside," Joshua invited as he unlocked the door.

The two men stepped into the darkened shop. Joshua flicked on a lamp, the kind with a bright glass shade that made colorful geometric patterns on the walls.

"Where did you find the card?" Joshua lowered himself stiffly onto a wooden barstool, gesturing for Matt to do the same. "Must have fallen out of my pocket."

"In the bush outside of Lizzie's old room," Matt said. "But why break into the house?"

"I didn't," Joshua responded quickly. "Not like you're assuming. Lizzie told me to leave the riddle with Aspen. She wanted it to be a surprise. No one was supposed to know it was me. I knew Aspen was gone, but I didn't know she locked the house because Lizzie never worried about that. Luckily, she'd left one window unlocked, but my old body couldn't climb through it. I guess I'm not as young as I used to be." A corner of his mouth turned up. "I lucked out though, because Aspen left a set of keys close by the window, so all I had to do was reach inside. Those keys got me through the back door. Unfortunately, I forgot to shut the window when I left."

"But why did Aunt Lizzie ask you to leave this riddle?" Matt wondered. "And what do you know about it?"

Joshua sighed, like the memory troubled him. "It's time you heard the entire story."

∾

THE NEXT DAY, when Matt stepped foot in the low-lit auditorium for the awards ceremony, a wave of anticipation rippled through him. After talking with Joshua the night before, he'd made a rash decision to follow Aspen to Las Vegas, even though he felt totally out of place.

The small venue was packed with guests in black ties and ball gowns. Women glanced his way and gave an appreciative smile as their eyes skirted over his suit. He tugged uncomfortably at the collar of his dress shirt. His neck itched. The jacket constricted his shoulders. He'd rather don his fireman's uniform any day than these duds. But he knew the positive effect of a well-dressed man, and he hoped it had the same impact on Aspen.

A woman approached him wearing a navy convention center coat.

"Can I help you, sir?" She offered him a glossy program.

"Do you know where the contest winners are? I'm here for Aspen Bradford."

"Unfortunately, they're all backstage and will be seated on stage the entire night. But I can find you a seat if you're alone." The usher motioned him toward the front row, where a few empty seats remained.

So much for surprising Aspen before the awards ceremony. He would have to wait until the end of the night to give his congratulations, if hordes of people didn't reach her first.

He followed the usher to a lone front-row seat in the center section of the auditorium. If Aspen missed his surprise visit, he'd not only have wasted a plane ticket to Vegas, but the opportunity to show her what he was willing to do for her.

After his conversation with Joshua last night, he hoped it would shed light on Aunt Lizzie's riddle and give her some answers about her future.

He pulled out his phone and sent Aspen a quick text.

. . .

Matt: Congrats on your win tonight. I'm so proud of you. Signed your biggest fan and solo cheering section.

He hoped she saw the message in time.

As the stage lights brightened and guests scrambled to find seats, a man with greying hair approached the podium and adjusted the microphone. "Welcome to the sixteenth annual *Hometown Heroes* contest."

A wave of applause rose from the audience. Matt propped his elbows on his knees and tried to glimpse Aspen backstage with no success. Where was she?

"Tonight, we are honoring the work of three photographers whose photos were chosen from thousands of entries to illustrate the dedication of those in our communities who've sacrificed their lives and earned the title of hometown heroes."

As the audience clapped in response, Matt shifted uncomfortably in his seat. He didn't feel like a hero, not after he'd made a mistake that nearly cost a child's life.

Before that, he'd been flawless in his work, mentally cataloguing every compartment, piece of brass, tool, and equipment, complete with drawings and labels. He checked every room in each house precisely. The importance of knowing exactly where everyone was remained critical to the safety of the people he served.

He thought that would always be enough.

Making an almost-fatal error with a child was nothing short of horrendous. Worst of all, he hadn't realized the mistake until a teammate had pointed it out. In the middle of fighting a house fire, the words had slammed into him: *One child was unaccounted for.* That's when his stomach had dropped. *There's a child still inside.*

He'd been the one who searched the bedrooms. Somehow

he'd missed a closet where a child hid, scared of the noise and the fire.

That mistake had cost him precious minutes and put a child's life at serious risk. Even though they'd been trained to search for hiding victims, his mental cataloguing had failed him. Because of his mistake, a child had been critically injured, and he still couldn't forgive himself.

Someone could have died because of me. He lived with that guilt every day.

Even now, sweat sprang up under his collar. He felt like a fraud, undeserving of the title of hero. He hadn't expected this contest would trigger the images of that day so violently.

He gripped the arms of his seat as the emcee introduced the third and second place winners. As the photographers explained the inspiration behind their shots, they displayed the winning photos on a giant screen.

Matt dug his fingernails into the plush fabric of his seat. Despite rescuing people from life-threatening situations, he'd never been so nervous in his life. He didn't seek the spotlight; he'd rather do the dirty work of putting out fires than stand in front of a crowd. Imagining his face plastered on the screen almost made him sick. *Some hero I am.*

A dreadful silence filled the room as the emcee stepped to the microphone. "Now for the winning photograph of the *Hometown Heroes* contest. Let's give a round of applause for our winner, Aspen Bradford."

Matt held his breath as his picture appeared on the screen and Aspen stepped on stage. Trying to tone down the rising panic in his brain, he focused on the beautiful woman before him. Just catching a glimpse of her face helped him to unclench his fists.

As much as he hated seeing himself heralded as a hero, in one shot Aspen had caught the tension of a critical moment in the men around him. Though she had featured him centrally in the photograph, members of his crew played an integral role in telling the story behind the picture. He wasn't a hero. But his team was. Somehow, Aspen had shown heroism as a collective sacrifice, not an individual one.

Even though he couldn't forgive himself for his mistake, his fellow firefighters kept going. They continued to serve, even when it was astonishingly hard. If any of them had made the same mistake, he'd have forgiven them in a heartbeat. But forgiving *himself*? That was another story altogether. He simply couldn't allow himself to.

Matt had been so distracted that his attention had slipped from Aspen's turn at the microphone. As she made her way to the podium, he suddenly couldn't tear his eyes away. Dressed in a black silk dress that was as tasteful as it was beautiful, he was overcome with pride. He'd always known how talented this stunning woman was. Only now did the world recognize all she had to offer.

Although he suspected she was quaking inside, her face glowed as she began to speak. Hands down, she was the most beautiful woman here.

"Ladies and gentlemen, I'm honored to accept this award and want to thank the entire panel of judges." Her eyes flitted across the audience. "But I'm not the one who should receive it."

Suddenly, her gaze fell on Matt, and a look of shock crossed her face. He hadn't considered that his surprise arrival might leave her speechless. Her cheeks deepened to red as she grasped for words. "I, uh . . ."

As she struggled to regain her focus, he offered his most reassuring smile.

She returned a shy grin and pulled her attention back to the crowd. "I want to honor the true heroes tonight: the team who makes up the Wild Harbor firefighters. Without their sacrifice, our community would have lost countless lives. They risk their health and safety every day so they can protect ours. This photo is one small way we can recognize their service, and it represents all the first responders across our country who save lives every day."

With her final words, her eyes locked on his. "We want to applaud every single one."

The crowd erupted in cheers as people stood to honor first responders all across America.

Matt slowly joined in, not only for his fellow firemen, but also for Aspen. As she stepped away from the podium, she mouthed *thank you,* and he knew it was just for him.

In an adjacent ballroom, a fancy reception followed the awards ceremony. As Matt entered, a jazz trio's upbeat tune floated over the laughter of the crowd. Even with the lights dimmed, he spotted Aspen surrounded by fans at the front of the room. He stood at a distance, not wanting to interrupt her moment in the spotlight.

Matt watched as a man with sun-bleached hair greeted Aspen with a wide smile. As he held his phone out for a quick selfie, he wrapped an arm around her waist.

Seeing another man touch Aspen caused Matt to surge forward like a bull. As he stepped into her line of sight, Matt pushed past the crowd.

"No more selfies this evening," he insisted, barging in front of other guests who were waiting to meet Aspen while nudging the blond man out of the way. Normally, he wouldn't intervene with this kind of forcefulness, but tonight he didn't care.

"Hey, it was my turn in line," the man insisted. "I wasn't finished taking pictures."

"You are now."

The man studied Matt for a second and then backed off. "Who are you anyway?"

He grabbed Aspen's waist, pulling her away from surfer guy. "Her bodyguard for this evening."

With his hand on her lower back and her body neatly tucked

against his, he guided her safely away from the crowd. He refused to let go until they found an empty corner where he could finally see her with no interruptions.

"Thank you for coming tonight, but I think you scared that guy," she murmured. "And my bodyguard? Really?"

He shrugged. "If that's what it takes to get you to myself, then I'm not sorry."

"You know I don't need saving," she reminded him gently. "I can take care of myself." She reached for a fruity punch drink from a server carrying a silver tray.

"More than capable." He moved closer, the scent of her intoxicating perfume overwhelming. "But say the word and I'm happy to shove off any blond surfer dudes who get a little too touchy."

Unsurprisingly, men were flocking to meet her. He only wished he could steal her away so he could have her to himself.

"I never guessed people would be so . . ." She searched for the right word.

"Enraptured by you?" he finished. "I'm not. You're stunning tonight."

Her cheeks heated. "You shouldn't say things like that. Not after last night's date."

"Jessica can't hold a candle to you," he told her.

She looked at him. "Stop."

"Stop what?"

"Making my heart do funny things," she said, waving her program like a fan.

He frowned, suddenly concerned. "Are you okay?"

"It's not like last time," she reassured him. "This is a good thing. A normal reaction when someone has made an outrageous compliment. I'm not used to it, actually."

"Well, get used to it," he said. "Because I'm not one to hold back."

Her mouth opened as if she wanted to say something more,

but instead, she downed her drink, then tossed the cup in the trash. "Do you want to sneak out of here? I'm tired of the crowd."

"Do I ever? I've wanted to steal you away ever since I saw you across the room." He grabbed her hand before they escaped through the door.

After searching for a quiet corner in the lobby and finding every seat taken, Aspen finally offered her hotel room as a place to talk. Winning first prize meant she'd received a special suite on the top floor, which included a huge balcony overlooking the city.

"It's not like I need all this space. It's a waste, really." She flicked on the light switch to the room, and the swanky suite sprang into view. A small kitchen opened into a large living room that held an enormous flat-screen TV. In an attached room, a king-sized bed faced a window that filled the whole wall. Across the city, lights glowed in the darkness. She slid open the patio door to a balcony where two patio chairs invited them to gaze at the scene below.

"I haven't used this balcony since I arrived. Seems a shame." She lowered herself onto a chair and kicked off her shoes. "These heels are killing me."

"Are your feet ticklish? Because if not, I've been told I give phenomenal foot rubs."

She frowned. "You don't feel weird about touching my feet?"

"Would I have offered otherwise?" He invited her to lift a foot.

She daintily pointed one toe, like she was posing for a footwear commercial.

"You can't stiffen your foot." He tried to bend her foot back and forth. "Relax and let me work the tension out."

He kneaded his thumbs into a tense spot while she melted in her seat.

"Wow, you really are a pro," she said. "How did you learn this?"

Touching her was so satisfying, he didn't even care if it was her foot. "Don't think I'm a weirdo. But you can learn anything from YouTube."

Aspen rested her head on the back of the chair. "Did you travel all this way just for me?"

"Of course I did," he assured her. "I wanted to be here for you."

She tilted her face toward him. "How did you know exactly what I needed?"

"A hunch," he admitted, grinning.

"Right before I went on stage, I had this lonely feeling in the pit of my stomach, which seems silly since I'm only away for one weekend. But traveling so far made me realize I don't fit in with these people. When I saw you in the crowd, I thought my brain was imagining it. That's why I forgot my speech. When I realized it was really you, I just wanted to cry."

"Which you didn't," he reminded her. "You brought the audience to its feet."

"No, *you* brought the audience to its feet. It was your picture that inspired people." She clearly didn't want any recognition, even from him.

"But there would be no picture if you hadn't taken it," he insisted. He gently lowered her foot to the ground. "I was pretty upset when you showed up at the fire that day. I'm sorry I came down so hard on you, especially if I triggered your heart issues." He still felt guilty over it.

She leaned forward and touched his hand. "It wasn't your fault, Matt. I forgot my medicine. I'm the one to blame."

"I was so scared of something happening to you." He shook his head, remembering. "I hated that I couldn't take you to the hospital myself."

"You were doing your duty," she assured him. "I didn't need you to take me to the ER."

A furrow settled into his brow. "You didn't? Because I felt just the opposite. I needed *you*. That's when I decided I won't let you out of my sight again."

"Well, you'll have to once I sell the inn."

He didn't want to talk about her leaving. As far as he was concerned, he needed to convince her that there was still some hope for them.

"There is another thing I wanted to tell you," he said, relieved to finally share the news. "Last night, I went over to Joshua's shop. I had a hunch he knew something, but I couldn't confirm it until I talked with him."

"About what?" She propped her elbows on her knees and leaned toward him.

"I found out Joshua was the one who delivered the riddle." Matt watched as the realization unfolded across her face.

"But why?"

"It wasn't a break-in. He was fulfilling Lizzie's wish."

Aspen's eyes widened. "So, *he* took the letter?"

"He didn't take it," Matt corrected her. "The letter belongs to him."

Her forehead creased with lines. "Wait a minute. Joshua was Lizzie's love?"

Matt nodded slowly.

"But that's impossible," she argued.

"Why?"

"Because they lived in the same small town their entire lives. If they once loved each other, why didn't they work things out?"

Matt shrugged. "I only heard Joshua's side of the story. I have a feeling that's why Lizzie left the riddle. She wanted to explain something to you when you solved it. Of course, I could be wrong."

Aspen sat back, stunned. "They could've been so happy

together." She twisted the sapphire, tugging until it slipped off her finger. "Joshua should have this back."

Matt folded his hand over the ring and tucked it in his pocket. "I'm not sure he'll want it. It's no use to him anymore."

"Give it to him anyway," she insisted. "To remember her."

"I think the letter served that purpose. Aunt Lizzie's apology gave him the closure he needed. What she didn't know was that he'd forgiven her already, long ago."

Aspen shook her head sadly. "Why wasn't she willing to work things out while she was alive? They may have had a chance together."

"I don't know. They were both as stubborn as mules. But at least she didn't hold a grudge forever. From what Joshua said, she visited him regularly at the shop. Over time, they became friends, even if they never found love again."

Aspen gazed into the bright, twinkling lights of Vegas, looking lost in a love story that would never have a happy ending. "Does Joshua know anything about the riddle?"

Matt shook his head. "The end is a mystery, even to old Joshua. The first person to figure out the riddle will be you."

Her shoulders slumped. "But I don't know where the key fits. If I can't find the lock, then it's pointless."

He leaned back and folded his hands.

She narrowed her gaze at him. "Why do I feel like you know something I don't?"

"Because I do, but I can't tell you yet," he said vaguely.

"Can't tell me?" She leaned toward him, ready to spring on him. "The riddle? The key? What is it?" Her hands were squeezing his shoulders now, her nails softly digging into his flesh.

"I can't tell you and—hey!" He lurched to the back of his chair as she pinched him a little too much. "When you squeeze like that, it tickles."

"I don't care. Out with it now." She stood over him, her lips curved into a mischievous grin. If she was trying to get him to cave, it was almost working. Her flirting verged on more than he could take. He leaned back in his chair. Even sitting, she wasn't much taller than him.

"Are you going to tell me yet?" She placed her arms on either side of him and leaned in.

"If I do, it'll spoil the surprise," Matt warned.

"I can pretend I don't know." She hovered over him, her hands resting on the arms of the chair, locking him between them. Her face was so close that with one brief move, he could kiss her. "Try me."

"But that's the thing. I'm not good at pretending. Especially with you."

With a swift motion, his hands pulled her body toward him. She didn't resist. Falling into him, their lips met, her warm embrace igniting a terrible and treacherous longing inside him. He didn't want to let her go. His hands climbed up her back as he tenderly kissed her cheeks, her jawline, her mouth, all of it.

He was willing to do anything for her. Follow her across the country. Leave his family. Whatever it took to be together.

Without warning, her lips broke away from him, and their moment together quickly crumbled. "What are we doing, Matt?"

"I think the answer is obvious, Aspen," he murmured with a grin.

"Let me rephrase that," she said, refusing to lighten the mood. She dragged her hand through her hair and closed her eyes, frustration lining the corners. "I mean, why are you confusing me like this?"

She climbed off his chair and backed away like he'd done something terrible. "We had plans for everything," she reasoned. "For the inn. My future. Jessica's. All the pieces are falling into place, and you keep upending the whole thing."

"I want to be part of your future, Aspen." Couldn't she see how much he cared about her?

"That can't happen." She shook her head.

He didn't know what was happening, but something inside her had shifted drastically. He wanted to fix it, to take her back to when they were kissing and everything was right between them. "But why not? I'll follow you wherever. Even if that means leaving Wild Harbor for good."

He could tell by her expression that it was exactly the wrong thing to say.

"Leave? Are you crazy?" she shouted. "I could never let you do that."

He stood to face her. "Why not? I'd do it for you."

"Absolutely not," she demanded. "Don't you understand? You have something many people don't. A family who loves you. You belong in Wild Harbor while my whole family is falling apart."

She turned away from him, grasping the railing of the balcony, her knuckles whitening under her grip.

"That's not true." He tried to touch her arm, but she flinched like he'd burned her.

Refusing to look at him, she murmured, "I need you to go."

"But what about us?"

Her eyes, once full of light, had grown dull. "There is no us."

CHAPTER EIGHTEEN

ASPEN

The next morning, Aspen woke, exhausted and heartsick, the weight of sadness heavy across her shoulders. Thinking about how she'd left things with Matt the night before twisted her heart like an old rag. She'd been undeniably cruel, all because he'd unleashed a relentless longing for something more.

Him. Them. Together.

She knew her future depended on sticking to her perfect plan—the line of dominoes that she'd carefully constructed over the past several months. Only her own selfish desire would ask Matt to leave a job he loved and rip him away from his family.

Plus, there was the issue of Jessica's future. Her sister needed Matt more than she did. Settling for a life without Matthew Woods was the best option, even if it hurt the most.

A slow anger settled in her chest as she tossed her clothes into her suitcase. She was angry that Jessica had returned to Wild Harbor and had decided to pursue Matt. She was angry at

Matt for confessing his love when it was too late to change things. And she was angry at herself because she'd been too afraid to tell either of them what she really felt. Because if she did, it would ruin everything.

She believed love meant sacrifice, and family should stick together, no matter what. But even if it was the right thing to do, why did it feel so wrong?

She zipped her suitcase shut and stumbled out the door, wiping hot tears from her cheeks. There was no way to fix things now. Not when so much was already broken.

As she checked out of the hotel, one of the staff waved her down. "Before you leave, someone left you a package."

She glanced at her watch. At this rate, she'd barely make her plane. The shuttle driver beeped his horn and motioned for her to hurry.

The hotel clerk brought her a small box. "The person who left it said it was urgent."

A note was attached to the box, but there was no time to read it. She shoved the package into her carry-on as she hurried to the waiting shuttle.

It wasn't until later, seated on the plane, that she saw the package at the bottom of her bag. Opening the envelope, she immediately recognized Matt's handwriting:

Here is your surprise. When I was in Joshua's shop, I saw this and thought you might be interested. No matter what happens, I'll never give up on you.
Love,
Matt

Her heart tripped and stumbled, like a skater slipping on ice. Had he written those words after their fight last night? Surely he would give up hope for a relationship after she had asked him to leave last night.

Since the man next to her was asleep, she slipped her finger under the taped end of the gift and then froze. She didn't want to open it. Not if Matt was trying to change her mind. If this gift was an attempt to win her back, she couldn't bear to open it.

She shoved the package into the bottom of the bag and promised that she wouldn't unwrap it until she left Wild Harbor for good. Until then, his gift would remain a mystery.

If she left, it would give him and Jessica the space to find out if they could make things work. In the long run, it would hurt less if she forced him to let her go now rather than prolong things between them.

But it wasn't just losing Matt that hurt.

Tears formed in her eyes at the thought of handing over her great-aunt's beloved inn to a stranger. It seemed a betrayal to Aunt Lizzie, who wanted nothing more than to keep it in the family. But now that the place was ready to sell, she dreaded letting it go. She was doing this for her sister and the baby. This was the only way to provide them with a secure future.

Or was it? What if she could find a way to keep the inn?

A tiny spark of hope warmed her chest, a rising feeling that her tie to the inn was more than nostalgia, and she should do everything in her power to hold on to the beachfront home.

Even if she couldn't have a future with Matt, perhaps there was a way to avoid selling off the one connection to her great-aunt. As crazy as it sounded, nothing had ever felt so right. As soon as the plane touched ground, she knew what she needed to do. She only hoped it wasn't too late.

As soon as Aspen opened the front door, Jessica nearly tackled her. "Well, it's about time. We were all wondering when you'd get in," she said with a forced smile. "Normally, I'd welcome you and ask how the gala went, but we have a guest waiting." She nodded toward the sofa.

Aspen noticed a bald man dressed in a suit sitting in the living room. *The investor.*

He sat stiffly on Lizzie's floral sofa, examining every inch of the room like he was appraising it.

"Am I late?" she mouthed to her sister, unloading her bags in the foyer.

"He's early," Jessica mouthed back.

Aspen's heart flip-flopped in her chest like it always did when her nerves shifted into overdrive.

She approached the man and offered a handshake. "I'm Aspen."

"I'm Ron, the one who contacted you about the inn." The man rose, towering over her with an expressionless face. He sized up her slight frame with the attitude of someone who was used to dominating the situation.

Even though her mouth had suddenly dried up, a tiny glow of determination blossomed in her chest.

"I'm sorry I kept you waiting, but I'm afraid there's been a change of plans," Aspen said, apologizing.

The man frowned, his forehead crumpling. "Another offer?"

"Not exactly." She hesitated and glanced at her sister.

"Aspen, what's going on?" Jessica approached her sister with a look that said, *Have you lost your mind?*

With her whirlwind trip home, she hadn't had time to reveal what she'd decided.

"Until yesterday, I was determined to sell the inn as long as you offered the right price," Aspen explained.

Ron interrupted with the air of someone who wasn't used to being told what to do. "I'm willing to offer a good price. More than the asking price. I'm very interested in this place."

"Your offer is not the problem," Aspen continued. "The inn is no longer for sale."

Jessica gasped. "What?"

Ron looked stunned. "What's the problem? I traveled all the way here from California." He narrowed his eyes, trying to figure out her game.

"There is no problem," Aspen assured him. "At least, not anymore. That's the reason I'm taking the inn off the market. I apologize if I've wasted your time."

"Aspen," Jessica pleaded under her breath. "Now's not the time to make rash decisions."

The man looked from Jessica to Aspen. "Did someone offer cash?"

Aspen shook her head. "We haven't received any other offers."

"Then tell me how I can remedy the situation," the man urged. "So I can change your mind."

"You can't," she answered boldly. "The inn is no longer for sale because I've decided to keep it."

"Aspen, what are you doing?" Jessica's gaze looked deadly.

The man's lips tightened. "I would have appreciated knowing this sooner."

"Believe me, I would have too," Aspen agreed. "Again, I'm very sorry for this—"

The man ignored her apology, grabbed his bag, and stormed out of the house.

"What in the world?" Jessica threw her hands in the air. "You should have consulted me about this decision."

"Before you get angry, hear me out," Aspen pleaded, trying to calm her sister down.

"I'm already angry," her sister growled. "What if I need this money for the baby? For my future?"

"I know that, and you'll get your money, I promise."

Jessica looked doubtful. "But you don't have *any* money. You don't even have a job!"

Her sister's words stung, but Aspen wouldn't back down

now. "Trust me on this, Jess. I didn't have time to tell you before the investor arrived, but I'm keeping the inn. It's what Aunt Lizzie would have wanted."

"I'm so confused." Her sister shook her head. "I thought you were traveling the world and pursuing your *dreams*." She did air quotes around the last word to make a point.

Aspen's dreams were ridiculous to everyone in her family except her.

Jessica's mocking tone hurt, but her sister had good reason for her frustration. Just as Aspen's dreams were being realized, her sister's were falling apart. No wonder she was livid over Aspen changing her mind.

"You were set on selling." Jessica crumpled into a chair. "I don't get it."

"To be honest, I don't fully understand it either. When I hosted the Richardsons, I felt this thrill of having people around. I'm like Aunt Lizzie. I prefer a table full of guests and making strangers feel welcome. Good old-fashioned hospitality. But I thought the inn wasn't mine to keep. Financially, I couldn't afford to run it. But this place is my connection to Aunt Lizzie and her legacy. Something I want to be a part of. If you're not interested in sharing it, I'm willing to buy out your half in time. Whatever I can do to keep it in the family and make sure you and the baby have everything you need."

"But how are you going to run the inn while traveling the world?" Jessica asked, her tone thick with exasperation.

Though she'd never admit it, Jessica sounded exactly like their mom: highly doubtful that anything Aspen planned would work out.

"I'm still working on the details, but Wild Harbor will still be home between trips. The awards ceremony provided a huge number of leads for paying gigs. This will secure some income for me while we operate the inn together. I'll pay you a full salary to run the place while I'm gone, which will give you money until the baby arrives. Then I'll rent an apartment so that we can book all our guest rooms. That means you can have my room as long as you need it."

She didn't want to explain what had happened in Vegas and potentially ruin any chance Jessica had with Matt. All she knew was living at the inn wasn't a possibility anymore—not when seeing Matt every day would rip up her heart.

"When the baby comes, my plan is that we'll have a small nest egg, so we can hire someone to run the inn," Aspen explained. "Aunt Lizzie would want us to keep the home so that your children can run around the place just like we did."

Jessica's face softened at the memory.

Aspen reached for her sister's hand and gave it a squeeze. "Trust me on this, okay?"

"I do," Jessica said, then stopped as if she were considering something. "With your big news, I didn't want to say anything yet. But I might not need a room here for much longer."

"You're not leaving?" Aspen's mouth fell open.

"Absolutely not," Jessica corrected. "A pregnant woman with no place to go? A terrible idea." She paused. "While you were gone yesterday, I told Chase the news about the baby. He was shocked, but after some discussion, he suggested we try again."

"Try what again?" Aspen asked.

"Our relationship. He wants us to go to counseling. Start dating again. And more than anything, he wants to be a dad to this baby."

"But what about the divorce?" Aspen said, stunned. A second chance with Chase seemed impossible at this point.

"What about it?" Jessica shrugged like this was a minor inconvenience. "We're not rushing into marriage, if that's what you're worried about. But if things work out, wedding number two is not outside the realm of possibility."

Aspen flopped down into a chair, trying to absorb this news.

"But what about your feelings for Matt?" She almost couldn't bear to bring it up. "And your date Friday?"

"He didn't tell you? It was a disaster," Jessica admitted. "I was sick from the pregnancy all night, and we had zero chemistry. He might be handsome, but Matt and I could only ever be friends."

"Oh," Aspen murmured, the crushing realization hitting her at once. He'd shown up in Vegas for her and she'd ruined everything between them.

Rather than give herself false hope, she'd pushed him away because she believed Jessica needed him more. Sacrificing her own happiness for the sake of her sister's future seemed like the only way. Not only had she destroyed any chance for them, she wasn't sure she could salvage what was left of their friendship.

Her sister narrowed her eyes. "What's wrong? You look devastated."

Aspen covered her face and shook her head. "I've made a mess of everything, like usual." She dropped her hands. "Matt came to Vegas for the awards gala, and I basically pushed him away. I don't know if things will ever be the same between us."

Jessica raised her eyebrows. "I'm no expert on men, and I've done a lot of dumb stuff when it comes to relationships, but if he's hurt, you need to go to him—as hard as that may be." Jessica put her hand on Aspen's. "No matter what happens with Matt, I'll be here for you."

"I'd do the same for you. Like it or not, I'm not leaving Wild Harbor," Aspen promised.

"That's good, because there's no way I'm letting you out of being in the delivery room with me."

"Really?" Aspen's heart swelled. This was a bigger honor than traveling the world or winning a photography contest.

"Yes, really. Goodness knows Chase is going to be freaked out by the whole thing. I need you cheering me on. You're my sister, and I can't do this without you." For a moment, Jessica's eyes met her sister's and Aspen could see the fear in them.

"I won't leave your side, even if you're screaming at me because you're in pain."

"Then I apologize in advance for everything I might say or do in the delivery room," Jessica said, holding up her hands. "Oh and one more thing." Jessica shot off the couch and riffled through a stack of mail. "The doctor's office sent you something." She offered Aspen an envelope.

Aspen's heart did an odd little flop as she stared at the mail. She didn't need any bad news today. Throughout her whole life, she'd been poked and prodded, measured and evaluated. Despite following the doctor's orders, her heart had mapped out its own stubborn path.

A unique heart for a unique girl, her great-aunt used to say as she gave her chin a gentle squeeze. But she didn't want her heart to march to a different beat. She wanted one that pumped steady and strong, even when love took hold of it.

She grasped the envelope, and a dull nausea washed over her. Her finger hovered over the seal. After everything that had happened in the last twenty-four hours, she couldn't take any more life-changing news. She tucked the envelope in her bag. Sorting through bad news required more than she could give right now.

Despite the fact her body ached with tiredness, Aspen needed to find Matt. Although she'd messed up things between them, she couldn't live with this tension in their friendship.

"Jessica, do you know where Matt is?"

"That's the other thing I haven't told you yet." Jessica twisted her fingers, like she was about to give bad news. "He arrived home early this morning. Then he packed a bunch of bags and left. I think he moved out."

"What?" Although she'd known he would be mad, she hadn't

expected this. Pushing Matt away last night had been the last straw.

"I'm sorry, Aspen. I didn't know something happened in Vegas. With the investor arriving, I was too distracted to talk him out of it."

Aspen mentally checked off the places where she could search for him—the fire station, his parents' home, the gym, the beach. But at some point, he would have to return for the rest of his things and face her.

"He has to come back, right?" Aspen asked, desperately needing some reassurance.

Her sister nodded weakly. Even Jessica wasn't sure this time.

Aspen rushed to Matt's bedroom and parked herself there. Even if she had to stay all day, resolving the issues between them mattered more than anything now. She only hoped he could forgive her.

She settled in the middle of his bed cross-legged, his pillow cushioning her back. Outside, she could make out the rippling lake waters and a string of sailboats bobbing along in the distance.

As she sank into his sheets, his familiar scent brought a thrill of pleasure, reminding her of their kiss. She loved his smell. The way his hair laced through her fingers. How her body nestled into his. With the wind drifting through the open window, she let her thoughts swirl away like clouds on a summer day. Then she shut out the world, replaying their kiss until she felt heartsick.

Until now, she'd never let herself dream about Matt in that way, afraid her feelings would taint their friendship. But now it didn't matter, since she'd completely wrecked any future for them.

Because of her mistake, she'd have to live with the memory of that kiss, to sketch it out from a thousand angles until she could draw it blind. That was what love was. To know someone so well you recognized them without seeing them. Instead, you knew them by the sound of their laughter, the scent of their skin, the way they felt under your fingertips. And more than anything, how they made you feel like the most extraordinary person in the world.

Only now, she'd never get the chance to know him that way again, and that was what hurt the most.

CHAPTER NINETEEN

MATT

As Matt finished his final lap in the lake, his breathing grew ragged and his muscles burned. There was nothing like a good workout to rid your mind of the person who'd upended your life. But when the pain was gone, a different ache surfaced: a longing for the one thing you could never have.

It had only been two weeks since he'd left the inn and moved in with his parents, but he missed Aspen like mad. He'd heard Megan and Lily mention her in whispered conversations. She was back in town, and the inn was no longer on the market. She'd probably concocted another crazy redecorating project and would have it up for sale in no time.

His muscles trembled with exhaustion from the workout, but he hardly noticed the pain. The cold water had brought every frustration to the surface. Aspen was so wrapped up in selling the inn and leaving town, she didn't realize how terrible it felt to be left behind.

He was fighting a mix of emotions: a sinking sensation that

his time with Aspen was running out and regret over losing what he'd always wanted.

As he wiped his body down with a towel, he spied a young couple sitting under a sun umbrella, gazing at each other with goofy, lovestruck smiles. The woman sat between the man's legs as he rubbed sunscreen on her shoulders. His touch was so tender, she closed her eyes, then leaned into the man for a long, slow kiss.

Matt turned away. He shouldn't be watching this private moment that was obviously not meant for him. Their intimate kiss left a longing to have that same sort of relationship, but not with just anyone. He wanted Aspen. And he couldn't have her. The finality of that statement angered him so much he wanted to punch something.

On their last night together, she'd made things clear—there was no future for them, ever. Even though his desire to see her again was almost painful, he needed to accept his new reality. She didn't want him in her life.

He'd spent his time trying to plan every detail, and in the end, he'd failed at the most basic thing of all. His mistakes over the last year should have taught him that he couldn't control everything. But here he was, aggravating old wounds.

Losing her had left him completely broken, and his body sagged under the weight of grief. He'd stopped going out and avoided talking to friends. Even Chief Larson had been concerned and told him to take a break. Instead, Matt had worked extra hours at the fire station and doubled down on organizing supplies and truck checks. It was the one thing he could control. Maybe the only thing.

But this wasn't about forcing things to go his way. He'd already learned there was only so much you could do before life threw you a curveball and shattered all your plans. For once, this was about letting go of his future and finally forgiving himself for what was out of his hands. Shame had forced him to reach his tipping point, but only forgiveness could help him move on.

He picked up his phone and checked his messages. Aspen had tried calling again, but he ignored it and threw the phone into his duffel. Any response would probably make their situation more tense. More than likely, she would give him a good verbal lashing for what had happened in Vegas, and he was already feeling defensive about it. He wasn't even sure he could forgive Aspen for the way she'd humiliated him that night at the hotel.

To be fair, he didn't have a suitable reason for why he'd kissed her, other than the fact he was crazy about her. But he'd also felt like she wanted him. He'd sensed it in her kiss. How could he have been so wrong?

He glanced back at the couple who'd been kissing under the umbrella. Now they were laughing about something, a private joke only they shared. A surge of longing and jealousy shot through Matt with powerful force. He would never have what they did. *Never ever.*

Just as he rose to leave the beach, a text appeared, this time from Jessica.

Jessica: Aspen can't get in touch with you, so I thought I'd try. We need you to pick up the rest of your stuff. If you're moving out of here, we can't hold your room forever. Swing by today. The door is open.

Jessica's words felt like a punch in the gut. The sisters were kicking him out of the inn. *Not surprising.* After what had happened, it was clear Aspen didn't want him around anymore.

Eventually, she would sell the place and leave for good, and nothing would ever be the same. How would he go on once she left? He had no idea. But learning to live without her would be easier than forgiving her for rejecting him. He might as well face that reality now.

As he pulled up to the inn, he tried to fight the urge to turn around and drive away. No matter how much he hated it, Jessica was right. Moving out was the only option.

His gaze swept across the property, and a bittersweet feeling washed over him. Weeds consumed the beds and the grass needed a trim. He resisted the temptation to pull out the mower and give it a quick spin around the yard. This wasn't his job anymore. She wasn't his anymore, either.

The spot where Jessica parked her car was vacant. When he entered the house, the place was eerily quiet.

"Anyone here?" he called. Only Lester welcomed him, rubbing his tail against his legs.

Leaving while the house was empty would make things easier. He could move out without confronting Aspen. Rushing to his room, he halted in the doorway. Aspen was tucked under his blanket, sound asleep, her curls spread across his pillow. If he could wake up next to that beautiful face every morning, he couldn't imagine ever wanting more.

An envelope had fallen on the floor next to the bed. He picked it up, his eyes skimming over a letter from Aspen's doctor.

"What are you doing here?" A sleepy voice startled him. Aspen frowned as she rose up on one elbow. Her gaze drifted from the letter to his face.

He set the envelope on his dresser and kept his distance. "I'd like to ask you the same thing. You're in my bed. *Again.*" His defenses were up. No matter how he felt about her, he had to put up walls between them.

"I'm sorry," she stammered, struggling to untangle her legs from his blanket. "Are you going to rip into me again? I more than deserve it."

"Maybe." He crossed his arms. "Why don't you sleep in your

own bed?" Never mind that she looked adorable in his. He had to keep his feelings out of it. He wouldn't let her humiliate him again.

"I don't know," she mumbled, embarrassed. She paused and her eyes swept over him. "You look terrible. Is everything okay?"

"Thanks for the compliment." A bite of sarcasm colored his tone as he rubbed his unshaven face. "Just doing what you asked of me." He dragged his hand through his tousled hair. "I'm here to pick up the rest of my stuff and move out."

"Oh." Searching the floor, she raised her eyebrows. "For good?"

"Isn't that what you want?" He didn't know why she was asking for confirmation, but she seemed confused by this news.

In Jessica's message, she had made it clear—they wanted him to leave as soon as possible.

"Not really." She rubbed her palm in the hollow of one eye. "But I understand why you'd think that." She played with the edge of the blanket. "Listen, will you let me say something first?"

"There's nothing to say," he responded abruptly.

"I made a horrible mistake by asking you to leave at the hotel. I was so rude to you."

"You were rude," he agreed, his bruised ego wanting a fight. He'd never felt so humiliated in his life.

"I don't even know what to say, other than how sorry I am for pushing you away."

"You're good at pushing me away," he added. "Like you enjoy it."

Her mouth twitched almost imperceptibly. "For what it's worth, I don't. I feel awful about it. I just hope you'll forgive me."

He clenched his jaw. Forgiving her was the last thing he wanted, but her tortured look wouldn't allow him to flat-out refuse her.

"Why should I?" he shot back.

He didn't want to offer cheap grace. If he was going to forgive her, he needed to know why it mattered. He wanted it to cost something. Otherwise, forgiveness was only a numbing agent, making the pain go away, but not really doing the agonizing and gut-wrenching work of changing your heart toward the other person. If he was offering forgiveness, he didn't want it to come with conditions. He wanted it to demolish the walls he'd put up to protect himself, to burn all their hurt down to dust and ash so they could rebuild something new. Was their relationship worth anything less?

"I know I don't deserve your forgiveness," she said, looking down at his bed. "The way I treated you was horrible. I did it to protect myself because I was convinced my sister needed you more. I loved you so much, the only solution was leaving. So I pushed you away, hoping I could push away my feelings and spare myself some pain, but I ended up hurting you more. That was the worst part. When you wound someone you care about, it causes more suffering, not less."

She finally braved a look at him, her eyes rimmed with tears. "I've been miserable and sick over losing our friendship, Matt. If there's anything I could do to make it up to you and become your friend again, I'll do it. But please don't leave here without making things right, because it's killing me."

The way she pleaded for him—*for them together*—was enough to shatter the walls he'd put up between them. No longer did he wonder whether forgiveness and grace cost them something. It was clear that both of them were miserable without the other.

"Aspen, I forgive you," he whispered, lowering himself onto the bed. As soon as the words escaped his lips, she reached up and wrapped her arms around his neck in a fervent, almost desperate hug. He'd never known how good forgiveness felt.

In that moment, he knew he not only needed to forgive her,

he also needed to forgive himself. For too long, he'd carried the shame and guilt for past mistakes.

"You don't know how relieved I am," she said, her face buried in his shoulder. He could feel the joy splitting his rib cage in two. "I've wanted this ever since you walked out of my hotel room. I blame myself for everything that happened."

"Everything? You're not the only guilty party here."

"But the difference was you were honest about your feelings and I wasn't. I hid my emotions and pushed you toward my sister even though it killed me. But instead of telling you, I kissed you back."

"You regret it?" He could feel the next question before he said it. The same one he'd asked her after every date: *Is he the one you want to be with forever?*

She shook her head. "I'd never stop kissing you if you let me," she admitted.

Something was building in his chest that he couldn't contain.

"The truth is"—she paused, swallowing hard—"my feelings scared me because the last thing I wanted when I left was to hurt you."

"Too late for that." He pushed down the thought of what she'd done to him.

"Leaving or falling for me?"

"Both," he confessed.

"Then you haven't heard the news?" she asked incredulously.

He shook his head, confused.

"I'm keeping the inn," she said. "It's what Aunt Lizzie would want. This place is meant to remain in our family and I'm going to do everything in my power to hold on to it."

"But what about the money you need to travel? That was the point of selling."

"I'm scraping by. I've got some photography gigs coming up, and I'm hoping to fill the inn with guests as much as possible. But I'll be honest, I'm scared. What if I have an awful month?

What if I lose the inn because I can't pay the bills? It's a massive leap of faith trusting that this is all going to work out."

Matt could see how tired and worried she was. He wanted nothing more than to wrap his arms around her and assure her that everything was going to be okay. But was it? Their relationship was already on shaky ground. If she lost the inn, he'd lose her for good. One more blow could cause everything to fall.

"Did you unwrap the box I left at the hotel?" he asked. "The one from Aunt Lizzie?"

A look of surprise crossed her face. "It was from Aunt Lizzie? Not you?" She shook her head. "I promised I wouldn't open it until I left. But when I returned, I put my bag away and forgot all about it. Did you open it beforehand?"

"Of course not." He was offended she would think otherwise. "It was yours alone to open."

She ran to her room and returned with the gift, sliding it from the wrapping paper as they sat together on the bed.

A small carved box was underneath, modest enough to hold some coins or even a ring. The lid revealed three tiny clock faces. Etched on the bottom of the box were the words, *Time is short.* A memory clicked into place. Aunt Lizzie's riddle. *The answer lies under three clocks*

in the shape of a box.

Aspen flipped the box over, searching for something. "This is the next clue, but where is the lock? If the last clue gave me a key, wasn't I supposed to use it?"

She pulled the lid off the box. Inside was a note, penned in Aunt Lizzie's hand, along with an official-looking document. She opened the letter and began reading it aloud.

Dear Aspen,

Congratulations, my dear. I had no doubts you would solve the riddle, but also left instructions with Joshua in case you struggled to figure it out. You might wonder what it all means and why I left it for you after my passing.

Although I've lived a frugal life as a single woman, every year, I've taken a small amount and invested in stocks that have risen considerably in value. A year ago, I cashed them in and stored the payment in a locked safe in Joshua's shop. I knew that my time was nearing the end, and my plan had always been to leave this inheritance to you since I have no heirs. The document gives you the rights to the money, and the key will unlock the safe.

If there's anyone who reminds me of myself at a younger age, it's always been you. You're fiercely independent, determined to make your path, no matter what other people say. I've always liked that. But being an unmarried woman with ambitions means there's never a safety net to protect you if your dreams fail or life doesn't turn out as planned.

I have no regrets about my choices. Running an inn as a single woman was rather unconventional for my time, but I earned the respect of the town eventually and treated my guests like family. Living in the community and entertaining strangers who became friends has turned out to be the best gift of all. Wild Harbor was where I belonged, even when I didn't fit the mold. One thing I deeply regret, however, was giving up a relationship that meant a great deal to me. When I was a young woman, I became engaged to Joshua, and he meant the world to me. Unfortunately, we sharply disagreed over an important issue and could not resolve it. I won't go into what that issue was, because it's not important now. I always thought that there was no hope for us, but now I see it was my own foolish pride that kept me from repairing old wounds. Joshua and I eventually became friends again, but we waited too long for anything more.

Although forgiveness should never have a limit, I wasn't even willing to forgive him once for the hurt he'd caused me. I've had to come to terms with that and learn to let go of what could have been.

If there's one thing I discovered, it's that love is a beautiful and fragile gift. I realized this the hard way. Love takes a lifetime to build, but can be ruined in a moment.

The money I've left you will not make you happy. Nor will it give lasting satisfaction. Only love can do that. That is where the riddle ends. *Love opens the door to answers and more.*

All my love,

Aunt L

The tears rolled down Aspen's face, streaming like rain, dripping off her chin, dotting the letter Aunt Lizzie had written.

Setting the letter aside, she carefully unfolded the official document that revealed the amount of money in the safe. Aspen's breath caught as her eyes skimmed the paper.

"What is it?" he asked.

She turned it around so he could see for himself.

If this document was accurate, Aspen had suddenly become a much richer woman. So wealthy, in fact, that this could change everything concerning her future.

He shook his head, trying to make sense of it all. "This is enough to fund all your dreams, Aspen. The inn and your photography career. You could travel the world and never return to Wild Harbor." A bittersweet sadness tugged at the raw edges inside him. Why would she ever bother staying now?

"That's just it. I don't want to leave for good. What I've always wanted was a home, a place where I belonged. It took going to Vegas to realize that if you want something to grow strong, you don't need to look for it somewhere else. You must let it take root." She searched his eyes for some understanding. "I'm not giving up all my dreams. I just had to realize what my dreams really were, and if there's any hope for us."

He rolled her words around in his head, afraid of voicing his reply. "You mean friendship or something more?"

"Something more," she replied carefully. "If you want to—"

"*If* I want to?" He didn't even let her finish. Instead, he grabbed her waist and pulled her into his arms as he fell back onto the bed. They toppled together onto the bedspread. "Of course I do." His arms locked behind her back. "I was waiting for you to realize it."

"Oh, I've seen the light," she assured him. "I just didn't think you'd really want to date someone like me."

"What do you mean, *like you?*" He held her at arm's length, his gaze roving over her face. "You're perfect, Aspen. So perfect, it drives me crazy."

"Except for my malfunctioning heart." She rested her hand on her chest. "You know that surgery is probably in my future. As well as a lot of doctor visits. Even the uncertainty kills me. Do you really want to take a chance on that?"

His eyes studied her carefully. "I'll take a chance on you, Aspen Bradford, any day, no matter whether or not your heart is perfect. Judging by your latest test results, it sounds like we'll take it a day at a time."

She pushed away from his arms. "What are you talking about?"

"You mean you haven't read it?" he asked. He pulled it from the top of his dresser.

"I was too scared to read it," she explained before she tore open the paper and skimmed the page. "My heart tests were only slightly out of range," she said. "I need to follow up with the doctor in one year, and he didn't mention surgery." She tossed the letter to the bed and threw herself into his arms. "That's good news, right? I can forget about this for a year."

He spun her around, her feet dangling in the air. "For a year, yes. As long as you promise to tell me if anything is wrong. And if you ever get bad news, I won't leave you to go through this alone. From now on, good or bad, we get through it together."

When he lowered her to the floor, he had the sudden urge to draw her close again. His eyes drifted to her soft lips while his heart barreled through his chest like a wild horse.

"Why are you looking at me like that?" she asked, a curious grin playing on her lips.

"What way?" he asked innocently, trying to calm the wolfish intensity rising inside him.

"Like you want to kiss me again," she admitted with a smile, a secret only between them. "You've got your bodyguard eyes on again."

How could he argue with the truth? "Because I do want to kiss you," he said, lowering his voice. He took her palm and turned it over. "Right here," he whispered, kissing the back of her hand. "And right here." His lips grazed over the tips of her fingers. "And especially right here." He kissed the inside of her wrist, trailing kisses up her arm.

"We really shouldn't be doing this now." She closed her eyes as her breath caught. "In case"—she swallowed—"someone walks in."

"I don't really care who walks in," he whispered, kissing the hollow spot near her collarbone, then trailing kisses down the other side. "I've waited a long time for you. For this. And I'm not waiting anymore."

His body melted with hers, turning him into liquid heat as his lips caressed hers. Even though he didn't want to stop, he forced himself to pull away.

She leaned her forehead against his shoulder, her breath sounding as ragged as his. "That"—she tried to catch her breath—"was the most amazing kiss I've ever had. If I died now, I'd be satisfied."

"Well, I'm not satisfied. I've been saving these kisses for over a decade. We need to make up for lost time." He gave her earlobe a gentle nip before she wrenched away.

"First, that makes my knees weak," she warned him.

"That was what I hoped."

"Second, we need to tell my sister. And your family. Megan's going to kill me when she finds out."

"No way," Matt assured her. "She's been asking me for years if we'd finally kissed yet."

"She what?" Aspen's eyes widened.

"She was onto us long before we even realized it."

"And she never told me?" Aspen acted offended.

"You're not her sister." Matt paused. "At least, not yet."

Aspen stared at him gravely. "Don't start teasing about that. This is only our first day together."

"We've been together our entire lives," he replied. "Today, we're just making it official."

"Which is why I want you to treat me like we only started dating," she explained. "You don't get to skip all the romantic stuff. Flowers, chocolates, the grand gestures—I want it all."

"You want it all?" he repeated.

"Sure do," she shot back with a smile.

"Then I'll give it to you. Whatever you ask. Your wish is my command."

"Let's start with photographs on the porch swing, since I know how much you love getting your picture taken."

He gave her a look. "On one condition."

"What's that?"

"Answer my question," he asked, suddenly serious. "Am I the one you want to be with forever?"

He didn't have to ask her twice. She closed the distance between them in a few steps, grasped his shirt in her fists and pulled him to her.

She didn't say a word. Her kiss was all the answer he needed.

EPILOGUE

THREE MONTHS LATER

ASPEN

Aspen glanced at her checklist as Cassidy took notes on her phone. "Are you sure you don't have more questions? I'm gone for two weeks."

Aspen had covered dozens of scenarios to ensure that the inn ran smoothly while she was hiking the Grand Canyon. Somehow, she'd made it through the marathon list and hadn't scared Cassidy away from serving as a temporary host.

Matt's youngest sister already worked at the bookstore, but when Cass had found out Aspen was looking for someone to oversee the inn while she was on vacation, she'd heartily volunteered.

"Don't worry about me at all," Cass assured her, biting into a banana muffin Aspen had baked fresh the night before. "I'll be fine. You have a fabulous time on the trip and don't think about anything here."

"Jessica's only a phone call away if you have a question, and Matt, of course," Aspen added.

"I won't bother Jessica unless it's urgent. Not after just getting married."

Only a week ago, Jessica had remarried Chase in a beautiful but small ceremony attended by a few friends and family. At six months pregnant, her round belly popped out of her lace dress, and she glowed with a beauty that couldn't be recreated with makeup. She and Chase had worked hard on their relationship, attending counseling and making sure they didn't rush things.

But now that Jessica had moved out of the inn, Aspen needed a regular backup to help with hosting. She couldn't place everything on Matt's shoulders since his job could call him away at a moment's notice.

Aspen peeked at her watch, sensing the minutes sliding away until she needed to head to the airport. "Sorry for rushing through things today. This trip has frazzled my nerves, and I don't know why. I should look forward to it, but instead—" Her gaze drifted toward the shed where Matt was. The sunlight caught the sharp lines of his shoulders. He'd spent the entire week working on a surprise project with strict instructions that she couldn't peek at his progress.

"Top secret," he'd told her with a gleam in his eye.

What was so important about a garden shed? She'd seen dozens, and they usually reeked of dirt and lawnmowers. But Matt seemed intent on presenting it to her like a prize-winning piece of art.

Whatever his motivation, she hated saying goodbye even though he'd encouraged her to travel. Her heart was here. When she left, it was like leaving a piece of herself behind.

"I'm going to see if Matt is almost ready to take me to the airport."

As she approached the shed, Matt wiped his hands on his faded jeans and dark blue T-shirt that fit him like he belonged in a movie trailer. No matter how hard he was working, he never failed to draw attention. Even the ladies at the local nursing home loved when he stopped by to check their smoke alarms. They'd pat his hand or pinch his cheek, anything to get his attention. Matt endured it with an awkward smile. Aspen would just have to put up with it, knowing that he was hers alone. Even the word *hers* choked her up. She didn't deserve such a good man.

"Just in time." He brightened at the sight of her, setting a shovel to the side. Her entire collection of garden tools lay scattered on the grass outside the shed.

"Shouldn't we put these away in the shed? Time waits for no man . . . or airplane departure." She turned to pick up a spade when he grabbed her arm and tugged her close to his body. His lips brushed the top of her head.

"Which is why this project has been top secret. I knew you'd try to undo all my progress," he teased before stealing the spade and throwing it in the yard like it was as light as tissue. "The garden tools are getting a new home. They'll move temporarily to the garage until I get a new storage shed built."

"Mercy, you've worked hard on this rickety shed. What's all the fuss about? Have I been good enough to get a glimpse before I leave?"

"You can convince me with a kiss."

"If that was all, I would have come out a long time ago and planted one on your cheek."

"Those kinds of kisses are for grannies. I want the real deal."

"The real deal, huh?" She gave him a wicked smile before leaning into him and planting her lips hard on his.

When she tried to pull away, he wrapped his arms around her like iron bands and forced her closer to him.

She could barely wrench away to catch her breath. "Goodness, Matt. You're going to make me lose my mind."

"That's the idea," he said, walking over to the shed door.

Already, the exterior of the building looked a million times better than before. He'd sanded and repainted the paint-flaked siding and even scored a beautiful old door from Joshua's shop to replace the rickety one. The outside reminded her of something from a lavish home and garden magazine.

"This shed is amazing compared to how it appeared a week ago," she told him.

"Ready to see inside?" He slowly turned the door handle, excitement building in his eyes.

"Why do you look like a kid on Christmas Day? It's a garden shed."

"Not just any garden shed. A *she-shed*."

"A what?" Aspen was unsure what Matt was up to.

"She-shed. It's like a man cave, but for a woman. You've mentioned your wish for a photography studio, but the inn doesn't have the space. Until now."

As she stepped inside, the room flooded with natural light from two new windows. He had refinished the entire interior with bright white paint and beautiful furnishings. One end was reserved as a working studio to accommodate her clients' wishes, while the other side held a simple Scandinavian-style desk for editing photographs.

He'd covered the walls in some of her best work, including her prize-winning picture from the *Hometown Heroes* contest. He'd also snagged one of Megan and Finn's engagement pictures and his parents' portrait on the porch swing. The giant photographs were a montage of family and friends, and the word *home* reverberated like a church bell. The girl who had planned to travel the world had finally found her place in this small town. Not in some exotic locale or wandering the countryside, but in the middle of a quaint community where there was always more room around the table.

"You turned a garden shed into a photography studio?" she

asked wondrously, an overwhelming flood of emotions rising in her chest.

"A she-shed. A garden shed definitely doesn't sound as cool."

"Well, I've never been one of the cool girls, anyway." She shrugged, thinking back to her high school years when she'd rather have her nose in a book than anything else.

"Cool girls are overrated," Matt said, coming up from behind and pulling her close. He gave her neck a tender kiss.

She spied a book sitting on her new desk called *The Inns of Lake Michigan*. On the front was a picture of The Red Poppy Inn and underneath were Ted and Lisa's names.

"Is this the book?" She rushed over to it. "Why didn't you tell me it came in the mail?"

"I wanted it to be a surprise," he said, grinning like a Cheshire cat. "Before you open it, I have to warn you. Lisa shared more than the inn's story. Our entire love story is there."

Aspen's mouth fell open. "She did what?" Aspen flipped through the pages until she found the chapter on The Red Poppy Inn. Her eyes skimmed over the words and a laugh escaped her lips. Lisa had even included the picture of them kissing.

Matt peered over her shoulder. "It's a good thing our relationship worked out, or we'd have a lot of explaining to do."

Aspen closed the book and looked around the studio. "I don't deserve this, but I'm truly grateful. Why did you do it?"

"Because I didn't want you to let go of your photography dreams because you're running an inn now. You have a special gift for seeing beauty in things I'd never notice. The last thing I want is for you to stop using your talent because you live in Wild Harbor and not at the international airport terminal. You made a sacrifice, but you don't have to give up what you love."

"But I'm not giving up what I love. I have you." She squeezed his hand. "Now that I own the inn, I've found my true calling, and it's given me a confidence I didn't have before. I was even brave enough to call my former employer and tell him it was unfair to use my photographs without permission. Mr. Hartford apologized profusely, and get this: he agreed to pay me double for them. I never would have done that before. I only wish I wasn't leaving you behind on this trip."

The corners of his mouth curled up like he was hiding something. "That's the other thing I wanted to talk to you about."

"What do you have planned?"

"Grab your luggage. You're about to see."

She followed him to his truck as he took her bags and tossed them in the back, like they weighed nothing.

As he opened her door, he had an envelope waiting in the seat.

"What's this?" She pulled out a note.

"It's my second attempt at a riddle." He cleared his throat. "Except I'm still a rotten poet."

"I bet your sisters would be shocked to know you're a poet."

"Please don't show them. I'll never hear the end of it."

She held up his handwritten rhyme:

You've won over my heart,
so now we can't part.
If you accept your fate,
I'll be your travel date.

She glanced at him. "What's this about?"

"It means I never want to be away from you." He slowly lowered himself to one knee and opened a jewelry box with Aunt Lizzie's sapphire in it.

She looked from the ring to him. "You're kidding, right?" she asked incredulously. "You're proposing now, right before I leave?"

"Does it look like I'm kidding?" he laughed. "I love you,

Aspen, and want to be with you forever. You'd make me the happiest guy ever if you'd be my wife."

"Yes," she whispered, blinking back the tears before cradling his face and kissing him hard on the mouth.

She held out her hand so he could slide on Aunt Lizzie's sapphire. "But what about Joshua? Didn't he want the ring?"

Matt shook his head. "He wanted you to have it. The man couldn't stop smiling when I told him I was going to ask you to marry me."

After everything that had happened, she only wished her great-aunt could see that love had a happy ending after all.

She admired the ring before grabbing his hands. "But were you always planning on asking me before I left?"

"Originally, the plan had been to pop the question at the Grand Canyon, but I couldn't wait."

"You're going on the trip with me?" she asked slowly.

"As a surprise," Matt admitted. "I booked a seat on the same flight."

"But how did you arrange this, and where are you going to sleep?" She seemed baffled he could plan this behind her back.

"Where do you think?" he asked, his eyes dancing.

"Um, if you expect this is our honeymoon—"

"As much as I'd like to, that will have to wait until after our wedding. I have a buddy near the Grand Canyon who offered his couch to me."

"Oh, so you're dumping me for him?"

"Not a chance. I'm staying with you forever, if you'll have me."

She nestled closer to him. "Is that a promise you plan to keep?"

"You better believe it." He backed her into the door of the truck and flanked her head with his arms, pinning her down. With a playful intensity, he stroked his hand across her cheek.

"Aspen, you've played the longest game of hard to get, and there's no chance I'm letting you go. Not now. Not ever."

"*Never ever,* huh?" A smile spread across her lips, remembering when he'd used those words before.

"That's right. *Never ever,*" he repeated, kissing her forehead.

"That's the first time I've liked hearing those words from you." She wrapped her arms around his back as he touched his lips to her nose, then her cheeks.

"You can hold me to it," he vowed, as his lips met hers, sealing his promise with a kiss.

He was too logical, too handsome, too daring, and otherwise not who she'd imagined in her wildest dreams. And yet, he was everything she'd imagined. Now that he was hers, nothing could ever convince her to let him go.

Get a bonus scene or chapter one of the next book by joining Grace Worthington's newsletter.
Get it at graceworthington.com.

Did you love this story? **Leave a review on Amazon!**

Read on for a sneak peek of *A Wedding in Wild Harbor.*

A WEDDING IN WILD HARBOR

SNEAK PEEK OF BOOK FIVE

She needs a hero to save her beloved bookshop. He needs a fake engagement to satisfy his mother's dying wish.

Can they work out the perfect deal for a happily ever after? Or will a plot twist they didn't see coming ruin everything?

If Cassidy Woods could make one dream come true, it would be to save her struggling bookshop from closing its doors.

So when wealthy investor Liam Henry announces he just acquired—and is shutting down—her store, Cassidy will do anything to change his mind, including becoming his fake girlfriend, even if she'd rather die first.

Liam Henry is running out of time. His mother's final wish is that he'd meet the girl of his dreams and get engaged before she dies. But Liam doesn't stand a chance without some kind of help. No woman can see past his grumpy exterior to get to know the soft teddy bear underneath.

When his mother threatens to advertise his search for a girl-friend on a Times Square billboard, Liam makes the best, worst plan of his life: Ask the first woman he sees to become his fake girlfriend.

Too bad that woman is Cassidy Woods, the ridiculously optimistic bookstore owner who's about to get axed from her job by him.

Cassidy's sunshine is the perfect opposite to his grump, forcing Liam to make an outrageous trade-off he's destined to regret: If Cassidy will be his fake fiancée, he'll keep the bookstore open.

Now everybody's happy, except the mismatched couple who are headed toward a bumpy road that unravels every tightly constructed argument they've put up against love.

In the end, only one of them can win. When they're thrown together in a race against time, who'll be left with a happy ending?

Or will they discover that in fooling everyone, the only person who's fallen for it is themselves?

A Wedding in Wild Harbor is coming soon!

A NOTE FROM THE AUTHOR

If You've Ever Believed in Love, You're Not Alone

I've always loved reading books with happy endings. It doesn't matter if I've guessed the ending before it's done or if I've already figured out how the couple is going to get together. If there's a happy ending, I'm here for it. One hundred percent.

When I began thinking of Matt and Aspen's story, I wasn't initially thinking they would become a couple. In earlier stories, they were friends. I was okay with leaving them as such. But several readers asked me about it. *Are Matt and Aspen next?* I could tell they wanted them paired up and that started the wheels turning in my head.

The friends-to-lovers trope is such a satisfying one because I love a good, slow burn where they've been holding a flame for the other in secret. A love that starts as friendship is a strong foundation, not only in fiction, but in real life too. It allows us to mine the characters' backstories and explore how they've wanted the other person for such a long time we can't understand how they haven't gotten together before this moment. This kind of story isn't insta-love. It's a slow-growing relationship we know is going to last. As Matt says, it's "the longest game of hard to get." No wonder we can't stop cheering for them.

As I fleshed out their backstories, I made new discoveries about the characters, things that gave them juicy layers and struggles, just like real people. Matt struggles with forgiving himself. Aspen struggles with finding her place of belonging. In the end, love forces them to deal with these inner wounds, even if that means giving up the other person. Since every sweet love story leads toward a happily ever after, they find their way back. Love wins after all.

At first, this might seem unrealistic. No one gets a happy ending like that. Or do they?

When we're moved by a story, it's our longing for a complete and satisfying love that compels us to keep reading. Though we're given human relationships to satisfy that desire, I also believe it's a spiritual longing that goes much deeper. We want unconditional love from someone who'll never let us down. I believe our longing for unconditional love comes from the one true source of love in Jesus. So when I write these happily-ever-afters, I persevere in the hope that someday we will feel every longing fulfilled and grasp hold of the love that is better than all loves.

~

My email list is the best way to stay in touch and it's where I share bonus epilogues and free novellas. Plus, every week I include great book deals and new releases! Join it at graceworthington.com.

You can also join me on Instagram or Facebook @graceworthingtonauthor.

ACKNOWLEDGMENTS

Thank you to my husband who was my friend before he was my love. You're my first reader and I'm so grateful for every ounce of your encouragement.

Thanks to my children who continue to inspire me with their own creativity. Someday you'll understand why these stories matter.

Thanks to my editor, Emily Poole, and my wonderful beta readers who give me such valuable feedback, Leigh Ann Routh, Joy Martz, Heidi Lanter, and Michelle McCubbins. Thank you to Judy Zweifel for giving this story a final proofread and Kristen Ingebretson for the beautiful cover design.

To my readers, you're the greatest gift any writer could ask for. I hope you love this series as much as I've loved writing it.

ALSO BY GRACE WORTHINGTON

Love at Wild Harbor

Summer Nights in Wild Harbor

Christmas Wishes in Wild Harbor

The Inn at Wild Harbor

A Wedding in Wild Harbor

ABOUT THE AUTHOR

Grace Worthington writes clean contemporary romance novels because she loves giving readers a happily ever after with heart. She has a degree in English and resides with her husband and two children in Indiana.

Get a free stories and more when you sign up here.

Sign up for it at graceworthington.com and get notified of sales on Grace's books and other great deals.

Made in the USA
Middletown, DE
21 April 2022

64601075R00154